PRAISE FOR THE NOVELS OF CYNTHIA SMITH
FEATURING
PRIVATE RESOLVER EMMA RHODES . . .

Misleading Ladies

"Enchanting . . . a one-of-a-kind series with universal appeal. All mystery enthusiasts will clamor for more Emma Rhodes stories."—*BookBrowser*

Impolite Society

"I have been charmed right out of my high-heeled sandals by Cynthia Smith's *Impolite Society* . . . a refreshing delight."—The *Washington Times*

Noblesse Oblige

"Fast . . . clever . . . charming."—*Publishers Weekly*

"A sparkling debut of an original sleuth."
—*I Love A Mystery*

"Globetrotting, high-society sleuth Emma Rhodes makes her debut in this classy whodunit. Aristocratic suspects and European locales make this charmer a welcome addition to the amateur sleuth category. Readers will eagerly await captivating Emma's next case."—*Gothic Journal*

SILVER
AND GUILT

Cynthia Smith

BERKLEY PRIME CRIME, NEW YORK

SILVER AND GUILT

A Berkley Prime Crime Book / published by arrangement with
the author

PRINTING HISTORY
Berkley Prime Crime edition / June 1998

The Penguin Putnam Inc. World Wide Web site address is
http://www.penguinputnam.com

ISBN: 0-425-16382-2

Berkley Prime Crime Books are published
by The Berkley Publishing Group,
a member of Penguin Putnam Inc.,
200 Madison Avenue, New York, NY 10016.
The name BERKLEY PRIME CRIME and the BERKLEY PRIME CRIME
design are trademarks belonging to Berkley Publishing Corporation.

PRINTED IN THE UNITED STATES OF AMERICA

10 9 8 7 6 5 4 3 2 1

For the girls of Palm Beach:
Gert Reich, May Burrows and Ria Simon

ACKNOWLEDGMENTS

According to most of my writer friends, only one acknowledgment for research help is required today—the Internet. But I still operate the old-fashioned way—I talk directly to people and not to a machine. I find that conversing enables me to get the benefit of their opinions and not just the facts. Thanks to Joseph L. Schwartz, esq. of Hollywood, Florida, who guided me through the legal labyrinth of Florida statutes. And to the Palm Beach Police Department for details on their procedures. Inspector Jane Perlov of the New York Police Department was also extremely helpful. Winchester, England was brought alive to me from walks around that beautiful city with James and Sonia Malloch together with Dennis Howe, whose encyclopedic knowledge of the city's history was invaluable. And, as always, thanks to my wonderful agent, Judith Riven, whose comments on my manuscript are invariably helpful.

SILVER
AND GUILT

I

ONE HAS TO be very still when attending an auction at Sotheby's. The first time I attended one of these fascinating events, I inadvertently scratched my sunburned nose and found I had become the possessor of a grotesque armless 17th-century Spanish chair which they told me was designed by someone named Tirazo but I think owed its provenance to Torquemada. I keep it in my New York apartment where I use it for seating insurance agents and other purveyors of boring but necessary services in order to ensure the brevity of their presentations.

When I'm in residence in my London King's Road flat, I always check out Sotheby's catalog to see if there's anything on current sale that could add to the visual pleasure I derive from any of my three abodes (I also have a villa in Portugal). The Emma Rhodes style of home decoration could be called ''Impetuous Collective''—if it grabs me, I grab it. I cannot understand people who must consult their decorators before daring to alter wall, window, or floor arrangements. Living in a place that someone else furnished would be like spending your life in a motel. But some people do not trust their own tastes and thus are doomed to accept the dictates of whomever they hire to furnish their homes. I wondered who would bid for the black sarcophagus that stood in the back corner of the room and could just imagine a decorator explaining enthusiastically to a client how this important piece in a foyer could set a unique if a trifle morbid Egyptian theme. The Madame Recamier-style chaise longue I noted on the side of the room would require an extensive wardrobe of suitably diaphanous gowns.

Right now, I'm after a lovely small oil painting the catalog describes as done by a "Follower of Fragonard" being offered for 500 to 800 pounds. I inspected it two days ago and fell in love with it, not only because I like Fragonard but probably because it depicts a little girl carrying flowers and wearing a white dress with a blue sash just like the one I had to wear as a flower girl at my nasty cousin Candace's wedding. The child has the same secret smile I had when I realized I looked adorable enough to outshine the bitchy bride.

The room was packed with many dealers whom I nodded to. One gets to know the regulars. A busy auction is like live theater and it looked like today would be a lively event. There is absolute silence in an auction room when the bidding begins, denoting the seriousness of the business being transacted. You can spot the professionals immediately by their totally impassive faces. They never betray the slightest interest in any piece being offered. The only sound you hear is the turning of catalog pages; the only action you see is the waving of green paddles to make their bids. I like to sit in a back row so that I can get a full view of the performance. Suddenly I realized the attendants were setting up "my painting" on the platform while the auctioneer began to describe it. I felt that frisson of excitement I always get when entering into action. I had mentally set myself a ceiling of 800 pounds which, as every seasoned bidder knows, is the only sure way to avert the disaster of auctionmania whereby the heat of competition drives you into imprudent insanity and you end up paying a thousand dollars for a brass spittoon worth sixty bucks or $200,000 for Jackie-O's *faux* pearls.

Suddenly I felt rather than heard a whooshing movement and a woman dropped down heavily into the seat next to me.

"Pardon me, terribly sorry, but have they brought in the Louis XV silver candelabra yet?"

I was about to cut her off sharply when I saw she was in the throes of acute distress. A handsome blonde woman of about forty-five, her brown Valentino suit was misbuttoned and the bow of her silk Liberty blouse had come open. Her diction said upper class and her clothes indicated wealth. Since the self-control of the English well-born is legendary, she was uncharacteristically distraught and panting heavily as though having run a distance. She looked vaguely familiar.

"Yes, the gavel went down on it about five minutes ago," I answered. "I believe it went for the hammer price, one million pounds."

She emitted a small scream and keeled over in a dead faint. I helped two Sotheby employees carry her outside to a sofa. She came to in minutes.

"I am so sorry to have caused this trouble," she said, trying to sit up. "What a very foolish thing to do."

"Shall we fetch a doctor, Lady Margaret?" asked one of the employees anxiously. Obviously they knew her. Now so did I.

She shook her head firmly. "No, not necessary. I'm fine—just a momentary thing. I shall be all right. You may go," she said in the dismissive tone with which the aristocracy have subjugated generations of the lower orders.

"Not to worry," I said to them as they stood there uneasily. "I'll stay with her ladyship."

She smiled at me thankfully. I held out my hand. "I'm Emma Rhodes."

"I'm Lady Margaret . . ."

"Duchess of Wykeham—yes, I know," I said. "We met at the Duke of Sandringham's some months ago."

Her eyes widened. "Of course, you're Lord Mark's friend—the one who does that extraordinary type of detective work. Dear God, how absolutely perfect to meet you here and now," she said fervently. "I am in desperate trouble—my marriage, perhaps my whole life is in jeopardy. Let me tell you what's happened and you'll see why I need help urgently."

Here we go again. People tell me things. There's something simpatica about either my face or manner that seems to engender confidences from even the most restrained and reticent individuals. It isn't just gratuitous outpourings to indulge themselves in the luxury of venting. They seem to sense that I can help them. And they're right. I can and will—for a price. I learned a number of years ago that my unusual talent for evoking confessions of dire personal *tsuras* from people, together with some other inborn qualities such as keen insight plus solid common sense backed up by a 165 I.Q., enabled me to find solutions to people's problems—quickly. I also discovered that these fortunately endowed traits can be the basis of a fine, lucrative profession.

I am a Private Resolver. It's a job title that's uniquely my own and is not listed in the yellow pages, which is why my parents have such difficulty explaining it to their friends. Don't confuse it with that struggling group of Private Eyes who have been portrayed in endless books as working on the side of the gods but living in a hellishly seedy state. Mine is a hugely satisfactory career that amply provides for my penchant for designer clothes and high living plus a personal freedom that is the envy of all my ex-colleagues whose seemingly extravagant compensation packages produce an actual yield of $18.75 per hour when you compute the eighty-hour weeks they're forced to put in for the hot-shot law firms that enslave them.

I heard the gavel come down in the other room and I sighed—there goes my little almost-Fragonard. Oh well, perhaps this visit to Sotheby's will increase my exchequer rather than deplete it. If I take on Lady Margaret's case, instead of paying out 800, I'll end up taking in the 12,500 pounds that is my regular fee.

"Why oh why did I ever go into the back of that closet," moaned Lady Margaret. "I was getting things together for our regular Sotheby's sale." Without a trace of embarrassment, she explained that the family periodically sold off items from their extensive accumulation of furnishings and works of art in order to pay the enormous taxes on Medthorpe Hall, the huge manor in Winchester that had been the ducal seat for over two hundred years. They were fortunate in thus being able to maintain the estate without having to resort to the extremes of other noble families who were forced to open their homes semi-weekly to charabancs of paying visitors who tramped through the place while the family huddled in a far corner hoping no curious wanderer found the doors that connect to their private apartments and wiped their hands on the crested linen towels.

"Gerald—that's my husband, the Duke, has been off shooting at Bodysgallen Hall in Wales for the past week, so he left it to me and Wilford, our butler, to sort out and prepare the shipment. I'd never done it before, you see, and

I was dead keen on doing it right," she said sadly.

I remembered hearing the seventy-three-year-old Duke had brought home a young wife last year to the chagrin of his mother, the dowager duchess who had been his hostess for the ten years since his first wife died. The marriage was widely regarded as a coup for Margaret, the well-born widow of a lesser member of the nobility. Her late husband, peerless in polo but a bust in business, had become a Rolls Royce salesman after squandering what small inheritance he had.

"Wilford and I had put together all the bits and pieces for Sotheby's pickup. Gerald had given me a list of the articles to go. They were in two closets in the east tower room."

"What sort of items?" I asked.

"Mostly large silver serving pieces. Gerald had explained to me that what with the servant problem and the huge cost of heating, the formal dining hall is rarely used now. The small informal family dining room is more suitable to our current simpler style of entertaining."

Don't get visions of them having to scale down their guest lists drastically. From my experience, the landed gentry's idea of a small dining room is about the size of two split levels in Scarsdale.

"When I saw that massive silver candelabra in the back of the closet," she continued, "I thought Gerald must have missed it since it was somewhat hidden. It was obviously totally useless since how can one use just a single candelabra?"

Beats me. It's not the sort of problem I get to deal with too often.

"So I had Wilford pack it up and include it in the shipment. Sotheby's came and took everything away a few days ago."

She began to unconsciously pull at her fingers in a way that told me the major source of agitation was about to unfold.

"Last night Lady Sibyl asked for the consignment list. She's the dowager duchess, my mother-in-law. She keeps the file because she has been doing it since Gerald's first wife died. You see, she had been Gerald's hostess during his widowed years and he did not want to make her feel *de trop* now that I'm there. She could have lived in the dower house, but Gerald felt she is too elderly to leave her apartment in the manor with us."

I got the feeling that the only one made to feel *de trop* by the marriage was the new wife.

"When she saw the candelabra on the list, she became absolutely apoplectic. Good heavens, she turned so red I thought she was about to have a stroke. She ranted and raved at me as though I was a scullery maid who had burnt the toast," she said bitterly. "And in front of the servants!"

Unforgivable.

"The way she carried on, you would have thought I sold one of her precious Corgis. She lavishes more attention on them than on members of the family."

Meaning you, poor dear. I can believe it. The English treat four-legged creatures with the unreserved love and affection that they seem unable to display to the two-legged varieties.

"When Gerald arrived home late last night, she was at the door to regale him with the details of my horrifying transgression," she said resentfully.

I guess a bitchy mother-in-law is a bitchy mother-in-law, no matter how charming the accent.

"What is it about this candelabra that makes it so special?" I asked.

She sighed. "As it was explained to me, there was a set

of four made in 1735 or thereabouts for King José I of Portugal by Thomas Termain, official silversmith to Louis XV and reputed to be the finest craftsman in the world. There was some war or other and a member of my husband's family performed a heroic service for King José who gave him two of the candelabras in gratitude. He sold one of them to raise enough money to buy extensive lands that started him on the way to great success. Shortly thereafter, he was granted the dukedom and the vast estates that went with it. Apparently the family regards and reveres the remaining candelabra as a sort of talisman that brought them good fortune and it has been passed from generation to generation as though it were the holy grail. The way Gerald and his mother talk about it, you would think the most dire consequences will befall the family unless that piece of silver is returned.'' She shook her head in disgust. ''The whole thing is incredible—why, it's just an old wives' tale!''

''Superstition is a funny thing,'' I said. ''Actually, it's a belief that a thing not logically connected to events can influence their outcome. It's the faith that omens can control our fate. If you think about it, isn't that the basis of many religions—usually someone else's?''

''But how can intelligent educated people hold with such nonsense?'' she asked.

''Nancy Reagan, Shirley MacLaine, anybody who knocks on wood, won't walk under ladders, or reads daily astrology charts. None of us has the right to question another's beliefs. If your husband's family feels the candelabra is endowed with unique properties, then you must honor it.''

''I know,'' she wailed. ''So please, please—you must get that infernal piece of silver back for me. My marriage depends on it!''

"What was your husband's reaction when he learned you had consigned it for sale?"

"You mean you didn't hear him?" she asked with a laconic smile. "I thought his bellowing would have carried from Winchester to London."

"I did hear some ear-splitting racket last night," I said, "but I figured it was the rock concert down at the docks." We both laughed. She had calmed down and her very pleasant personality was emerging.

"Sotheby's won't allow a seller to withdraw property at this late date," she said, "not after it's already in the catalog. So I arose at six this morning in order to be here and buy it back. I didn't want to risk having Thompson drive me in—the traffic from Winchester can be fearful—so I took the train. There was a derailment that held up all rail traffic into London for three hours. I sat there in agony for all that time," she said in a voice of abject misery. Then she looked at me with a face filled with hope.

"Finding things and solving delicate problems are what you do, isn't it, Emma?" We were now on an Emma-Margaret basis. "Lady Catherine told me you're a miracle worker . . . that you've resolved sensitive matters for some of her friends and they all praise you to the heavens. Perhaps God felt my pain and sent you here at this time."

I always find it amusing how some people envision God as running a sort of divine taxi service.

"You want me to retrieve your candelabra?" I asked.

"Please—oh yes."

I never accept a case unless I can be reasonably certain of fulfillment within two weeks. It's not ego that demands a 100 percent score record, which I have—it's economics. I require no money up front, no expenses, which means I don't make a nickel unless there's a successful outcome. The two-week time limit is self-imposed because of a personal character flaw. You see, I may have been blessed with a high I.Q., but I'm burdened with a very low threshold of boredom. If I can't reach a solution to any problem fast, it's instant ennui and I'm out of there. It used to drive my teachers up a wall until I told them I suffered from Minimal Focal Facility, a clinical term I made up to get them off my back when I couldn't show enthusiasm for subjects I found deadly dull and utterly useless.

I won't mention which courses because there are bound to be some of you who adored the disciplines I detested and may be making a fine living today working in just those fields. It's amazing how educators can be snowed by psychobabble. Perhaps it's because of the threat imposed by our litigious society and parents who might sue if you do not respect their darlings' so-called learning disabilities. I wonder what creative individual came up with Attention Deficit Syndrome?

Since I get no fee unless I fulfill the client's directive, I cannot afford to spend time on a potential loser. Which means I must do some research before I accept the matter.

I told Lady Margaret my terms—she didn't blink an eye at the 12,500 pound fee; that kind of money will only mean a few less frocks this season. I also told her I would have a yes-or-no decision within the hour.

I checked immediately with the desk to find out the name of the candelabra's buyer. Luckily it wasn't one of those guaranteed anonymity deals where the purchaser has asked to remain unidentified. Even better, it was a dealer whom I knew.

"Marcus—how are you?" I asked the tall sandy-haired mustached man who was sitting at an unsold French desk in the outer salesroom doing the paperwork on his just-completed purchases. He looked up and his face broke out in a broad smile.

"Emma, how lovely to see you. I noticed you inside—did you get what you came for?"

I shook my head. "It was that follower-of-Fragonard painting."

"Shame. Were you outbid?"

"No—I never got a chance. There was a little to-do in my row and I got involved."

"Oh yes—I heard the duchess popped off her seat. Unlike some of the other members of our so-called good families, she's not known to tipple heavily with the cooking sherry, so perhaps it's PMS. Ladies seem to attribute all sorts of bizarre behavior to that condition."

"You know Lady Margaret?" I asked.

"Certainly. Most dealers are familiar with members of the Wykeham family. One or the other is often around flogging ancestral objects. What the laws of primogeniture did to save our vast estates, the laws of taxation are working to destroy." He shook his head sadly.

"But isn't that what keeps you antique dealers in business?" I asked with a smile.

He laughed. "Quite right, my dear. I've always admired your perception as well as your beauty."

"Case in point: you just bought the Wykeham's candelabra, didn't you?"

He eyed me shrewdly. "Do I detect an interest? A bit over your usual, isn't it, Emma? I've never known you to get into the seven-figures category. Did some auntie die and leave you pots of money? However, it's not for sale—even to you, love. I bought it for a client, one of your country folk actually."

"An American? Probably one of those New York yuppie types."

"No, but she lives quite well in that posh enclave, Palm Beach, thank you very much. Matter of fact, I have a good

number of clients there. Most of them are trying to create
instant backgrounds for themselves. You know, they tell
their friends that the pair of chenets I bought for them are
old family heirlooms and the Bombe Regence Walnut
Commode circa 1730 has been in the family for generations. When I send them the bill, besides giving them the
provenance of the objects, I have to be sure to tell them
how to pronounce them. But this particular client is different, thank heavens. She collects only seventeenth- and
eighteenth-century silver very selectively and money is no
object. In other words, a perfect client.''

"Oh? What's her name, Marcus? I have so many friends
there. I probably know her.''

He shook his head. ''Sorry, love, can't divulge. It would
be a violation of confidence. Sort of like a lawyer or priest,
you know.''

No matter. I knew. It could only be Bootsie Corrigan. I
met her ten years ago in Vancouver BC when the law firm
I worked for sent me there to handle details of her husband's complex far-flung holdings. After he died, she took
his vast fortune and moved to Palm Beach where her ec-
centricities have become as legendary as her collection of
eighteenth-century silver which covers tables and myriad
niches in her sprawling beachfront mansion and keeps a
staff of four polishing daily. I know a lot of eccentric people. Of course, they're loaded. When you're poor, peculiar
behavior labels you as a loon. But if you're a rich oddball,
you're termed an eccentric.

I told Lady Maragaret I would take the case and would
get back to her within two weeks. She was relieved and
delighted, but then a shadow crossed her face.

"Whatever shall I tell Gerald in the meantime?'' she
groaned.

"As my father always told me, the truth is the best lie.''

II

THE WEATHER WAS warm, but not half as warm as my welcome. Bootsie nearly knocked me to the tiles in her palazzzo-like entry hall as she threw the considerable weight of her body at me and wrapped me in her arms.

"Emma—sweetie! It's great to see you!" Her bright red hair was tied back in a ponytail which somehow seemed perfectly suitable to a woman of her sixty-some years. She was one of those beautiful heavy women who are fortunate enough to have their weight confined only to their bodies and have no jowls or double chin to mar a smooth neckline. On anyone else, I would have suspected plastic surgery, but Bootsie was one of those "take me as I am" people who is totally unselfconscious about cosmetic shortcomings. Born on a farm in Louisiana, she was perfectly comfortable with her humble roots and reveled joyously in the good fortune of marrying a man who became a billionaire.

"Now don't tell me you're here for just a week—it's the height of the season and you absolutely must stay until the festivities are over. I need you—you'll give my parties real class. I'm sick of all those scrawny face-lifted blondes

talking in that whispery voice they think is Jackie Kennedy
Newport but sounds more like Madonna with laryngitis.
Not only are you naturally gorgeous but you have a brain.
It'll be refreshing to hear conversation other than who's
fucking who and why the latest divorcée just had to have
her husband's private jet in the settlement so that she could
fly to Madison Avenue to have her hair done every week.''

The chauffeur had picked me up at the airport in one of
Bootsie's Bentleys—she regarded Rolls Royce as the ostentatious choice of rock stars and considered the absence
of the bird hood ornament on the Bentley a sign of under-
stated elegance. As we turned into the driveway of her
sprawling pink stone beachfront mansion on Ocean Boulevard, the profusion of colors provided by what looked like
thousands of vividly toned tropical flowers against the turquoise Atlantic and a cloudless blue sky made me gasp with
pleasure, as always.

I visit Bootsie whenever I feel the need for beach and
sun attendant with the totally sybaritic luxury of a private
suite facing the ocean, a personal maid who actually draws
baths and irons your clothes, and four-star cuisine. Bootsie
is the perfect hostess: she adores having guests, gives you
a rousing welcome, the run of the house and grounds, and
then blissfully ignores you for the rest of your stay.

Like many other Americans, I used to fly off to some
Caribbean island to get away from winter's ice and cold.
Florida was strictly for the cane-and-wheelchair set. Then
a few years ago, Bootsie invited me to stay for one memorable week in February and I discovered I didn't need steel
bands playing ''Yellow Bird'' in order to enjoy a vacation.
When I want out from the winter blues, I want palm trees,
beach, sun, wall-to-wall luxury, and total indulgence.
Which is why I love staying at Bootsie's.

This stay, of course, will be work and not just play—but

what a way to work. If I haven't mentioned it before, do I have the best job in the world or what? My former colleagues who continue to toil in the repressive canyons of Wall Street will look enviously at my tanned skin and tranquil stress-free mien and gripe that I have all the luck. Bull crap and balderdash, I say, and then I treat them again (and you, too, if you've read my earlier books) to the Emma Rhodes Conveyor Belt Theory of Life. It states that during one's lifetime, everyone has a number of opportunities that pass before them. The person who has the keen perception to recognize the potential of an opportunity, the guts to take the risk of acting upon it, and the ability and drive to make a success of it is inevitably labeled as ''lucky.'' One makes one's own luck. I did.

My *momento de verdad* was a chance meeting with a troubled wealthy English woman on a hydrofoil voyage from Copenhagen to Malmo, Sweden, when I suddenly realized I could solve her problem and make twenty thousand dollars for ten days work in doing so. To the horror of my friends and parents, I threw aside the big-bucks job of associate in a major law firm. To the world at large, I was indeed the personification of a successful young attorney who had it made. But I was never one to care about outward appearances. The reality was I just couldn't see the purpose of working eighty-hour weeks to make a huge salary with no time to spend it. So here I am living a positively hedonistic life on a billionaire's Palm Beach estate, working at my own free and easy pace. All this and I make money yet.

I didn't bring up the subject of the candelabra until the next evening. To have done so earlier would have been pushy, bad taste, and downright stupid. We were having dinner in the glass-walled dining room that faced the exquisite gardens kept blooming by an army of gardeners—

not your usual untrained laborers who just arrived in this country yesterday and can't distinguish a weed from a prize *Duchesse de Brabant* pink rose but a well-trained cadre supervised by a skilled horticulturist. Bootsie's hospitality rules ran to come-when-and-if-you-wish buffet breakfast from eight to ten, lunch from twelve to two. Dinner was a sit-down affair which you were expected to attend unless you notified the kitchen accordingly. Casual dress, of course, but Palm Beach casual which precluded jeans and required jackets but no ties for men.

The room was approximately forty-five by twenty-five feet with an antique mahogany refractory table that had at times accommodated sixty but was now closed down to cozily hold four of us. The table was set with pink Wedgewood and James Robinson silver. Bootsie's house was a rambling mix of pink stone and glass built by a local architect who knew how to site the house suitably for sea and sun. Being familiar with the problems of tropical living, he didn't make the error of putting large expanses of glass facing west which would make the interior a broiling oven until sunset. The dining room faced east which offered a cheerfully sunny room for breakfast and a lovely cool one for lunch and dinner.

Besides me and Bootsie were her nephew and heir, Jonathan Carswell, and her charming titled Portuguese live-in lover, Count José do Figuera. I had met Jonathan many times and liked him enormously. He was a tall man with the broad shoulders and muscled physique of a swimmer and athlete. He wore his curly brown hair slightly long and I noticed some gray in the sideburns but he was forty-one and entitled to some signs of maturity. It looked good next to his tanned skin and bright blue eyes. There was a sweetness in his face that reflected the idealism that made him take up the career of high school science teacher rather than any of the high-income professions that his scholastic standing would have permitted. He was graduated magna cum laude from MIT and had a Master's degree from Harvard. Jonathan was the only son of Bootsie's sister who, along with her husband, was killed when the boy was fourteen. Bootsie, who had no children, took him into her home and brought him up lovingly. It was always a delight to be with them since they obviously had great affection for each other.

The Count, however, was a complete stranger to me. He was the present incumbent consort, with a long line of predecessors. Bootsie was known for her lusty tastes and I had not always agreed with her choices but this time I approved. Count José had that unusual mixture of tan skin and green eyes that makes Portuguese men so attractive, and was one of the reasons I had bought my villa in the Algarve. Of medium height, he carried himself regally in a way that gave the impression of a tall stature. His English was only slightly accented and his manners were impeccable. All and all, the ideal consort if you could afford it. No reference was made to his business or profession, so I guessed that his tan linen Armani blazer, beige silk shirt and slacks, and olive-colored Hèrmes scarf had been charged on Bootsie's American Express card.

"I see you are admiring the candelabras," said the Count.

"Yes," I answered. "They're extraordinarily beautiful. I don't think I've ever seen anything like them before."

"Damn straight," said Bootsie. "José tells me there are only four of them in the world. They're Portuguese."

"No, *querida*," he said with a smile. "They were made by a French craftsman for the King of Portugal. Their provenance is French, but they *belonged* to the Portuguese."

"And now they're mine," she said with delight.

Somehow I sensed this wasn't the time to bring up the reason for my visit.

Jonathan looked puzzled. "Didn't you used to have only one?" he asked. "I seem to remember seeing it in the center of the table at Thanksgiving. I was so proud that you put me facing you at the foot of the table. But I remember bouncing back and forth in my seat to try to see you over the candelabra."

Bootsie smiled at him fondly. "You were my man of the house, Johnny boy. That's why you sat at the foot of my table and me at the head."

"Not any more," he said with a smile, looking at Count José who now occupied the host's place.

"Quite right, darling. I'm no longer your number one honeybun either. Let's see, there was Squiffy Huttendon when you were fifteen, followed by Muffy Morgan when you were sixteen, then you went into your exotic ethnic stage and we had Conchita Melendez followed by Rosie Velasquez. Then there were those troops of unmade-up long-haired lovelies who looked interchangeable. I think they owned one Indian-print dress among them and never had time to wash it. And now we have Melissa. When the hell are you two going to get married? You've lived together for two years, for God's sakes."

Jonathan smiled patiently. This was obviously a much-discussed point.

"Don't you think it's time they tied the knot, Emma?" she asked me.

"If you're looking for corroboration you're asking the wrong person, Bootsie. You don't see any band of gold on my finger, do you?"

She looked surprised. "I wouldn't expect to, Emma—you're having too great a time having lovers all over the world. You'd be crazy to tie yourself down."

"You mean marriage is only good for old sticks-in-the-mud like Melissa and me?" said Jonathan sardonically.

"Don't be silly, darling. You two are lucky enough to have found the right one with whom you want to spend the rest of your life. It's time you admitted it and formalized the deal. Marriage to the right person is the most marvelous way to live. My years with Buck were the happiest anyone could experience. There's a sense of oneness and mutual commitment that makes the present wonderful and the future exciting. I probably sound like a Hallmark card, but there's no more joyful and satisfying life than one a young married couple faces together, if they're right for each other."

Jonathan leaned over and kissed her. Count José sat looking quiet and thoughtful. Bootsie put her hand over his.

"You and I are too young to die and too old to be newlyweds. I think it's perfect this way."

He kissed her hand and smiled. "I am quite content, my darling Bootsie."

"How long are you staying here, Emma?" asked Jonathan.

"I'm not quite sure. It depends on if and when I accomplish my mission."

Bootsie shrugged. *"Mi casa es su casa, love,"* she said. "There's no one waiting on line to get your room. Stay as long as you like. You know I love having you."

Count José's somewhat bushy eyebrows went up quizzically. "You have a mission here, Emma? You are perhaps raising funds for some fine and worthy cause?"

"You bet," said Bootsie with a laugh. "Emma raises money for the best cause in the world—Emma Rhodes."

He looked confused. "Excuse me. You must be of the new breed of career women I hear about but seem to run into rarely. All the young and beautiful women I see here in your Palm Beach spend their time either giving parties or going to parties for some charity or other. May I ask what you do?''

Bootsie leaned back in her chair and laughed. "Go ahead, honey. See if you can explain it to him. I sure as hell never could.''

"I'm a Private Resolver.''

He looked dumbfounded.

"I resolve touchy situations for people who have gotten themselves into troubles they wish to keep private.''

"Is this something like those Private Investigators you are so fond of in your American films and books?''

I've been forced to go through this sort of explanation many times and it's a pain in the ass. But one must be patient and not rude. Besides, since I don't run ads in the yellow pages, I must depend for business solely on recommendation or as they call it, word of mouth. So it's important that I put the right words in the right mouths.

"Sort of. But I don't just investigate, I resolve the situation.''

"In just two weeks, for twenty thousand dollars. And she never fails,'' said Bootsie proudly.

The Count looked at me admiringly.

"You are most certainly a *unica*, Emma. In my country, that's what we call a person who is one of a kind.''

"She sure as hell is special. I hope you're staying until Thursday, darling. That's the Red Cross Ball—the highlight of the season as you undoubtedly know. I've taken my usual table and there's plenty of room. Goddamned table cost me a quarter-of-a-million bucks so I like to see every seat filled.''

Today being Tuesday, I was fairly sure I would be here through then.

"If you need a ball gown, I'm afraid you're shit-out-of-luck if you want to borrow one of mine." She looked at my size eight figure and down at her robust size eighteen and giggled.

"No need, Bootsie," I said. "I always consider the social customs as well as the climate when I pack. When I travel to Nairobi, I take carry-on luggage filled with chinos, shirts, and shorts. When I go to Palm Beach, I take a suitcase filled with ball gowns."

The butler came in with a huge silver coffee service.

Bootsie arose from the table. "Rivers," she said, "I think we'll have our coffee on the terrace."

"Yes, madam," he said with a Michael Caine accent.

"I'm afraid I can't stay, Auntie," said Jonathan. "I have to pick up Melissa." He turned to me. "She's a school psychologist and tonight's her parent conference night. She'll be finishing up soon." He kissed me and his aunt goodbye and left.

Bootsie looked after him proudly. "They're two wonderful kids. They care about people, not things. Their only concern is to help."

"That, my dear, is a luxury for the rich. It is only the financially secure who can enjoy the pleasure of doing for others," said Count José.

"That may be true. But Jonathan has never been concerned with possessions or acquiring, or luxuries," said Bootsie as we strolled out of the room. "With the money I settled on him when he was twenty-one, he could be living a helluva lot better than that small house in West Palm Beach, and he could drive a Mercedes instead of a Toyota and have a wardrobe from Georgio's instead of getting everything mail order from Eddie Bauer. A big dining-out evening for him and Melissa is Charlie's Crab. The young, loaded Palm Beach crowd of Jonathan's age are happy to contribute tax-free money to dance the night away at glamorous benefit balls that raise money for the education of underprivileged youth, but they'd cross the street in horror if they came anywhere near one of them. Jonathan and Melissa live among them, teach them, and befriend them."

She put her arm through his. "I know you saw a lot of poverty in Portugal, and didn't always have an easy time of it yourself so maybe you can't find anything admirable about someone who was lucky enough to never have to struggle. I wasn't exactly raised with a silver spoon in my mouth. There were five of us on the farm, my sister and brothers and my mom and dad, so we only had five spoons, five forks, and five knives. And they were tin. It wasn't till I was seventeen and got my first job and ate at a lunch counter that I found out that forks had more than two tines and spoons didn't necessarily have to be unbent every time you used them. We had no choices, we just tried to survive. But kids like Jonathan and Melissa have choices—and they choose to live simply and give to others rather than only to themselves."

The Count turned to her and hugged her. "You are a good woman, Bootsie. Which is why I admire as well as love you." And then he kissed her deeply on the lips.

"Will you ladies excuse me?" he asked. "I have some correspondence to take care of."

It was a beautiful evening. We settled into comfortable rattan chairs and sipped our coffee in quiet contentment. Bootsie's home was furnished like no other Palm Beach home I had visited. She hated fashionable decorators.

"I can't see paying a fortune for some ratty-looking old tables and chairs and then spending another fortune to have them stripped and repainted and re-upholstered. And their color schemes—I can tell what year a house was 'done' by the colors. One year everything was turquoise and salmon, another year it was avocado and gold. Then those peculiar doodads they put all around to give your home 'character.' Whose character? Sure as hell not mine. I'll fill my home with my own *chatchkas*, thank you very much. Everything you see here is either a memento of Buck's and my life or something I chose and wanted. Every single piece makes me feel sentimental, or proud, or just plain happy.''

"Like that exquisite Aubusson rug hanging in your entry hall?" I said with a smile.

"Yeah—ain't that a beauty? I just love the silky look and the reds they use to make those flowers.''

I looked at it admiringly. "You have a good eye, Bootsie. This is one of the best Aubussons I've ever seen.''

She looked at the rug with proprietary pride. "Damned straight. Bet you can't tell me what that darling rug is worth.''

"In the neighborhood of two hundred thousand dollars, I'd say.''

She laughed in delight. "Fantastic. Exactly right. When I first heard the price, I can tell you even I was shocked out of my gourd. I saw it at Milo Pachurian's shop. He's my neighbor and owns probably the two fanciest rug shops in Florida—one in Hobe Sound and one on Worth Avenue. But I thought hell, it's only money and I really like the thing and it ain't going to change my lifestyle if I buy it. But that dirt-poor little farm girl still sits on my shoulder, Emma. I can't buy a pig in a poke. So I did a little research. Did you know they were all handmade in the little village of Aubusson from the 14th century on? Louis XIV, XV, XVI, Marie Antoinette and Madame de Pompadour owned them and Napoleon loved them—he had them in all his palaces.''

"I'm impressed, Bootsie," I said. "You really did your homework.''

"Before I spring for that kind of money, honey, I damned well have to know what I'm getting. I used to be one of those buyers salesmen love. I'd believe every word they'd tell me. Then Buck took me in hand. 'In God we trust' he said—'no one else.' He taught me to question everything."

Her face took on a smug, canny look. "So I did a bit of wheeler-dealer stuff with Milo, and believe me, I paid a lot less." She eyed the rug with pleasure. "I did OK, right?"

"I'd say you did fine. And you can always resell it for the same price or more. That's the great advantage of antiques."

When the building of her house was completed, she spent a week in Bloomingdale's and a few days in Burdine's and then filled in with Pier 1. The result is a wonderful and inviting mix that reflects her *joi de vivre* and unpretentiousness. It's a home, not a showplace and is a delight to live in and visit.

"I see Rivers is still with you. He's the only English butler I know who speaks with a Liverpool accent. Have you ever thought of sending him to Berlitz to improve his diction?"

"What the hell for? Most of the phonies down here couldn't tell Liverpool from Louisiana. He's the faithful family retainer and I couldn't do without him. Though I must admit he's getting a bit long in the tooth—which means he's moving slower and forgetting faster."

"I remember him in Vancouver. There was some story as I recall about Buck finding him in the streets."

She smiled fondly. "Not quite. He came into the soup kitchen with his little boy where Buck used to volunteer two nights a week. My Buck was one of those no-nonsense saints who helped anyone he could without making a fuss about it. I remember it vividly—it was 1977 and we had a terrible winter there. Buck came home and told me about this poor fellow who was intelligent and educated but had obviously been in some sort of trouble and was now forced to live in the streets with his little boy who was retarded or something. He wanted to bring them home—we had a big house—and was that all right with me. Rivers worked for us and was wonderful from day one. He took over right away. Lord, I just don't know what I'd ever have done without him.''

"What happened to the little boy?"

"He was a dear little thing. He lived with us for a while until it was time for him to go to school. Buck found a special school for him and he went to live there."

"Where is he now?"

"Well, I don't really know. I think in some special place for folks like him."

"I wonder if you would be so quick to do that today. I mean, bring a strange man into your home, no references, totally unknown to you," I said.

"References!" she snorted. "Call someone for references and you think you get the truth? Even if the sucker broke all the china and was caught pawing through madam's jewelry, you think they're going to tell you? They're glad to be shot of the bastard and are afraid to say a bad word about him for fear he'll come after them or sue for defamation of character. If you ask them why they let this paragon go, they tell you some crap about their lifestyle change no longer requiring his services. The best references are your own eyes and ears. Buck was a good man and a wonderful judge of people."

"He must've been," I said. "He picked you."

She roared with laughter. "Girl, you got that wrong. Why, I chased that man half across Louisiana until I let him catch me. He didn't have a pot to piss in, but I knew a good thing when I saw it."

After a few minutes of silence as we listened to the marvelous sounds of the waves, I brought up the object of my visit.

"Bootsie, I mentioned my mission before. It involves you."

She looked surprised. "Me?"

"You and your lovely candelabra."

I told her the entire story. She listened quietly.

"So you're here to persuade me to sell the candelabra back to Lady Margaret."

"Yes."

"Then I'm afraid this is the case that will break your 100 percent record, honey. Don't bother telling me you'll up the price and give me a tidy profit. You know the money doesn't matter to me. I love you dearly, Emma, but I won't sell it."

"Why not? "I asked.

I wasn't troubled by her negative response to my initial overture. To me, "no" is merely the beginning of any negotiation.

"I like the way the pair looks on my table. You heard Jonathan—we used to have only the one which I bought maybe twenty-five years ago. It never looked right standing there all by its lonely. So when José saw it in the Sotheby catalog, I called Marcus in London and told him to buy it for me. José tells me the original set was four, and I've told Marcus to keep an eye out for the others. They're bound to come on the market sometime."

I nodded in understanding. I know many collectors and they are a fanatic, tough and determined breed. But Bootsie has a soft edge which I was counting on.

"To you, Bootsie, this candelabra is just a decorative

object that you enjoy having. But to Lady Margaret, it can mean the total disintegration of her marriage.''

"I gotta tell you, Emma, it's really tough for me to whip up any sympathy for any of those snotty British aristocrats. Prince Charles keeps some horses at the Jockey Club. A lot of them come over here to play polo, you know, and I run into them often. They have a healthy respect for wealth, all right, but if you're not of the landed gentry and God forbid you made your money in trade, you're rated two steps above the garbage collector. Believe me, if the positions were reversed, she wouldn't give a shit for me.''

I kept quiet. Not only because I happen to agree with her, but I have always found that silence is the best position to take when someone is spewing their anger. I was depending on the fact that Bootsie has a very soft heart.

"And what were they doing keeping this gorgeous piece of silver—a work of art—tossed in the back of a closet?" she fumed. "They weren't even enjoying it, or displaying it to let others enjoy it. For them, it's just a lucky charm, like a goddamned rabbit's foot. They don't deserve to have it.''

I sipped my coffee and looked at the lovely star-studded sky and the flickering lights of a liner anchored offshore.

"You're right, Bootsie. But a piece of silver, no matter how lovely, is only a piece of silver. For you, it means just another addition to your vast collection. Having it or not won't change your life any. But to Lady Margaret, it has a far greater significance that will in effect change her life drastically. Ridiculous as it may seem to us egalitarian Americans, the English nobility attribute tremendous importance to ancestral elements. To the Duke and the Dowager Duchess, the fact that Margaret was responsible for the loss of a vital cog in their family history would weigh against her forever.''

Bootsie snorted. "You mean that tight-assed lord husband and his bitch of a mother would put Maggie on their permanent shit list if she didn't bring it back?"

"You got it," I said.

"Say, I'm finding it a bit chilly out here," she said. "I think I'll go inside and watch a little TV."

That was her way of saying "No more talk. Let me think about it." The first step in my campaign was completed.

III

"PARDON ME, MISS Rhodes—there's a call for you."
It was Rivers, the butler. He handed me a portable phone.

"Emma, *bubele*, I can't wait to see you. Is your bikinied bod already gorgeously tan or maybe you've gone topless and the viewing is even more glorious?"

I smiled. "Abba! Where are you calling from?"

"Right around the corner—just down the road apiece," he said triumphantly.

"What are you doing this far from the Negev?" I asked.

"They sent me here on an Israeli Bond tour. There's enough fucking money in this garden of gelt to equip the Israeli Air Force and the house I'm staying in could accommodate all of them."

I laughed. "You on a bond tour? Making speeches to convince people to buy bonds? Somehow I can't picture you hat in hand pleading for contributions."

"First place, with us Jews the hat's always on the head. Secondly, I'm an absolute knockout. I come on stage in my uniform, the one with the bulletholes in the hat—you know, the man of action. They're already awed by this hero. Then

I thrill them with tales of dangerous Mossad activities—and by the time I'm through, they're so excited half the men have to change their underwear and with the women, there isn't a dry eye in the house.''

Abba is my best friend and favorite person in the world, right after my parents. He's a Brooklyn-born boy who ended up as a top officer of the Israeli Mossad. He's the only person I would trust my life to unequivocally.

"How did you find out I was here in Palm Beach?" I asked.

"Surely you jest, my good woman," he answered. "Have you forgotten I am a member of the finest spy organization in the world? We have our top secret methods."

"How?" I asked.

"I called your mother''—and he roared with laughter.

I invited him over for dinner the next night. I knew Bootsie would love to meet him. Abba is five feet nine, weighs 250 pounds, has a keen intelligence and an ebullient personality that make him the darling of every woman he meets.

When he arrived, Bootsie's eyes were shining with delight. "Abba, you're a treat. You look like a teddy bear, but I bet you charm the pants off women."

I groaned. "Bootsie, don't get him started. His conquest list goes into double digits and I can attest to the validity of his claims."

Abba beamed expansively. "Except for Emma, whose constant rejections have kept me humble."

"Isn't that what friends are for, dear?" I said sweetly.

He had elected to come in his uniform which gave him a distinctive élan that could never be achieved in mufti. His first greeting to Bootsie when she came into the living room wearing a colorful silk caftan made of numerous saris with her red hair done up in a smooth French twist, was "Ma-

dame, you are absolutely dazzling. And if not for the daunt-
ing presence of this gentleman to whom I presume you
have more than a casual attachment, I would start by kissing your hand and probably never stop.''

She gave a hearty shout of delighted laughter.

"Lord love ya, I adore a man who bullshits with style!
Abba, you're a man after my own heart.''

"Ah, my dear—but that's not the only part of you I'm
after.''

"Abba,'' I said with mock annoyance, "you sound like
Groucho Marx. Bootsie, I apologize for the behavior of my
friend.''

"Are you kidding?'' said Bootsie. "Emma, this is the
best gift you've brought since you shipped me those
twenty–five-pound bags of andouille sausage and vidalia
onions.'' And she put her arm through Abba's and said,
"Won't you lead me into the dining room, kind sir?''

Dinner was a hoot. There were six of us—Jonathan
brought Melissa. Abba had them laughing and talking and
even the usually quiet Melissa was animated.

"Mmm, what is this marvelous soup?'' asked Abba as
he started his second helping.

"José made it,'' said Bootsie proudly. "He's a fantastic
cook.''

"It is from my country,'' said Count José. "It's called
Acorda com Ameijoas and is made with clams, lobster, and
chourico sausage.''

"Omigod,'' said Bootsie, putting her hand to her mouth.
"It's not kosher. Abba, I'm sorry—I didn't think.''

"Not to worry, *motek* darling—we Jews are a nation of
many opinions and points of view, even in the way we deal
with our religion. Me, I observe *kashruth* in my home but
outside, the world's my oyster—which, by the way, isn't
kosher, nor are clams. In other words, I can't cook it, but

I sure as hell can eat it," he said with relish as he dunked bread into his bowl.

"You can't ask for the recipe, Abba," I said, "but I can. José—would you kindly give it to me?"

"If it's one of those all-day-slaving-over-the-stove jobs, forget it," said Abba. "Emma is a great cook, but it's got to be strictly fast foods."

"I just can't see spending a whole day preparing anything that's consumed in ten minutes," I said. "When I look at a recipe, if the list of ingredients is more than an inch long, and the prep time takes more than an hour, I'm out of there. I'm not one of those hostesses who believes in conspicuous competence. I have friends who take three weeks to whip up a dinner party for six. They use words like infused oils, minceurs, and lemon grass and they'd rather walk stark naked into Le Cirque than be caught serving iceberg lettuce. They gave up serving radicchio before I learned how to pronounce it. I have one friend who serves marvelous food but makes eating it a chore for the guests because she serves every course with an apology. If you try to assure her that it's delicious, she looks at you with disdain because obviously you have a peasant palate. But if you agree with her statement that something didn't turn out right, she's a basket case for the rest of the evening. My ego is not tied up in my cooking. So yes, please—I would love the recipe."

José smiled with pleasure. "I think you will find this very simple. I will tell you only ingredients and procedures— quantities are up to you, depending on how many people you wish to serve. You fry clams together with cut-up chourico sausage. When done, pour them with their juices into a large pot where you have been sautéing in olive oil, garlic, green pepper, chopped parsley, and cubes of good heavy bread. Then put in pieces of lobster to brown. Add salt, pepper, and then water as needed. The proportion of water to ingredients depends upon the pocketbook of the cook. I shall write it all down for you, Emma.''

"No need, Count," said Abba. ''That computer brain of hers has it all down. She could recite it back to you exactly as you said it.''

"Truly?'' asked the Count, looking at me curiously.

I hate showing off. My parents used to ask me to perform feats of memory for friends and family until I rebelled when I was twelve and embarrassed them by coming in with our dog's leash and collar around my neck. ''If you want a performing pet,'' I said, ''then I should dress like one.'' They never did it again.

"Go ahead, *ahuvati*," said Abba teasingly. ''Show the nice people how smart you are.''

I looked at him balefully. He knew the story.

"Go ahead, Emma," said everyone at the table. ''Can you really remember the recipe word for word?''

What the hell. So I did.

Everybody clapped, so I stood up and bowed.

"Ain't she the smartest gal ever?'' said Bootsie in delight.

"Fuckin' A,'' said Abba proudly. ''Oops! I beg your pardon," and he looked apologetically at Bootsie.

She laughed. ''You can't be apologizing to me, Abba honey. I grew up on a farm. Fucking wasn't a word, it was a barnyard activity. And Melissa works at one of those inner-city schools where that's probably the kids' adjective of choice. José, though, he's a gentleman—you may have offended him.''

Count José waved his hand. ''Not at all. I have been in the United States long enough to become used to the use of that word. In the movies, on television. Actually, when I had first come to this country someone took me to see a

play by your famous playwright, David Mamet I believe
his name is. I was puzzled by the constant use of the word.
We have a word in Portuguese—'pois'—which we use all
the time. It really means not too much, like 'then'—sort of
as a comment one makes during pauses in another's conversation, much as you use 'uh-huh.' So I assumed that
perhaps was what 'fucking' meant. Well, I used it just that
way at a dinner party I was taken to and the silence at the
table told me right away I had done something very
wrong.''

We all laughed at his story, Abba the loudest.

''Profanity gets to be a bad habit,'' he said. ''I try to
curb it.''

''But not very hard, I've noticed,'' I said dryly.

''How long are you going to be in Palm Beach, Abba?''
asked Count José.

Abba shrugged. ''Another week, at least. I think I'm off
to Fort Lauderdale then.''

''Wonderful!'' said Bootsie. ''Then you can join us at
the Red Cross Ball.''

''What's that?'' he asked, looking at me.

''It's the biggest charity bash of the season. Everyone
who's anyone in Palm Beach will be there.''

''Ah yes,'' he said. ''One of those affairs where everyone assuages their guilt for their gelt by paying what for
me is a month's salary for a ticket which they feel entitles
them to dance and drink the night away in gowns that cost
another month's salary.''

Jonathan became serious and Melissa took on the self-
righteous look of those committed to causes.

''He's absolutely right, Aunt Bootsie,'' said Melissa with
humorless intensity. ''Those balls are truly decadent.
Abba's disapproval is to his credit.''

Bootsie looked at them with a fond smile and then turned

to Abba. "Abba, would you like to go as my guest?"

"You bet your ass I would," he said enthusiastically. He turned to the earnest young couple. "A little depravity is good for the soul. It keeps your values straight. Besides, why should those fuckers have all the fun?"

After Jonathan and Melissa had left, pleading the need to attend a community meeting regarding the closing of a much-needed neighborhood playground to make way for yet another luxury condominium, Bootsie looked after them and shook her head. "I admire their dedication, but I wish Melissa would lighten up a little. I sympathize with Jonathan's concern for people and justice, but I wouldn't want him to turn into another Ralph Nader and spend his life living in a third-floor walkup wearing shiny seventy-dollar suits."

"I wouldn't worry, Bootsie *tsotskele*," said Abba. "They're young. The saying goes that if you're not a liberal when you're young, you have no heart and if you're not a conservative when you're old, you have no brain. My communist sister-in-law wouldn't accept a decadent diamond engagement ring from my brother, but three years later when she got pregnant and quit her city job, she used her payout pension money to buy herself the biggest, longest mink coat you ever saw. It's easy to scorn bourgeois luxuries when you live high on your emotions. Give them a few more years when the class struggle begins to pall and they'll be out shopping for BMWs like the rest of the yuppies."

"You are indeed a sage, my friend Abba," said the Count with a smile.

Abba shook his head. "Moses was a sage. Jesus was a sage. Me, I'm just a kid who grew up in a neighborhood that wasn't a melting pot, it was a smelting pot. Everybody was boiling with emotion. We believed the landlords were the enemy and the rich got that way from exploiting the poor. And you never trusted Authority because they were out to shit all over you if you didn't fight them every step.''

"Then somebody took him to Lutece for dinner and his philosophy changed overnight," I added.

He laughed. "I learned that a lot of the rich got that way by busting ass and being smarter than the next guy. And I stopped assuming that a guy's a putz just because he wears a Rolex."

"My husband had a little hardware store in Bogalusa, Louisiana when we got married," said Bootsie. "Then for our honeymoon, we went to visit his brother in Vancouver and he saw Asians moving in, taking their money out of Hong Kong in preparation for the Chinese takeover. So he hocked everything we had, and started to buy land, mortgaged one piece to buy another and soon he owned half of downtown Vancouver. He was the sweetest man you'd ever meet, he never hurt a soul." She sighed. "He had a lot of years to enjoy his money—but not long enough." Her eyes filled with tears and José put his hand over hers.

"I remember Buck vividly, Bootsie," I said, "and he adored you. For sure he's looking down and getting a big kick out of watching you enjoy his money."

"So what do I wear to this hoo-ha ball? I didn't pack formal dress, matter of fact, I don't own any," said Abba. "So I figure I can come as I am and look colorful instead of just handsome."

"With your beard and that uniform, they're liable to think you're Castro and if word gets to Miami and Hialeah, there may be fireworks that the hosts didn't plan on," I said.

He shrugged. "It's a Red Cross Ball—aren't they trained to handle casualties?"

"Nonsense," said Bootsie, "I think he looks cute. Besides, with the money I've paid for that table, any guest of mine could wear a diaper and come as Gandhi and no one would dare say a word.''

Abba's eyes lit up. ''Don't tempt me.''

''Somehow I don't think you could carry that off, Abba,'' I said.

''Why not?'' he asked. ''Just because Gandhi was clean-shaven?''

''I know you fast every year on Yom Kippur, my love, but one day of starving hasn't exactly given you that lean emaciated look. Besides, this isn't a costume ball.''

'Maybe I should wear a patch over my eye and they'll think I'm Moshe Dayan.''

''He died years ago,'' I said.

''You think these goyem know that?''

''No, and they undoubtedly don't know who he was anyway.''

Abba looked surprised. ''But he was an internationally famous Israeli hero.''

''This crowd's idea of heroes are Gordon Liddy and Ollie North.''

''Then it's settled,'' said Bootsie. ''Be here tomorrow evening at eight and come as you are.'' She clapped her hands delightedly. ''Boy, for the first time, I think I'm gonna have a ball at the ball. Usually these things are deadly boring. The women look around wondering how much each other spent on her gown and face lift. And the men look around trying to figure out who they're gonna boink next week.''

COUNT JOSÉ LOOKED every inch the aristocrat with his impeccable white dinner jacket on which he wore his decorations. Bootsie floated by in yards and layers of beige chiffon which went beautifully with her red hair. She was wearing the single-strand emerald, diamond, and pearl 19th-century necklace I had seen in Maria Grazia Baldan's Sardinia shop which bore, as I recall, a price tag of $135,000. Around her wrist was a Stefan Hafner 2.33-carat diamond and white gold bracelet.

"Don't bother looking for the label, honey," she said to me when I commented on her lovely dress. "Those shit-head designers only make clothes for size-three anorexics and shriveled old bags who haven't eaten a decent meal in twenty years. I have everything made for me by a darling little Cuban girl in West Palm Beach. Now you look smashing—whose name is in that gorgeous nothing of a gown?"

"Herve Leger," I answered.

It was a slim black tube of horizontal strips of black silk and lace that started just above the cleavage and hugged the body the rest of the way down. Around my neck was my favorite white gold and diamond necklace I bought in Rome last year from Cesare Barro in a wild moment of self-indulgent extravagance. I carried my antique Van Cleef and Arpels gold evening bag which matched my Manolo Blahnik sandals.

Abba arrived in a freshly laundered and ironed uniform. He "oohed" and "wowed" quite satisfactorily over how beautiful we ladies looked.

"Abba, did you have to wear the hat?" I asked.

He looked surprised. "Are you kidding? I told you it's my hero hat. The bullet holes get 'em every time."

"Are they really from bullets?" asked the Count, obviously impressed.

"You bet your sweet ass they are, Count Baby," said Abba. "They sure as hell ain't moth holes."

"Then you have my permission to keep it on all night, Abba," said Bootsie, linking his arm in hers.

I groaned.

"Listen, sweetheart," he said to me, "at these bashes, everyone's out to stand out and we all use whatever weapons we have available. I'd say that minimalist piece of fabric you're wearing with the strips of see-through stuff displays your merchandise pretty effectively."

"He's got you there, honey," said Bootsie. "Let's go—" and the Count took my arm and led me out to the waiting Bentley.

IV

"STEP CAREFULLY, ABBA," I said as we walked up to the Breakers that was ablaze with lights. "You're walking on a million dollars." The entire front path was covered with oriental rugs.

"Holy shit!" he said when he looked down. "These fuckin' things are genuine!"

"Milo Pachurian is the chairman of the ball and he lends us rugs from his stock every year," said Bootsie.

"From this he makes a living?" said Abba. "The rug merchants I know in Israel peddle them off their backs."

"The ones in New York have stores but you can never see rugs because the windows are always covered with big 'going out of business sale' signs," I said.

Bootsie laughed. "Not our Milo. You can't have four beachfront acres on Ocean Boulevard and two Rolls Royces and be suffering too much financially. He's married to a real lady. I understand her daddy is some sort of lord or other. She invited us over for tea day after tomorrow. I told her I had a gorgeous young thing staying with me, Emma, and it seems she has a cousin visiting, Lord or Earl something or other, and thought it would be kind of nice for him to meet you.''

As we crossed over the threshold into the club, Abba muttered to me, ''Just what you need, another asshole aristocrat.''

We all gasped when we entered the ballroom. You had to—the effect was sheer fantasy. This year's theme (one *must* have a theme) was angels. A drop ceiling had been installed that looked exactly like pure blue sky with white clouds that moved slowly—a stunning pictorial effect conveyed by strategically placed computerized cameras. Suspended angels flew across the sky lazily, and skillfully directed lights caught the movement of gossamer-winged figures that floated over every table. The designer was obviously a lighting genius—small pin lights had also been placed in candleholders on each table to pick up the glow of the pink iridescent tablecloths.

Abba was enchanted. ''Who created this fairyland?'' he asked.

''As I understand,'' said Count José, ''local interior designers vie for the privilege of doing it.''

''The guy must charge a fortune,'' said Abba admiringly. ''It's worth it—and from all the Rolls Royces and Bentleys I saw being parked, this crowd could afford it.''

''Charge? Are you kidding?'' I asked. ''Any designer with a brain would bribe or kill to get this gig. Do you realize what it's worth to get the chance to showcase your talents to wall-to-wall billionaires who relieve their ennui by refurbishing bi-annually? I bet you most of them would sell their children, who they probably never see anyway, for a chance to get into *Architectural Digest*.''

''It's true,'' said Bootsie. ''Every designer who's done the Red Cross Ball has become very successful. Around here I'm considered an oddball because I haven't changed a thing in my home since I moved in. Susie Van Doran over there redoes hers every other year; alternate years she redoes her face. Karen Lee Potter over there has her place redecorated every year. She says she likes the excitement of change. I think she likes the excitement of having all those young muscled workmen around the house. If you have all the money to do anything you want, it's amazing how soon there's nothing you want to do.''

"Do you think maybe I could help break the sad monotony of their lives by getting up on a table and pitching Israeli Bonds?" said Abba, grinning.

"Hey, I think that's a great idea," I said. "I can see the headlines in the *New York Times*: 'Pogrom in Palm Beach.' ''

Abba looked around the room. "I don't know much about women's clothes, but even I can tell that some of the dresses these broads are wearing have to cost hundreds of dollars.''

Bootsie and I laughed. "Try thousands, honey. A good number of the gals around here took their husbands' private jets to New York last month to pick up about a dozen gowns for the season at about five thousand a pop.''

"How many gallons of high octane polluted our air in order that these *nafkas* make an impression on each other? If I was fifteen years younger and in my radical mode, I would have recommended Palm Beach as the ideal place to start The Revolution,'' said Abba with a grimace. "And they say the masses are revolting.''

"If you're looking to stir things up, Abba, how about taking me for a dance?" said Bootsie. "That's a tango they're playing and if you know how to do it, honey, I think you and I could create quite a spectacle.''

"Can I tango? Baby, you're in for a thrill. I'm a regular John Travolta.'' And he led her out to the dance floor.

The Count and I sat down at our table and watched them. As Bootsie predicted, heads quickly turned toward them. Abba's tango owed more to Arnold Schwarzenegger than John Travolta—it was big on action—but I was surprised to see that he really knew the steps.

"They make quite a colorful couple," said the Count with a smile. "Bootsie seems to be enjoying herself immensely."

"How long do you two know each other?" I asked.

I liked José, but he was a figure of mystery to me. This was a good chance to get to know him.

"We met three years ago in Estoril. She was visiting at my cousin's palace in Sintra."

"She seems quite fond of you," I said.

He looked at me with a quiet smile. "And you think maybe I am one of those impoverished titled Europeans who seek to live off some rich American lady."

"Are you?" I asked.

"Appearances to the contrary, I am not. My first reaction when I met Bootsie was—what an unfortunate name. I never understood why you Americans cling to your childish nicknames that seem so unsuited to an adult. My second reaction was to be utterly charmed by her spirit. My wife died five years ago, you see. She was a fine woman but of a very serious and rather lugubrious nature. When I met Bootsie, her zest and élan enchanted me. I am fifty-five and am not the sort who is captivated by some twenty-year-old to whom I would have nothing to say. I find being with a younger woman only makes me feel older. The physical contrast between her nubile body and my maturing one I find depressing. And the mental contrast between her frames of reference and mine I find distressing. When Bootsie invited me to visit with her in Palm Beach, I thought it would be an enjoyable episode. But as I spent time with her, I became more and more attracted to her honesty and straightforwardness. I had never before met a woman like this and I soon found myself quite in love with her." He smiled. "So I stayed on."

"So you have no designs on her?" I said with a smile.

"Only on her silver. That is the one area in which we both share the same passion."

I felt my antennae tingling.

"I think Bootsie's collection is exquisite," I said. "I especially admired the candelabras."

His expression changed and his face darkened, literally. It was as though all light left. I obviously struck a nerve, but which one? I was about to pursue the subject when a loud roar made us both turn around. It was the crowd applauding the bowing Abba and Bootsie at the conclusion of the tango. They both approached the table, flushed with success and followed by a crowd of admirers. Bootsie plopped down in her chair, panting with exhaustion, but Abba stood up chatting. When his audience finally faded away, he sat down.

"Wherever did you learn to tango like that, darling boy?" asked Bootsie as she struggled for breath.

"In South America."

Count José looked puzzled. "But that is so far from Israel."

"But not so far from Nazi Germany. We call South America the Fourth Reich. I've had reasons to visit there fairly often."

"Bootsie, that was just marvelous," said a woman who had approached our table. A burgundy Valentino gown hung from her spare figure, matched by a simple but lovely ruby and diamond necklace. She was accompanied by two men, the older one darkly handsome and the younger tall and fair.

"Lucy, honey—you look just divine," said Bootsie with a big smile. "Emma, these are my friends and neighbors, Lucy and Milo Pachurian. This is Emma Rhodes who is my favorite houseguest and that man over there panting to catch his breath is Abba Levitar, my favorite tango dancer. Emma, you should see their marvelous vegetable garden— they're always sending us the most delicious fresh peas, beans and carrots."

"I can't take credit for that," said Milo. "It's Lucy who is the serious gardener in our family."

"She's more than that, why, she's a scientific horticulturist," said Bootsie. "She actually has a little laboratory where she does the most unusual things with plants. But then Milo is very creative in his own way, too, aren't you, darling? I tell you, they're quite an innovative team. Perhaps someday they'll have some kind of showing. I've been thinking of arranging one," she said, looking at them with a smile. Then she turned her attention to the young man standing next to Milo. "And who is this handsome chap?"

"This is my cousin, Alfred Wittington, Earl of Crandon," said Lucy. "Actually, he is the son of my first cousin, Gerald, which I guess makes him my second cousin."

"Where I come from, I think we'd call him your first cousin once removed," said Bootsie. She eyed him appraisingly. "But if you were my cousin, I don't think I'd want you removed even once."

The Earl and I looked at each other and were both obviously pleased with what we saw. He was over six feet tall with a full head of sandy hair, a lock of which fell over his very dark brown eyes. He had a strong nose and a great smile which he at present aimed at me. I smiled right back. This might make the time pass more pleasantly. Abba, who missed nothing, rolled his eyes up as if to say "Not again!"

"Would you like to dance?" the Earl asked me.

He was a good dancer and we moved around the floor as one because he believed in the body-to-body style of dancing. This is most pleasant when the guy's attractive and probably barf time if he's a schlunk. But I wouldn't know because I'd never dance with a loser. I usually scare off unappetizing types with the excuse that I can't dance because I have a hanging uvula. Don't be embarrassed if you don't know it's the little lobe that hangs down in the middle of the back of your throat; most people don't and it makes the dorks back off in confusion without having to undergo the pain of rejection.

"Are you here on holiday?" I asked.

"Not entirely," he answered, somewhat cautiously.

"Then you have business here," I said.

He hesitated. "Well, it's more of a mission, I'd say."

"If you've come to get Palm Beach to secede from the United States and become a British colony, you might succeed. Most of them are devout anglophiles so they'd probably love the idea. And all of them are filthy rich so with your slipping economy, the Chancellor of the Exchequer would be panting with desire."

He laughed. "What a marvelous idea. I do love the climate and the polo facilities. But I fear it's nothing so imaginative."

Obviously he intended to leave it there. But he reckoned without my dedicated nosiness.

"If I get three guesses, I've only used up one," I said as we moved slowly around the floor."

"I've always admired that about you Americans," he

said. "Even the well-bred ones are quite ready to push you to the wall if they want information. An English lady would have given up at the first sign of hesitation."

"Hesitation only whets my desire for more information," I said. "And it creates mystery. I'm a sucker for a good mystery."

He sighed. "I give up. But I don't think you'll find it all that fascinating when you hear it. Actually, my business is with your friend Mrs. Corrigan. She has something my family wishes to acquire."

I stopped dead in the middle of the floor. "Your father wouldn't be the Duke of Wykeham, would he?"

He looked stunned. "Yes. How on earth did you know that?"

I took his hand and led him out of the ballroom into the lobby where I found a quiet corner and sat us down.

"You're looking to buy Bootsie's candelabra, right?"

He was wide-eyed. "Yes. But how did you know? By chance you're not out to buy it as well? Good lord, Father will be beside himself."

"Relax, Junior. I'm not foe, I'm friend." And I told him the entire story.

He looked stunned. "You are a private detective?"

"No—I'm a Private Resolver. I know I look like a ditzy debutante—well, postdebutante, very post. But my job title explains what I do—I resolve dicky and sticky situations for people who need them done and need them done privately and quietly. I find things for people, and sometimes people for people. I'm circumspect and I'm very successful. Results are guaranteed."

"And your fee?"

"Also guaranteed. I guarantee the fee is nothing, zip, unless I produce results—and within two weeks."

He shook his head in wonder. "Margaret never mentioned a word."

"She probably never told your father about our arrangement," I said, "because she was terrified of him."

"Not of him, but possibly of Grandmama," he said with a grim smile.

"Is *she* the power behind the throne?" I asked.

He grimaced. "More like a destructive force. Father is a pussycat. Not that he isn't a strong, reasonable, and very admirable man whom I respect enormously, but he's very good-hearted. It's Grandmama who is making his and Margaret's life a living hell about that damned candelabra. She's the one who sets great store on that nonsense about it's being vital to the future of the family. I came because I thought I could help set things right again by offering to buy it back."

"Why does your father pay attention to such silly voodoo?" I asked.

He smiled ruefully. "Maybe because there are two things he desires desperately and wants to give them every chance of happening. And he's afraid that perhaps there is something to Granny's idea of there being a hex on the family without the candelabra."

"You mean he's like the praying man on the sinking ship who exhorts the Protestant, Muslim, and Jew to get down on their knees with him because he's not sure who really has the direct pipeline to God."

"Exactly. He doesn't want to overlook anything that might work to bring about these two events and to eliminate anything that might cast the shadow of deterrence on them."

"You already know I'm nosy and pushy. So I feel perfectly free to ask you what are the two events?"

"First, my elder brother who will inherit the title has

three daughters and his wife is pregnant. She swears she will give up trying after this baby. If she produces another girl, the title will pass to me. I'm forty-two and my father has no faith in the possibility of my marrying and producing an heir. In which case the title will pass to his repellent Scottish cousin Rodney who, when he visits periodically, makes Father apoplectic when he seems to be taking careful visual inventory of the contents of the house.''

I looked at him appraisingly. ''Why doesn't he think you'll ever marry and produce a line of heirs? You're not gay.''

''How do you know?'' he asked.

''We just danced together rather closely. Your interest in women was shall we say pointedly apparent.''

He laughed. ''Ah yes, we men are at a disadvantage that way. Our bodies betray our emotions. But actually I *am* gay, but in the old-fashioned sense—I'm what used to be called a gay blade. I'm the classic bachelor of British literature who adores women, late nights, dinners at the club, and the quiet peace of his own very comfortable living accommodations. I've seen marriages of all sorts—and I have never found the whole idea attractive. As for offspring, I find small children untidy little leaky things and older children rude and demanding buggers. From what I see, the job as parent is one from which one can never resign or retire and I don't fancy that sort of lifetime encumbrance. Which is why my father's poor opinion of my ever being the provider of an heir to Wykeham is quite accurate.''

''So he wants desperately for your sister-in-law to have a boy child. Now what's desire number two?''

He looked uncomfortable. ''It's about me. I studied Greek literature at Oxford and then took a degree in political science at the London School of Economics.''

"You've become interested in politics," I said.

He nodded. "Lord help me, yes."

"And Daddy wants you to run for Parliament."

He nodded again. "Very much. But he has absolutely no political connections. Nor do we have the sort of free capital to spend on a political campaign that would make me attractive to the party. We are not impoverished, but our wealth is in land which fortunately generates enough to maintain itself. And there are a few other problems he and I have about the matter."

"So he's waiting for some sort of bolt from heaven that would suddenly make you an M.P. and your sister-in-law produce a male child. Which means he now never walks under ladders, always crosses the street when he sees a black cat, tosses salt over his shoulder if he spills any. And he is totally vulnerable to your grandmother's nagging."

"Quite."

"Well, I can understand his and your concern to recover the piece of silver, but I don't think you have a chance."

"Why not? Mrs. Corrigan seems like a nice woman who would listen to reason."

"She's a great woman whom I've known for years. But your cause doesn't move her in the least. I've already discussed it with her."

"But I thought you Americans were awed by English aristocracy. She might respond differently to pleas from the son of the Duke of Wykeham."

I waved my hand grandly. "Then I suggest you give it a shot."

He eyed me narrowly. "Why do I feel you're inviting me to step off a precipice?"

"Well, to give you a hint, snotty British aristocrats, and I'm quoting, do not rate high on her list of favorite people. But I don't want you to think I'm trying to discourage your

efforts because I might lose a fee. I'm in the lovely position
of never being short of cash or clients. However, I've already taken the first steps toward trying to convince Bootsie
to sell Margaret the candelabra and I believe I will succeed
in time. But even more important, if I retrieve it under
Margaret's aegis, she'll get the credit for its return. Whereas
if you do, she'll be on Grandmama's shit-list forever. And
that would be a shame because it could ruin what might
have been a happy marriage for her and your father.''

He looked thoughtful. ''This is the sort of work you do
regularly?''

I smiled. ''Actually, I'd say I do things rather irregularly.
But it gets results.''

''All right. Perhaps I'd best leave it to you. I'm usually
pretty good at convincing women to do what I want, but I
must say it has never involved the acquisition of any tangible object but me. I'm not sure the same methods would
be effective.''

''Hmm, but they sure as hell might be a lot of fun for
Bootsie. I may be depriving her of the pleasure of your
efforts,'' I said.

We heard the sounds of a loud fanfare. ''I think dinner
is being served. We'd better get back to our tables.''

''When will I see you again?'' he asked.

''I think your cousin has invited us to tea the day after
tomorrow.''

''Capital!'' he said, and he led me back into the ballroom.

As I approached the table from one side, Abba was ap-
proaching from the other, trailed by a bevy of starry-eyed
dowagers.

''Abba honey,'' said Bootsie admiringly, ''you sure do
have a way with women.''

''What do you mean 'women'—I just sold one hundred

thousand dollars' worth of Israel Bonds to their husbands,''
he said triumphantly as he dropped into his chair.

"How ever did you convince that pack of tight-assed
Presbyterians to contribute a nickel to a country of people
they won't even let into their clubs?" asked Bootsie.

"I just explained that the survival of Israel is the only
way to protect their holy places like Bethlehem and Jesus'
walk from disrespect and possible destruction by the infi-
dels. Unlike the Arabs, Jews don't have holy wars and *ji-
hads*. We don't proselytize, we respect all other religions.
All sacred Christian sites are preserved in Israel. That's
why we have pilgrims coming at Easter and Christmas. We
are always aware of our responsibility that Israel is the Holy
Land for people other than Jews."

The Count looked thoughtful. "I had never thought of it
that way."

Abba smiled. "You bet your butt those *fahcockte* anti-
Semites never did either."

I shook my head. "Abba, you're almost unscrupulous."

"Now wait a minute—that means unprincipled. I sure as
hell have my principles. They may not be the same as
yours, but you Americans have luxuries we don't because
you're big and secure while we fight possible extinction
every day."

"The man's right, Emma love," said Bootsie. "On the
farm where I grew up we shot foxes because they killed
our livestock. Now I'm on the committee here to eliminate
fox hunting because it's cruel to the poor animals."

"Perhaps it is that principles are determined by survival," said the Count. "And thus they are formed by our
needs at the time."

He looked at me and smiled. "Now you're thinking
maybe there is more to this person than being Bootsie's
fancy man and maybe he also has a brain."

I don't often blush, but this time I felt my face getting hot. "Are you also a mind reader?" I asked.

"No, just a face reader. You treated me to a look of approval which I had not before seen."

"Don't make the mistake of underrating José here," said Bootsie. "He's sharp as a tack besides being a very educated man."

"Where did you get your degree, José?" asked Abba.

"My undergraduate years were at the University of Coimbra. I also have a degree in Scottish history from the University of Edinburgh, one in Medieval History from Cambridge University, and one from the Wharton School of the University of Pennsylvania. The last one was for my father's sake who hoped I could save his businesses but it was too late."

"Boy, that's better than Brooklyn College," said Abba as he dug into the quenelles that were placed before him.

"What were his businesses?" I asked.

"The family had cork trees, olive groves, and even a sardine cannery in Setubal. In earlier years under Salazar, large landowners were protected and even supported. But after the revolution in 1974, competition arose and skills were needed. Enterprises like my father's that were run by absentee managers, who spent their time in the casinos of Estoril and racing their Porsches along the Côte d'Azur under the foolishly blind assumption that those favored conditions would last forever—these began to fail. We lost everything and my father died a sad and poor man."

"Where I grew up, the only gambling you could afford was Bingo at the Temple on Saturday nights," said Abba. "As for cars, I never knew people bought cars new—we only had used Chevvies. José, maybe it's better to have lived and lost than to have never lived at all."

"Please," said José urgently. "I did not mean to complain or look for sympathy. But sometimes it's hard to not feel some bitterness when I pass the property we used to have and see it in other hands.''

"That's understandable," I said.

"You may have lost some things," said Abba, "but your basic treasure they can never take from you."

"What's that?" asked José.

"Your intelligence and your education. The reason education is so stressed in Jewish families is because throughout history, our properties and possessions were constantly confiscated. The only thing no one could take was our knowledge, skills, and brains. So Jewish children are always driven to perform in school and to become as educated as possible. You've had a great education and for that you should be grateful to your parents."

"The wisdom floating around this table is very impressive," said Bootsie, "but let's not forget this is a party. So let's lighten up and have fun. José, sweetie, they're playing a waltz in between courses—how about us having a go around the dance floor? Wait until you see this man waltz," she said to us as José pulled out her chair. "He makes me feel like a queen when he whirls me around. Just watch."

"The guy moves like Fred Astaire," said Abba admiringly. "Your friend has good taste." Then he looked at me. "But I'm not sure about you, *bubele*. Haven't you had enough of those toffee-nosed Brits? Look at that outfit— what kind of fancy dinner jacket is that he's wearing? It looks like double-breasted but it only has three buttons instead of four. And what's with those cuff buttons—they have button holes! Why would you need to unbutton your jacket cuffs?''

"The reason you've never seen the like of that jacket before is Savile Row is located in London and not Brooklyn. His dress coat has been custom tailored—that's the

London version of double-breasted. The cuff buttons with buttonholes are the traditional mark of English tailoring. The tradition began years ago when it is said they were demanded by Harley Street physicians who needed to un-button their jacket sleeves so that they could push them up when examining or operating on patients.''

"Tradition!" thundered Abba, sounding like Zero Mos-tel.

"Right," I said. "As far as Lord Alfred goes, my interest is business, not personal."

His eyes widened. "You're here on a case?" He shook his head. "For once I thought you might be on vacation. Don't you ever take a rest?"

"I always mean to—but I seem to get into these con-versations with people in the oddest places, and one thing leads to another . . .''

"I know—you turn on that *simpatica* face and they start to pour their hearts out to you and you're hooked."

"I don't turn on anything—it's always there. I was born with a receptive face. It's part curiosity and part concern."

"In other words," said Abba with a smile. "A *yenta*."

"Wrong," I said. "As I understand it, a *yenta* probes for information for the joy of knowing something no one else knows and offers unsolicited advice. I do none of the above. And more important, I don't just listen—I do some-thing about their problems."

"OK—so you're an activist *yenta*. What's the gig this time?"

Abba is the one person in the world with whom I discuss my work. His Mossad training has made him intensely alert to the nuances of human behavior and a rock of discretion. His comprehension is instantaneous and his brain is incred-ibly nimble and fertile. And most valued of all, he is my best friend. There are Hollywood types who refer to a person they met last week who agreed to put money in their film as their "dear friend." Then there are the New York types who claim to be your friend with the statement "I'll always be there for you" which promises interest but offers no activity. My definition of a friend is someone who is supportive and loyal and can be depended upon to respond to a call for help immediately and without question. That's Abba.

I told him the entire story about Lady Margaret and the silver candelabra.

"They got a million pounds for it and they want it back? My grandmother Bubbie Sadie had a lucky charm, a small cameo from her mother. It was pricelessly precious to her because she felt it warded off the evil eye and kept her family safe. She brought it with her from the *shtetl* all the way across the ocean to America. But she sold it to a sailor on the ship for four oranges for her children. She was an ignorant woman, but she understood that survival supersedes superstition. These idiots have endowed a piece of silver with greater importance than their marriage." He shook his head. "Sometimes I despair of the perpetuation of civilization."

"I know it seems hard to work up a case of sympathy for so frivolous a cause," I said. "But to Lady Margaret it means everything. She has no skills, no ability to make a living. All she's been trained for is to marry well. She finally did after one disaster, and now the whole promise of a secure and golden future is threatened. As I've said to you many times, Abba, the problems of the rich may seem frivolous compared to those of people who scrounge for a livelihood, but pain is pain and you can't scorn it just because you don't respect the reason."

Bootsie and Count José returned to the table and we told them how wonderful they looked on the dance floor.

"José is such a divine waltzer, he makes me look like Rita Hayworth. Oh, I've invited Lucy and Milo with her cousin to dinner tomorrow night. Won't that be jolly?" asked Bootsie. "Of course you must come too, Abba."

V

BOOTSIE WAS IN her element. She dearly loved to host parties and her table was always a creative tour de force. Tonight, the silver candelabras were at either end of the table, with a line of votive candles and rose-filled bud vases meeting them. The centerpiece was three exquisite yellow and pink hybrid orchids from her incredible garden and hothouse where all sorts of rare flowers were grown by Manuel, her gardener. The silver and crystal picked up the reflections of the candlelight and made the room look magical. She beamed when we all complimented her on the stunning effect.

"Not bad for this little old farm girl who didn't know until she was sixteen that people sat down to meals. In our house, when you were hungry, you just dished yourself up a helping of whatever was on the stove and ate on the run."

"Auntie has marvelous taste, doesn't she?" said Jonathan fondly as he pulled out the chair for Melissa.

"Yes," said Melissa, "and fortunately the money to indulge it."

"Honey," said Bootsie, "isn't that what it's for?"

"Here, here," said Milo Pachurian, "that's the attitude that puts bread on my table and allows me to shop in Ralph Lauren." He looked splendid in a pale blue linen jacket, white slacks, blue and white print chambray shirt and a red and white silk scarf. His wife was simple and elegant in a lime green raw silk sheath. Her cousin was right out of Savile Row in a navy blue wool blazer, cream wool slacks, and an Eton tie.

The first course was asparagus in a balsamic vinaigrette served on Flora Danica plates.

"Bootsie, these dishes are exquisite," I said.

"Yeah, they're pretty. My fancy aunt Rosie had a set like this," said Abba.

I looked at Bootsie and we smiled. When I told him later that Flora Danica plates cost thousands of dollars each, he roared. "Rosie got them for giveaways from the Brooklyn Paramount theater."

Rivers and Eunice, Bootsie's personal maid, served us the entrée.

"This is the cutest little chicken I ever ate," said Abba. "And it's delicious."

"It's not chicken," I said, "it's Rock Cornish Game Hen."

"No wonder it's so small. It lost weight flying here all the way from the Cornish coast. And what's in this great stuffing?"

"That's my special recipe," said Bootsie. "It's got the andouille sausage and vidalia onions that Emma sent me."

Suddenly she made a strange noise. Her face, hands, and arms turned bright red and she began to gasp for breath. I jumped up and ran over to her with Abba close behind me. Everyone else just sat frozen.

She clutched her chest, and slipped to the floor.

"Call the doctor. She's having a heart attack!" screamed someone.

Abba, I, and Jonathan bent over her. Her eyes were closed and she was gasping for breath.

Abba took command at once. "Rivers, get the hell to the phone and call 911 and her doctor. Jonathan, does she have a history of heart trouble?"

"No, never," said Jonathan, who was now white and obviously trying to control the panic that his eyes showed.

I was getting no response. I stopped for a moment. "Does she have asthma? Is she allergic to anything?" and continued my ministrations..

"Yes, no—I don't know," said Jonathan weakly.

"Peanuts," screamed Janet, the cook who had come running in from the kitchen when she heard the commotion. "She can't never touch them—she told me they could kill her."

"Does anyone have an Epi-Pen Kit? Is there one in the house?" asked Abba. When he saw everyone's uncomprehending faces, he shouted, "It's the antidote."

Janet stood wringing her hands. "But I swear, there weren't none in the food. Why would I put in peanuts?" she said, sobbing.

Count José was kneeling at her side and everyone else was standing around paralyzed.

"It ain't the food, I swear," sobbed Janet. "I make this all the time—it's one of her favorite dishes!"

I heard the siren approach and a policeman was at the front door in minutes. All 911 calls go to police headquarters as well as the fire aid stations, and since police cars are always on the move, there's usually one nearby to dispatch quickly whereas the emergency people are waiting at fire aid stations which could be miles away. The patrolman dropped to the floor and pushed me aside to take up the

CPR. A few minutes later, the emergency medic team came rushing in and took over. The lead E.M.T. looked at her and immediately reached into his bag, pulled out a tube and injected her. Then he took her pulse, pulled out a stethoscope and listened. We all stared at him for what seemed like an hour.

"Don't let her die, please God," I said silently. "Please."

We waited. After about five minutes, he took off the stethoscope and folded it away. Then he looked at me with a face filled with deep sadness and shook his head. "She's gone."

I felt tears streaming down my face and I saw José holding Bootsie's hand and sobbing quietly. In spite of my own emotion, my professional instinct went into drive and I quickly surveyed the room. Jonathan was sitting on the floor next to his aunt staring at her in shock while Melissa had her arms around him trying to comfort him. Lucy was leaning on her husband and crying. Alfred looked stonily serious. The other servants who had come in all had tears streaming down their cheeks and Rivers was trying to quiet Janet, who at this point was hysterical.

The officer pulled his phone out of his belt and spoke quietly into it. Then he spoke.

"Everyone please sit down."

"If it's all right, officer," I said, "perhaps it's best if we all go into the living room. I don't think any of us wants to stay at the table and besides, I think your lab people won't want the plates to be disturbed."

"Right, they'll want to check out Mrs. Corrigan's food," he said.

"I'm sure they'll want to check out everyone's food," I said.

He looked at me quizzically.

We all filed into the next room and we heard the front door open. The Medical Examiner hurried in.

We all took our places. Abba and I sat on a loveseat that faced the dining room so that we could watch the proceedings. I was trying to maintain my professional *sang froid* but as I heard the sounds next door and knew well they meant my beloved friend who a few minutes ago had been a warm, vital, marvelously alive being was now being converted into a body, an object to be probed, cut into, and investigated, I started to shake. Abba put his arms around me.

A woman walked into the room and looked around at us. She was in her early thirties, a little less than medium height, had curly black hair, a straight small nose, and what my father calls a determined chin. She was pretty and pleasant looking and wearing a chino pantsuit and pink blouse.

"I'm Detective Sergeant Berkowitz," she introduced herself. I felt Abba react and I smiled to myself. "I will be the lead detective on this case and I'd like to talk to each of you." The uniformed policeman joined her.

Her eyes went immediately to Abba who was dressed in his usual Israeli uniform.

"You must be Abba Levitar," she said. "You're here for the bond drive. I'll talk to you first."

He looked at her and said, "I'd be happy to, Detective. But might I suggest that you speak first to Emma Rhodes here?"

"Why?" asked the detective.

"I think her knowledge of the people involved and the situation is far greater than mine and I believe she would be more valuable to you."

Detective Berkowitz eyed him calmly. Then she looked at me in my yellow Versace linen suit with the bare midriff and the lime Christian Laboutin pumps. OK, lady, I thought, here's where we find out if you're one of those insecure fools who look upon all advice as a threat to your authority, or an independent woman strong enough to make your own judgments.

She looked at him for a second and then turned to me. "OK, Miss Rhodes, I guess you're number one."

I felt rather than saw Abba relax and smile. He too now felt we were in capable hands. There's nothing more painful for professionals like Abba and me than being forced to watch, let alone be part of, an investigation being run ineptly. Law enforcement officers are highly trained to follow specific procedures and to understand and handle every possible situation that may arise in criminal investigations. Their training may be the same, but they are not. Some are intelligent, insightful, and subtle while others come on like bulls. Each approaches his work differently and evolves his or her own style. No matter how much they are taught to be impersonal and unbiased, everyone carries personal emotional baggage that must affect judgment. Some are overimpressed with their own power and impose it heavily. Others are more laid back, Columbo style. Some are soft and pleasant, some are offensive and unlikable.

We got lucky.

Detective Berkowitz pointed to me to go first. "You know the house—where do you suggest we settle down?"

I led her to the small sitting room with a door that can be closed so as not to be heard by the people in the next room. She turned to the uniformed policeman.

"Come in with me and take notes. Tell McCarthy to get names and addresses from everybody."

She sat down facing me and looked appreciatively around her. "This is a lovely room. It's what my mother would call an eclectic mishmash, but it works."

I liked her immediately.

"That's about the best description you could give about Bootsie Corrigan," I said.

"What was the nature of your relationship with her, Miss Rhodes?"

I looked at her with a small smile. "A question right out of the textbook, Detective."

She colored slightly.

"Then I'll answer it that way. I am—was—her friend."

"OK," she said, "suppose you tell me just what happened here tonight."

"It was a simple casual dinner party," I looked down at my clothes "for which one dresses in Palm Beach pseudo-simple casual." She smiled. "'The cast of characters were me, her houseguest—we've known each other for many years. I met her in Vancouver when I was doing work for her husband."

"What kind of work was that?" she asked.

"Legal."

I could see the changing expression on her face. First she had me pegged as a socialite airhead—now I'm a lawyer. I wondered which she considered the lower animal. I didn't want to get into my work story since I make it a habit of not lying to the police and I surely didn't want to go into my Private Resolver explanation or we might be here all night. So I changed the subject.

"The young man is Jonathan Carswell, her nephew and his fiancée, Melissa—I don't know her last name. Then there's the charming Portuguese gentleman, Count José do Figuera, who lives here with Bootsie. Lucy and Milo Pachurian are friends and neighbors and the other young man is Lucy's British cousin, Alfred Wittington, the Earl of Crandon.

To her credit, she didn't look even a bit impressed.

"Abba you know. And then there's Rivers, the butler,

and Janet, the cook, who I believe have been here almost forever, and Eunice, a fairly new employee who was Bootsie's ladies' maid, I think they call it.''

"How was everything going at dinner?" she asked. "Everyone pleasant and smiling?"

"No disagreements at all, Detective. The food was too tasty to ruin with harsh words, and everyone was feeling mighty pleasant from the wines. You had to know Bootsie—she made everyone happy because she was so ebullient and just seemed to will everyone to have a good time at her table, in her home. It was like she was always making up for the deprived years of her youth. She had pots of money and reveled in spending it on anything she had a whim for."

I paused. "There was absolutely no warning at all. We were all chatting away, enjoying the delicious hens, when she just went into anaphylactic shock."

She sat up as I knew she would.

"How do you know that's what it was?"

"My mother is highly allergic to shellfish. I saw her go into shock once and recognized the symptoms. Fortunately for my mom, a doctor was at the table and administered adrenaline immediately and she survived. Bootsie wasn't so lucky. If only one of us were a doctor or carried an Epi-Pen, or if only she kept one in the house—if only, if only."

"We can't be certain of the cause, Miss Rhodes, until the M.E. completes the autopsy and gives the official statement. That most likely won't be for a few days."

"Still you are considering it a suspicious death or you wouldn't be questioning us this way," I said.

"Any death that's not a natural one is considered by the police to be suspicious until proven otherwise," she said.

"This dinner party was not a long-planned one," I said. "Verbal invitations were extended casually yesterday."

She looked at me with a slight touch of respect. "So that there was no time for anyone to make elaborate preparations for a murder—if that is indeed what it was."

I nodded. "Someone had to lace the food with peanuts on a spur-of-the-moment idea. It had to be in the stuffing because andouille sausage is a very strong spicy flavor and would easily mask the taste of pulverized peanuts. That someone had to know that it would be lethal only to Bootsie. In other words, it could well have been one of the guests."

"Including you," she said.

I nodded. "Exactly right. Except that specific someone had to have a motive—which I don't."

From her expression, I could see that she had already overlooked my $5000-on-the-hoof look and accepted the fact that I had a brain. So I pushed a little.

"At the risk of being offensive and tacky, let me throw in that Mrs. Corrigan endowed a Policeman's Fresh Air Camp for kids last year. She was a generous giver to the Policeman's Benevolent fund and just funded a complete emergency unit for your department. Her relatives and friends would be most grateful if you could use your influence to speed up the M.E. so that she doesn't lay around on a slab for days but can be buried next to her husband as soon as possible."

Then I pushed a little more.

"Colonel Levitar—he'd kill me if he heard I used his rank—he never alludes to it—can only be here for a few more days. He's a keen observer and could be a help to your investigation—which I gather really can't go into high gear until you have the autopsy results."

Bingo. I saw her eyes widen. She was impressed with Abba, everyone is. She didn't say anything, but I saw I had hit home. I really felt strongly about my bid for special treatment for Bootsie, but I also confess to a slightly self-serving motive. (I hope you've noticed that I never lie to you.) I've been on the candelabra case for four days which means I have only ten days to go. I can't afford to wait for some suntanned doctor to complete his eighteen holes before attending to his daily quota of cadavers.

Abba came in to be questioned by the detective as I was walking out. I think his reason for having me precede him was only a partial one. He wanted to spare me the sight of the body bag being removed. I've seen this many times, but I can never get used to the sight of a once-living person being reduced to what looks like a duffle bag of laundry. Especially someone I knew and loved. Abba is tough and hard as he must be in his work, but he has never become calloused to suffering and is actually one of the most sensitive men I know. By the time I came out, the body was gone. The CSEU (Crime Scene Evidence Unit) was at work in the dining room. The unit consists of an officer and two skilled technicians who go over everything meticulously. They have been highly trained and certified in order to qualify as expert witnesses in court, and if anything is there that could offer any clue to whodunit, they will find it.

Then I noticed Detective Berkowitz approach Jonathan and speak to him earnestly. He looked stunned, then reached into his pocket and handed her his keys.

"May I have your attention, everyone?" she called out. "I have a warrant here that permits us to search this house. I promise you our people are careful and will leave everything as they found it. Everyone is now free to go."

There was a buzzing among the servants. "Does that mean the servants' rooms as well?" asked Rivers.

"Of course," said the detective.

Abba was impressed. "Boy, she sure as hell didn't waste a minute. She got that warrant pretty fast. I'll bet if this happened in one of those condominiums farther down where all the old widows live, you wouldn't see a cop for hours.''

''In that neighborhood, death is probably a daily occurrence, so why rush?'' I said. ''And from what I've seen of the population, sometimes it's hard to tell if some of them are still alive. On the other hand, this is murder on the big bucks strip. That's bound to bring out the heavy artillery.''

Jonathan came over, looking somewhat dazed. ''They asked for my key. They're going to search my house. Why would they do that?''

I looked at him. Like so many academics, he may write brilliant papers but he couldn't find his way out of a paper bag.

''They're looking for anything that would indicate you killed your aunt,'' I explained simply, as one would to a child.

He looked stunned. ''Me? Why would I do such a terrible thing? I loved her.''

''We all did, Jonathan, but someone deliberately killed her.''

Melissa came over and took him by the arm. ''Come on, Jonathan, let's go home. Maybe the police will have gone by the time we get there.''

VI

ABBA AND I sat on the terrace. The Count had gone upstairs to bed and everyone else had left after being questioned by the police.

"She's good," said Abba.

I knew who he meant, of course. No Israeli profanity, no lascivious comments. This was a different Abba.

He looked over at me. "What, no snappy Sarah Lawrence remarks?"

"No."

"How come? You never missed out on a chance like this before."

"Because Detective Berkowitz is not in the same category as those blonde bimbos you collect. The only thing deep about them were their cleavages. This one is solid, smart, great-looking, and of the Faith. I never mock the genuine article."

"I think she likes me, too," he said in a faltering subdued tone. He sat up suddenly. "Sonofabitch! I haven't been this unsure of myself since my bar mitzvah speech. What the fuck's happening to me?"

I laughed. "Hey, Mr. Invulnerable. If I had a horn I'd be tooting it like Gabriel. Methinks someone finally broke down the walls. You just may be falling in love, my man."

He looked very serious for a moment. "Well, I guess she's worthy." And then he exploded into laughter.

I joined him, but felt a stab of apprehension. If this feeling wasn't requited, he'll be in for a bad time and I would hate to see him hurt. I just lost one good friend to death; I wouldn't like to see another suffer the pain of rejection.

I sighed.

"Was that *kvetch* for me or for Bootsie?"

"A little for you, but mostly for Bootsie. I can't believe she's gone—she was so vital one minute and then dead."

He looked somber. "In my business, we see a lot of that. If you want to know if you ever get used to it, the answer is never."

We were both silent for a few moments. "How come Jonathan didn't know she was allergic to peanuts? Or rather claimed not to know."

"Yes, I spotted that," said Abba. "Berkowitz shouldn't find this too tough a case. Only a few people had access to the kitchen. All she has to find out is *cui bono* and she's home free."

"The *cui* who *bonos* the most is Jonathan, her heir." Suddenly I jumped up. "Tom Blair, I must phone him! Lord, I don't want him to hear it on the news."

"Who's that?"

"Bootsie's lawyer and oldest friend in Palm Beach. He should be told. This is going to break his heart—he's had a thing for Bootsie since Buck died and I think he always believed she'd get tired of exotic younger lovers and turn to solid old Tom. What a hope. Bootsie was sixty-seven. Why would she want to settle into an existence where the only highs are high colonics and high-fiber breakfasts shared with a man who is probably now or soon to be impotent from prostate surgery when she could have caviar and champagne with a handsome lover offering fully functioning equipment?''

''Who says money can't buy happiness?'' asked Abba.

I reached Tom Blair at home. When I told him what had happened, he was silent for a moment. Then he said, ''I'd like to come right over.''

He arrived at 9:30. My God, just two hours ago we were sitting around the table laughing. How can life change so unalterably so suddenly? A tall slightly stooped white-haired gentleman, his usually tan face was ashen with grief. I put my arms around him and we stood in silence, just holding each other.

''Did she suffer?''

''No, it was almost instantaneous.''

''Tell me exactly what happened.''

I introduced him to Abba and he took the seat facing us as I described the events leading up to and the actual details of her death, including the comings and goings of the police. As an attorney, I knew he would want to hear all the details.

''Who's in charge of the investigation?'' he asked.

''Detective Berkowitz.''

He nodded approvingly. ''Excellent. She's the best.''

Abba smiled broadly.

''When will the coroner have results, did you say?'' asked Tom.

''The detective said within a few days but I asked for one.''

''I'll make sure it will be tomorrow,'' he said firmly.

''How can you do that?'' I asked.

He smiled grimly. ''Dr. Granat and I have a golf game tomorrow at 8:00. When I cancel at 7:30, too late to find a replacement, the lazy bastard will have to go to work.''

We chatted and reminisced about Bootsie. Rivers brought out a silver tray bearing single malt scotch, brandy, soda, and a silver ice bucket and glasses.

''Madam would never forgive me if I didn't extend the hospitality of the house to her friends,'' he said with tears in his eyes.

Tom sat sipping his drink. Suddenly he sat upright.

''Emma, I want to commission you to solve this murder. Your usual terms, of course.''

''Don't you have sufficient faith in Detective Berkowitz?'' asked Abba.

''In *her*, yes—but not completely in the Palm Beach Police Department. She is bound by strictures imposed by the hierarchy and bureaucracy and politics. I've lived here many years and am quite familiar with the situation. I'm not saying it's Claude Rains' 'round up the usual suspects.' But this town prides itself on elegance and wealth. We don't mind a few robberies—it only reinforces the pride in our coveted riches. Even an occasional accusation of rape is acceptable—you know, the reprobate young heirs taking advantage of the local peasant girls as in days of yore. But murder—after all, this isn't Miami. I'm afraid they'll try their best to solve it quickly, no matter how, in order to get it off the front pages.''

''It may sound tasteless to discuss at a time like this, Tom,'' I said, ''but this isn't some sleazy little crime of a stabbing in an alley or someone gunned down in a pizza parlor with blood mixing with marinara sauce on his shirtfront. This is a classy crime, committed with the upscale method used by noble families for centuries—poison. It shouldn't bother the town fathers one whit.''

''Don't kid yourself, *tsotskele*,'' said Abba. ''Murder is murder and no one feels safe in their beds until the villain is caught. It makes people aware of their own mortality and vulnerability. Especially when they're what you here euphemistically call 'senior citizens.' From what I've seen of this place, the mean age is 70 and boy, are they mean! I accidentally pushed my shopping cart ahead of some old gent at the checkout in Publix market yesterday, and if his cane had a sword tip I'd be well-ventilated by now.''

"He's right, Emma. The mayor's office will pressure the police to find a culprit, speed being the only goal. I want to know who killed my darling Bootsie and I want to see that killer punished. Will you take the case, Emma?'' he asked pleadingly.

I put my arm around his frail shoulders. "Of course, Tom. But I won't take your money. No fee.''

Abba's eyebrows arched. "I thought you never did pro bono, *ahuvati* my love.''

"I don't do pro bono publico—free for the public good. But I do pro bono amicus—free for the good of a friend.''

I turned to Tom. "OK—I'm starting. Who gets it all?''

He looked uncomfortable. A lawyer doesn't like to reveal the terms of a will unofficially. I could see him battling with himself.

"Jonathan Carswell. There are, of course, moneys left to charities and servants.''

"Anything for the Count?'' I asked.

He said, with a small amount of satisfaction, "Not a penny.''

"I am surprised. She seemed to genuinely care for him,'' I said. "And he really treated her wonderfully and although you may not like to hear it, Tom, quite lovingly. It's a pity—I gather he's not a wealthy man.''

"I'm afraid that's happened before,'' said Tom. "Bootsie was big hearted and filled with love and enthusiasm and good will. So she would put the gentleman *du jour* in her will and drop him out after he was dismissed. I'm afraid she just didn't get around to including the present incumbent.''

"So John-boy gets a sizable pile," I said.

"Oh yes, there's also a modest bequest for Rick Bolton.''

"Who's that? Bolton was Bootsie's maiden name, wasn't it?''

"Yes, he's a nephew.''

"I thought Jonathan was her only living relative.''

Tom shook his head. "Rick is unfortunately extant. He's always been trouble—he's the son of her dead brother. She only added him to her will recently.''

"And where does this paragon hang out?" I asked.

"I believe he was living in Vancouver but to my knowledge hasn't been in touch with Bootsie for years. Actually, the only time he ever contacted her was to ask for money. He is one of what I believe we used to call hippies or flower children.''

"You mentioned that this Rick no-goodnik is in for a piece of the will," said Abba. "A modest amount, I think you said. How much by you is a 'modest' amount?''

"$250,000.''

Abba whistled. "Is that like when those wine mavens take their first sip of some priceless bottle that's been in the castle cellar for fifty years and pronounce it a 'modest little wine'?''

"The term 'modest' is comparative, Tom," I said. "To a loser like the man you describe, this could represent a substantial fortune.''

"It ain't exactly peanuts to me either, if you'll forgive the choice of words," said Abba.

"You mean worth killing for," said Tom. "But he can't be a suspect. He's not here.''

"How do you know that?" asked Abba.

"Because if he were here, he'd have been to see Bootsie with his hand out, you can be sure. He doesn't know of the existence of his inheritance."

"I think we'd best wait for the M.E. results before I take any steps," I said. "Call me when you get them, Tom. Somehow I think you'll have them even before Detective Berkowitz. Come on, I'll walk you to the door."

As we opened the front door, we both almost fell back. The entire front steps were covered with large floral pieces.

"Good lord!" I said as I started to read the cards.

"Don't bother," said Tom dryly. "They're undoubtedly all from the Ghoul Brigade."

"What's that?"

"The Palm Beach real estate agents," he said sourly. "They know who died even before the undertaker. I'll suggest to Rivers that he set up the phone answering machine to take all calls for the next week or so."

I was stunned. "But Bootsie died just hours ago . . ."

". . . Leaving a house that sits on the most prime piece of real estate in Palm Beach," he said. "Buck had a phenomenal eye for land. On an island that is only twelve miles long and three blocks across at its widest point, he picked a spot that's smack-dab in the middle, which is the narrowest and most desirable beachfront area. Thirty years ago when he bought it, he probably paid under a million. Today, it could sell for between twenty and thirty million dollars to some New York money mogul like that trashy Trump or that pipsqueak Perelman who will raze the house and put up an ostentatious Paris-decorated palace which he will probably never visit. That ilk suffers from mansion-envy and they vie to outdo each other. The original Old Guard of Palm Beach regarded the north end as the low-rent district. But when the *nouveau riche* tried to move in, that's all that was available so they started buying there, but always moved south as soon as it was available. Perelman had a house in a north-end beachfront strip known as Raiders' Row, but he moved south as soon as the opportunity presented itself."

"With that sort of turnover at those prices, real estate agents must make a fortune."

"But at what cost? They're predators, pure and simple. As far as ethics go, money has pushed out morality." He sighed. "They'll probably soon be sending bottles of champagne over to Jonathan assuming he wants to sell."

"But they must know he's been arrested for the murder."

He shrugged. "They figure his money will get him off. The only good thing is that the ordinary people aren't hurt in this war—the participants feed on each other." I reached up to kiss him goodnight.

"Remember to call me with the coroner results as soon as you have them."

He phoned me at noon.

"Unquestionably anaphylactic shock." He sighed. "She wouldn't listen to me. I begged her to keep an Epi-Pen with her at all times, but Bootsie hated to display any sign of weakness or illness. She said she refused to be one of those old Florida farts who talked and thought about nothing but health."

"When is the reading of the will?" I asked.

"I notified all interested parties to be at the house today at 2:00."

COUNT JOSÉ SAT in a side chair. Jonathan was in front of the desk at which the lawyer sat with papers spread out before him. Melissa was next to Jonathan, holding his hand. Rivers and Janet sat in back of the room. There were two older women I didn't recognize who were identified as Pat and Meg McClintock, sisters who had been Bootsie's dayworkers for many years. Eunice, her ladies' maid, wasn't there but I realized she was only a recent addition to the household. I have had reason to sit in on will readings before and most often the only palpable emotions in the room are anticipation and greed. Not this time. You could feel the undercurrent of genuine sadness. Everyone loved Bootsie and the sorrow was real.

Jonathan and Melissa gasped when they heard the figures. He could be inheriting well over a billion dollars all told, plus the Palm Beach property. Rivers and Janet would receive enough to take care of them comfortably for the rest of their lives. The McClintock sisters were left five thousand dollars. Various charities received sizable bequests. A sentimental sidebar was that Bootsie had some years ago purchased the small farm on which she was born in Louisiana and left it to the family who were its caretakers.

Tom arose and began to pack up his papers.

"The silver—what about the silver?" asked the Count. He looked distraught.

"That's all included in the contents of the house and thus goes to Jonathan," said Tom crisply.

The Count looked stunned. "But she promised it to me always. She knew how I loved and appreciated her collection. She would always say, 'José, the silver is for you.' People even heard her say it, I am sure." He turned to Rivers. "You heard Madam say that, didn't you?"

I could see a flash of genuine pity on the lawyer's face. "I'm truly sorry. But unfortunately verbal commitments are not valid. Perhaps she meant to, but you know how Bootsie would make notes to herself and then forget. As things stand, the silver legally belongs to Jonathan."

The Count's face crumpled and he collapsed into his chair. He sat there mumbling "But she promised."

I walked over to Jonathan. "My condolences and my congratulations—it's sort of a mixed bag, isn't it? Would you like me to move out today?"

He looked confused. "No, no, Emma, of course not. Stay as long as you like, of course."

I looked over at the Count. "I assume you mean the same for José."

"Oh, for gosh sakes, of course. I'll go over and tell him he can stay in the house as long as he likes, the poor guy."

"Well, at least until you know what you plan to do with it," said Melissa.

"Thinking of turning it into a home for abused Inuit women, Melissa?" I asked.

She flushed. "No, of course not."

I shouldn't have done that but I couldn't resist. You can't joke with Cause people—they're always afraid to laugh for fear they'd be offending some oppressed minority or other.

"José was really wonderful to Auntie and I think she truly cared for him," said Jonathan. "Maybe I'd better include a small weekly allowance there, too."

Melissa looked disapproving, but then maintaining an idle fancyman would have no place in her black-and-white approach to life.

"I think that would be fair and proper," I said. "Your aunt for sure would be pleased."

He smiled.

"Also, don't you think you'd better let the staff know what to do?" I could see he was at a loss and not thinking things through. He obviously needed a little prodding and guidance.

"It's customary to keep the house open and the staff on at least until they get settled into their new lives and the will is probated and distributed. I'm sure Rivers will advise you on the financial details of running the household as he had full charge and your aunt trusted him completely."

He nodded gratefully. "Yes, thank you, Emma. I'll take care of that at once."

He went directly over to Count José who sat with his head on his chest. He was probably counting on a windfall for his years invested in being Bootsie's consort. Obviously new in the field, he was unskilled in the details of the job or he would have seen to it that his name was on the line in the will. A professional gigolo well knows that an oral commitment isn't worth the paper it's not written on.

I walked over to Tom. "One question, counselor. Did all the beneficiaries know about their inheritances?"

He grimaced. "Everyone except for Rick Bolton. Bootsie was a wonderful, generous woman. But we all have our little weaknesses. Hers was that she enjoyed gratitude."

"That little weakness might have killed her. It means everyone in this room had a reason to want her dead," I said.

He looked surprised. "Nonsense. Some of the sums were paltry."

"To you, Tom," I reminded him.

We were all milling around the room when the door opened suddenly. Detective Berkowitz appeared with two uniformed policemen and walked directly over to Jonathan.

"Jonathan Carswell, I am arresting you for the murder of Bootsie Corrigan. You have the right to remain silent, you have the right to retain a lawyer . . ."

We all froze in shock as they finished Mirandaizing him and slipped on handcuffs. Tom Blair spoke first. "Hold it there, Detective. I am his attorney," and he looked at Jonathan who nodded. "The murder was only just proven.

How can you possibly have accumulated sufficient evidence to charge Mr. Carswell?''

"We have, Mr. Blair," she said coolly. "You're welcome to come downtown with your client to ascertain all the facts."

"I'm coming too," said Melissa.

"That's your choice, of course, Miss Trabert. But you'll have to make your own way there and back and you may not come in with Mr. Carswell."

"I think it's best if you remain here, Melissa," said Tom Blair. "I'll come back here when we're finished downtown and report to you."

Melissa Trabert—I never knew her name. I wondered if she were related to the famous tennis player.

We heard the police car pull away. Everyone stood around looking confused. I sighed. OK, Emma, it's take-charge time again.

"Janet, why don't you start dinner? There will be four of us—I believe Mr. Levitar will join us."

She straightened up and her face immediately took on a look of contented determination. Everything's all right in the world—she had her job to do. Then I took Rivers aside and told him that financial arrangements for maintaining the house would now be handled by Mr. Blair who is executor of the estate and will be in charge until Mr. Carswell is able to take over (if ever, I thought). Rivers was always such a stalwart dependable rock that it never dawned on me until this moment that he was not a young man and was probably in his sixties. On hearing my assurance, the unfamiliar look of uncertainty disappeared and he instantly assumed his usual posture of authority. He walked over to the McClintock sisters, obviously instructing them to continue their duties. Eunice stood aside, apparently wondering about her current status. I heard him tell her to resume her work as there was still a lady in the house to be looked after—me—and she's to stay on until advised further.

It was a very quiet dinner table that evening. Even Abba couldn't get a conversation off the ground. We were a rather morose crew. Melissa picked at her food. The Count never looked up from his plate except to accept another wine refill from Rivers, which seemed more frequent than I remembered. Janet had provided a wonderful meal of melon and prosciutto followed by cream of watercress soup. The veal piccata was light and lemony, just as I like it, but everything seemed to taste like straw. The only one eating with gusto was Abba who, to my knowledge, has never encountered a situation that affected his appetite. We were on our salad course when we heard the front door open. In walked Jonathan with Tom Blair behind him. Melissa jumped up with a cry and ran over to her fiancé. Tom looked weary but triumphant. I looked at him and mouthed "Bail?" He nodded. Well, I didn't expect dismissal of charges.

"Have you eaten, Mr. Carswell?" said Rivers solicitously. "May I set up two more places at the table?" I noticed he no longer called him "Mr. Jonathan" but was now giving Johnny the full grown-up treatment as befitting the master of the house. The possibility that he may be the murderer of his former mistress made little difference. This is merely the normal process of succession and his job is to serve whoever is in charge. The queen is dead, long live the king.

"Yes, Rivers, please do. I know I shouldn't be hungry after all this. But I'm starved. Mr. Blair will join us, of course."

Tom nodded with a smile. "You might start calling me Tom. After dinner, perhaps we all ought to go into the library and I'll tell you all about it."

The Count looked up and said softly, "You will excuse me, please. I have some letters to write."

Either the man's a total gentleman who doesn't feel it is his place to attend such a meeting or he carries on a voluminous correspondence. Or perhaps he doesn't wish to be part of the cheering squad for the man who has in effect robbed him of his expected inheritance and possibly also of his benefactor.

We all settled into chairs and looked expectantly at Tom Blair.

"It seems our young friend here positively adores this particular stuffing."

Jonathan nodded. "It's that andouille sausage. I've always loved it since I was a kid."

"And when Janet makes it, he generally slips into the kitchen and nips a bit here and there."

"In other words," I said, "he's in and out of the kitchen all day with full access, making it a cinch to dump a load of powdered peanuts into the bowl."

Jonathan jumped up. "But I didn't do that—I wouldn't do that. Lord, I love her, she is my MOTHER. I don't need her money, I need her," he said, and he began to cry. You could see the first realization hit him that his aunt was gone forever.

Melissa ran over and put her arms around him protectively. "But everyone goes into the kitchen all day," she said. "Janet was never the kind of cook who doesn't allow people into her kitchen."

"Melly's right," said Jonathan. "When I was a kid, I'd come home from school and go straight in there. She'd always have freshly baked cookies and milk and we'd sit and talk. I loved being there, it was always so busy. People were trooping in and out—the maids, Rivers, deliverymen, repairmen. Whenever she made one of her special dishes, she'd always make lots extra for friends who would drop by or send their maids over to pick up their little Janet's CARE packages as we all called them."

"So everyone had a chance to lace the stuffing," said Melissa.

"True, but not everyone knew Bootsie was allergic to peanuts," I said softly.

"That's just what Detective Berkowitz said," said Tom Blair. "The police naturally questioned everyone and no one knew about the potentially fatal reaction. Which makes sense—I told you how Bootsie hated to reveal any physical weakness."

"Besides," I added, "it probably seemed like a very remote possibility that she'd ever encounter that humble little object in the haute cuisine around here. Macadamia nuts, maybe. But somehow I can't imagine the lowly peanut ever appearing on any table on Ocean Boulevard. She probably felt quite safe in not disclosing her condition."

I looked at Jonathan. "Why did you profess not to know about your aunt's allergy when I was giving her CPR?"

He was taken aback and I could feel Tom Blair stiffen. "I—I don't know. In the shock of the moment, I guess I just didn't remember. When you said allergy, I thought of those usual things people are always talking about—you know, ragweed, pollens, roses, penicillin. I'd forgotten completely about those damned peanuts. We just assumed that it wasn't ever going to happen." He sat down and put his head in his hands. "But it did."

I looked over at Abba and he shrugged. It was a reasonable answer. But certainly not a conclusive one.

"But, Tom, what's the basis of the arrest? You haven't mentioned any hard evidence against Jonathan," I said.

"They found bags of peanuts in Jonathan's kitchen," he said quietly. I fell back in my chair.

"And residue of ground peanuts in his blender," he said.
We all stared at Jonathan.

"It was all left over from the barbecue," he said, looking
distressed. "I had a cookout for my kids in my backyard.
We had popcorn, potato chips, peanuts, chili, and cokes."

"But why were peanuts getting ground up in the
blender?" I asked.

"For the chili," he said.

"You put ground peanuts in chili?" I asked in surprise.

"Sure, it thickens it. It's Uncle Buck's secret recipe. He
used to make it that way when I was a kid but he stopped
when Aunt Bootsie developed this allergy ten years ago.
She didn't always have it."

"I remember reading about a student at Brown University some years ago who died within minutes from chili
that was made with peanuts," said Tom. "Perhaps it's not
that uncommon an ingredient."

"Sure—now we know of two people who use it," I said.
"The reason that student died was because the presence of
peanuts in chili was totally unexpected and she had no reason to suspect it would be in the dish."

"Was this cookout a traditional thing, or just a spur-of-
the-moment idea?" asked Abba.

Jonathan looked puzzled. "I never did it before, no. This
was the first time." His face brightened. "It was great. The
kids had a swell time, didn't they, Melly?" Abba and I
looked at each other and both rolled our eyes.

"Melissa was there, too?" I asked. "Whose idea was
this event?"

Jonathan looked tentatively at Melissa. "I don't remember. I know Melly and I talked about it, but I don't remember who thought of it first, do you, Melly?"

"I think it was you, Jonathan," she said quickly.

She's lying.

"You explained all this to the police, of course," I asked.

Jonathan nodded, looking totally miserable. "But they didn't believe me."

No kidding. If I didn't know Jonathan to be such an ingenuous naif, I probably wouldn't buy his story either.

"You sure picked a lousy time for your peanut-packed picnic, boychik," said Abba.

"Detective Berkowitz might see it as a planned time. It sets him up with an alibi," I said. I looked at Tom Blair. "I assume you've placed a call to Kevin Birnbaum."

Tom Blair was great at handling estates for wealthy old ladies who adored him and was marvelous at taking care of their affairs honestly and profitably for all concerned. But when criminal charges were involved, he brought in Kevin Birnbaum, who was arguably the leading defense lawyer in the south.

"Who's Kevin Birnbaum?" asked Jonathan.

"The product of an Irish mother and a Jewish father?" asked Abba. "A truly winning combo—the great gift of language that's bred into every charming Irishman, and the clever *yiddishe kopp* that's enabled Jews to survive for thousands of years."

"He's one of the finest criminal lawyers in the country," said Tom.

Jonathan looked stricken. "Criminal! But I'm not a criminal—I swear I didn't do it."

"If you didn't, can you name a more promising candidate?" I asked. "You had the means and the motive."

I didn't like to hit him so hard between the eyes this way, but I didn't feel he was really fully aware of the danger of his situation. It's not unusual for accused individuals to feel calm and sanguine because they know they're innocent and just assume that this fact will become apparent in time. In the meantime the D.A.'s office is building a case and tightening the noose. It's important that a little fear enters their consciousness since that gets the juices flowing and often helps them remember points that may assist in proving their innocence.

He turned to me with a look of triumph. Good—maybe the element of fear is working on him and he'll recollect an important fact that would put him out of the running as the guilty party. Like maybe both his hands were in bandages with a severe case of poison ivy all that fatal day.

"That's it, Emma. You must help me. You'll find out who really did this terrible thing, won't you? Auntie used to tell me you were some sort of private investigator and you never failed."

I smiled. "True, but that's because I never accept a case unless I'm sure I can resolve it. I'm not sure about yours, Johnny. Besides, I am working on another case now."

Then I thought about it. He would have to be an absolute idiot to have poisoned his aunt in a situation where he would be the obvious suspect. If he wanted to get rid of her, surely there had to be many more private and obscure opportunities. He wasn't the egotistical grandstand type. And why would he want her billions? Knowing Bootsie's generosity, he must have a nice tidy income that keeps him living as well as he likes. He has never evinced any interest in becoming a tycoon. I knew Bootsie well, but I really knew little of her life and past. There may well be others who have reasons for not wanting her around anymore. My record has been aces because I don't deal in uncertainties. Most situations I run into may seem complex and often hopeless to the persons involved, but an outsider like me with the kind of brain that cuts to the core at once can usually see the way to a solution fairly easily. Of course, I never let that one out. My clients view me as some sort of cross between guru and genius, and I've never seen any reason to disabuse them of that opinion. They may be right. But this time I haven't a clue. The possibility of working on a case and failing to recover a fee was out of the question. Suddenly I had an idea.

"Jonathan, I'll take you on but with an additional stipulation. You may not know my terms—they are that I solve the case within two weeks at which point you pay me $20,000. If I don't, you don't pay me a penny."

I heard Melissa gasp. Welcome to the world of capitalism, my pet. You have entered the citadel of risk-takers and money-makers, which of course go hand in hand.

He nodded eagerly. "Sounds fine to me. What's the extra?"

"Whether or not I find the real murderer, you give me the right to make the disposition of the new silver candelabra."

"You mean you want it?"

"No, but I will take it from you and tell you to whom it must go and how."

He looked stunned. "That's it?"

I nodded.

His face lit up. He held out his hand. "Done!"

Tom Blair was frowning.

"Abba, Tom looks like he needs a little fresh air. Why don't you take him and Melissa out to the terrace for a bit?"

Melissa looked bewildered as she followed Tom, who wore a tight little smile. They silently walked out with Abba, who like a true soldier moved unquestioningly to follow orders.

I took Jonathan by the arm and said, "Follow me." I led him into the dining room and took the candelabra off the table.

"I'm taking this with me. It's not mine yet, but I want to be sure it's available when I am ready to take it."

He looked confused. "Why shouldn't it be?"

"Statute 732.802 Florida law states that no one convicted of murder may benefit from his crime. Most states have that rule. It means that in the unlikely event that the case comes to trial and you are adjudged guilty, you wouldn't be able to inherit Bootsie's estate and the candelabra would not be yours to give. Which is why I removed Tom from the room. He's an officer of the court and couldn't allow you to remove it. At this time, everything should rightfully be sealed by the court, but since that hasn't happened yet and no inventory has been taken, I see this as technically OK. And if not, who cares and who's to know?"

I went upstairs and put the candelabra into my suitcase. I don't break laws. I may bend them here and there when there's a fine line of uncertainty. Isn't that how all lawyers make their living?

When I came downstairs, I found everyone had left except for Abba who was still on the terrace.

He inhaled appreciatively. "The air, the flowers, the moon—it's marvelous here." For a moment I thought I'd gotten away with it. But Abba missed nothing.

"What a mind. You can't lose. No matter what, you get your twenty-thou fee for returning the silver to client number one—Lady Margaret. And unless the dastardly deed was really done by sweet-faced John-boy, you may well find the real killer and end up with yet another twenty thou." He shook his head in admiration. "Oy, could we use you in the Middle East Peace Talks. All they'd have to do is promise you twenty-thousand dollars, which is probably less than Arafat's weekly hotel bill, and you'd cut through all the fucking *bablat* bullshit and have the Arabs and Jews dancing the hora in Tel Aviv in two weeks."

I bowed my head in acknowledgment. "Thank you for your vote of confidence, my friend."

"So what's your next step, sweetheart?"

"Rick Bolton."

VII

VII

AS I WAS about to turn into the building on Comox Street and Denman where my friend Nancy Lagey lived, I looked over my left shoulder and stopped. It was easy to understand what drew people from all over the world to Vancouver. Where else could you see a foreground of tall green fir trees leading down to a beautiful sand beach and blue Pacific ocean waters against a background of spectacular mountains that appeared close enough to touch—all while you're standing on a downtown street?

The city has a vitality brought to it by the exciting ethnic mix it has attracted and the huge financial resources such groups have poured in. The Chinese appeared in the 1850s to find gold, which led them to name the city Gold Mountain or Gum Shan. They helped build the important Canadian Pacific Railway that, combined with the city's Great White Fleet of clipper ships, gave Vancouver a week's edge ahead of the California ports when shipping silks and spices from the Orient to New York. More recently the last few years have seen a huge infusion of Hong Kong money and people who are fleeing from the Mainland China takeover.

At this point, Vancouver's population is one-third Asian and it has become a multicultural World City. Forty-ninth and Main Street is called "Little Calcutta." As you walk around town, you can't miss the prevalence of supermarket signs in Chinese. The upscale suburb of Richmond is now one-half Asian. The city has grown so quickly that there is a helter-skelter architectural charm brought about by the juxtaposition of later Victorian, cobbled streets and huge glass monoliths that reflect the mountains and the often-turbulent skies.

Vancouver has a level of excitement that is kept on the *qui vive* by the dramatic weather changes that can suddenly transform the sky into swirling blue and black cloud formations, and the Pacific waters into frenzied whitecaps. It is a city of young people who are attracted to its spiritual quality created by the many religious faces presented. You can see them at the Sepulcher of Stanley Park, or enjoying the Gregorian chants at the Christ Church Cathedral built in 1895 with the exterior of an English village parish church and the rough-hewn interior of an American frontier town. The lively nightspots open to all hours are also a draw. The city abounds in marvelous restaurants offering a wide range of Asian dining spots established by the new wave of immigration from Vietnam and Korea as well as China. Vancouver has also attracted a large group of American retirees who are more adventurous than those who flock to Florida. The compactness of the downtown is appealing to people who have some difficulty getting around. And the excellent Canadian health care program is a major attraction to senior citizens, although the government is now getting tougher in imposing immigrant qualifications for admission to the system.

Nancy had moved to Vancouver fifteen years ago with her husband Joe who was a professor of sociology. It turned

out to be the last stop for Joe, a man who looked upon
roots as paralyzing rather than comforting and who reveled
in newness rather than familiarity. His restlessness kept the
family on the move and trained Nancy in the technique of
locating a doctor, dentist, lawyer, barber, cleaner, and Uni-
tarian Church in any town within two days. She was a li-
brarian—another wonderfully portable profession, and now
worked in Vancouver which meant she probably knew
everyone in town already. That's why I wasn't perturbed
when I didn't find Rick Bolton listed in the phone book.
His type doesn't always have phones since they're hard to
unload fast when there's a need for a quick getaway.

"Sure I know Rick Bolton. He's been a part-time worker
here at the library for the past month. He puts books back
on the shelves." She sighed. "He's eager, but we're going
to have to dump him soon."

"Why?" I asked. "All he would have to know is the
alphabet, right?"

"I'm afraid one needs more knowledge than that. Thomas Hardy does not get filed under 'T' and Charles Dick-
ens' *The Mystery of Edwin Drood* does not go into the
Mystery section. When someone asked him for *The De-
bacle* by Emile Zola, he led him to the correct 'Z' area and
then said proudly, 'We have all her books.' She looked
toward the door and then at her watch. "Here he is now—
half an hour late as usual." She sighed. "I hate it when
people are late. It's not their delay that bothers me, it's the
nuisance of having to listen to either their excuses of te-
dious minutiae-laden inane truths or convoluted but rarely
creative lies. I usually get the latter from Rick. When he
gets through, I'll introduce you."

He looked just like what he was—one of life's losers
who wore the continual expression of sneering resentment
at having somehow missed the gravy train he believed ex-

isted only for others. A walking cliché, he was in his early forties and wore his hair in a graying ponytail, the mark of the man who needed to proclaim his distinction from conventional folk. Of course, there was the usual ubiquitous outfit of worn leather jacket, jeans, and backpack.

When I told him I was a friend of his aunt, his face reflected such a fast succession of expressions that I almost couldn't keep up with them. Surprise, discomfort, happy anticipation, angry anticipation, fear.

"Why don't I take you to lunch when you're through here?" I asked.

I could see he was hesitant, yet curious. But it was the free lunch that got him.

"Sure."

I took him to Bud's Halibut on Denman Street. There are thirty-six restaurants within four blocks on Denman Street, offering a cornucopia of ethnic menus from every Asian nation. I chose Bud's because first, he has the best fresh fish and chips in town and I dearly love that English delicacy and mourn its disappearance from the streets of London. Second, their variety of beers is marvelous and I suspected that would be Rick's drink of choice.

I was on my second glass of New Castle Brown Ale which is so smooth, I think it's the closest thing to a malted milk, and Rick was on his fourth. We talked about Bootsie in the present tense and he was apparently totally unaware of her demise.

"She never liked me," he said truculently. "It was that little suck-up cousin of mine who got everything. She thought the sun shone out of his asshole."

"Maybe it was because Jonathan lived with her and became like a son," I suggested.

"Naa—I lived with her and Uncle Buck for a while, too."

"When was that?" I asked.

He shifted uncomfortably. "When my old man was away. I guess I was about fifteen."

"Where was your father?"

After a moment's silence, "In the joint. Two years armed robbery. The dumb fuck held up a 711 and forgot to fill the gas tank in his getaway car."

"Where was your mother?"

He shrugged. "Who knows? She took off right after I was born."

Either she wasn't the maternal type or one look at the ferret-face she gave birth to and she was out of there. It was the kind of sad little tale that defense lawyers throw out to juries to plead clemency for their clients' foul deeds. To me, it's simply an explanation, not an excuse.

Poor Bootsie. She sure had bad family karma. Her sister and brother-in-law get killed in a car crash leaving her with a fourteen-year-old orphan, and then her brother ends up in the slammer lumbering her with a semi-literate churlish teenager. The whole thing sounds like a song by Johnny Cash.

"Why wouldn't she like you?" I asked. Why indeed. Who wouldn't love such a darling boy? "You strike me as a pretty nice guy." So I lie a little. Just put it under the heading of "Techniques for Extracting Information." It beats the rubber hose.

As expected, this flattering and surely rare vote of confidence made him open like a flower. He slipped down in his chair and relaxed out of the stiff position that showed he had been on his guard. Body language is so eloquent and informative.

"Yeah—I don't know why she didn't seem to take to me. There I was, her brother's only kid who lived dirt poor always, and she's living high on the hog in that big house out here in Richmond when the place was still fancy before all those money-grubbing slopies moved in.''

Like I said, who couldn't love such a charmer?

"So maybe I didn't know how to eat and talk and dress like shit-faced Jonathan, but hell, couldn't she see I was more of a man? She threw me out when I was eighteen,'' he said, looking disgruntled at the memory of this great injustice.

Knowing what qualifies for manhood in his circles, I knew I wouldn't like the answer to my next question.

"Why? What did you do?''

He shrugged. "It was just one of those kid-bustin'-out things that any red-blooded young dude does. I took the car for a little joy ride without asking like I was supposed to do. Big fucking deal.''

"Where did you go?''

"Seattle.''

That distance qualifies for more than little joy ride status.

"You had a valid driving license, I assume?''

He looked at me with wordless scorn.

"How long were you gone?''

"Two, three days—I don't remember.''

"What did you do for money?''

His eyes took on a shifty look. "So I took a few bucks off Auntie's dresser. She never seemed to miss it.''

I'm not in the business of preaching morality. I leave that to ministers, priests, rabbis, and Jerry Falwell. I think even *they* might give up on this one.

"Did you ever go back to see your aunt?''

"Naa. I call her every now and then, though. Give the old girl a break, you know. I hear she lives like some queen in a fucking palace in Palm Beach.''

His face took on a bitter look and he took a long swig of his fourth beer. I hoped he wasn't one of those belligerent drunks. He was a big man and I flunked out of Karate I, but I've always found my knee-him-in-the-balls action highly effective.

"She'll probably leave everything to that suckface Jonathan," he said morosely. "But you can fucking bet Rick Bolton's not the kind who would fucking live with his face up anyone's ass, not for nothing," he said proudly and belched loudly.

His mother should win an award for 20/20 foresight.

He obviously knew nothing of Bootsie's death or bequest. He wasn't a good enough actor to carry off ignorance of something that big. Besides, why would he have to pretend no knowledge of his aunt's death if he had nothing to do with it?

He struggled to his feet looking for the room he needed to visit after so many beers, and knocked his backpack to the floor. We both bent to pick up the pieces of paper that had scattered and I was about to hand him a snapshot which I glanced at in passing and froze.

"Your girlfriend?"

"Yeah."

It was Eunice, Bootsie's and now my ladies' maid.

When he returned, I asked, "Does she live here in Vancouver?"

He looked puzzled. "Who?"

"Your girlfriend." I almost said her name.

"Oh, you mean Eunie. No, she's stateside, someplace down south. She calls me pretty regular, though. I don't have a phone, but she gets me at my friend Phil's place—in fact, tonight at 8:00. You could set the clock by her," he said. "She's crazy about me, you know."

Who wouldn't be?

"She's great but she's always at me to get married. She's older than me. She even once took me home to meet her folks in South Carolina. They were having some sort of soppy reunion, you know, some kind of family shit.''

"And you went? That was nice of you."

"Hell, why not? She paid for everything—even the hotel. It was kind of a blast."

"Where in South Carolina was it?"

"I remember because it had the dumb-ass name of Prosperity.'' He laughed. "Hell, the whole town had a population of about 700 shitkickers.''

There's going to be a big time at Phil's house tonight when lover boy here gets word of his windfall. They won't have to fire him from the library—he'll never show up there again. And the $250,000 will be just peanuts, if you'll pardon the expression. Because if Jonathan is convicted of the murder, the estate passes on to the next legatee as if the killer had predeceased the victim. In two words—Rick Bolton.

I had no desire to hang around for the upcoming celebration. I was on the next plane back to Palm Beach.

VIII

~~~

I'LL SAY ONE thing for Eunice, she had guts. There she was in my room, helping me unpack as any ladies' maid would do, acting as though nothing unusual had occurred when she had to know I had met Rick.

"I thought you seemed a bit out of character as a ladies' maid," I said. "What did you hope to accomplish here?"

She turned from hanging my clothes in the closet.

"Make money," she said simply, continuing to put things away. "I needed a job and Mrs. Corrigan hired me."

"You realize you're a prime suspect for her murder?"

She didn't even flinch. This was one cool cookie.

"Why? What do I get out of her death?"

"A rich husband."

She stopped what she was doing and looked directly at me. A tall woman of about fifty, with blonde hair worn in an oddly schoolmarmish bun atop her head, pale blue eyes, and a broad-hipped figure, she spoke in an educated voice.

"I understand you are some sort of investigator working for Mr. Jonathan or I wouldn't speak to you at all," she said. "I've been taking care of Rick for years—I love him and he needs me. I know you saw him in Vancouver and he doesn't make the best impression. He's really a good person who has lost his way because he never had anyone to love him. I felt if his aunt could just give him some security, it would be a start in the making of him. I came here to work for her so I could maybe get the chance to talk to her about Rick and help her to see what he's really like.''

"And did you get that chance?"

"Yes."

"Apparently you were quite eloquent. That bequest to him was recent."

She smiled. "Mrs. Corrigan was a very fair and kind woman.''

A neat epitaph. She was also a woman who understood the chain of poverty that can grip a family for generations. I could just see her thinking that for the sake of her dead brother who really never had a chance, she could possibly break the pattern of failure by giving his son a leg up. Perhaps she saw Eunice as the steadying influence that might get Rick on the right course.

I didn't share Bootsie's and Eunice's optimistic view. I saw no possible chance of reforming that little turd unless he shaved his head and became a Moonie. I looked at her sadly. Another one of those maternal women who pick up young losers in the belief that love will be the panacea for his difficulties and all that's been missing in his life is her. These misguided martyrs usually end up with the short end of the stick as the guy grabs the gains he has gotten through Mother Earth's labors and goes off into the sunset with some nubile chick.

"I know I'm older than Rick and you probably think I'm one of those desperate women who prey upon guileless young man to make a life for herself.''

"I'd never characterize Rick as guileless," I said dryly. "Gutless, brainless, and maybe a little heartless would be more like it."

She shook her head firmly. "You're wrong about him. I'll admit he's a little rough around the edges, but he's not a bad person."

"As compared to whom?" I asked. "OK, Nixon was worse."

"I'm not a complete fool," she said. "I would never give so much of myself to a real villain."

"I don't think you're a fool at all. In fact, you strike me as bright and educated. What did you major in and where?"

"English Literature at Emory. I visited Vancouver on vacation and fell in love with it and got a job teaching at the University of British Columbia."

I sighed. Another one of those victims of the Women's Movement who were told to fight for their independence until, too late, they realized that being independent usually meant being alone.

"Where did you meet Rick?"

"He took my course on love sonnets. At least, he attended a few sessions."

Just enough to meet women—that's why men like Rick took such courses.

"So you took him under your wing and decided to make a man of him."

She flushed angrily. "You make it sound trivial and stupid. It was neither."

"I'm sorry. It's just I feel you are wasting a good mind and soul on a wastrel who will never live up to let alone repay your efforts."

"That may be your view," she said firmly, "obviously it's not mine."

"How did he react when you told him his aunt had left him a quarter of a million dollars?"

She smiled at the memory. "To say he was overjoyed would be a bit of an understatement."

"And did you mention that his inheritance will be far more if Jonathan gets convicted?"

Her puzzlement looked genuine. But she was a very smart lady and may very well have played the lead in all her school plays. Both my professions require being a quick reader of facial expressions, but even the skilled cross-examining attorney or experienced Private Resolver can't outwit either a true psychotic or competent actor. Sure, Perry Mason and Matlock always spot the tell-tale flick of an eyelash that indicates the witness is lying. But they must have flawless insights since they only have sixty minutes to solve the case.

"Why would that matter?" she asked.

When I told her about Florida Statute 732.802, she looked genuinely shocked. Then I could see a look of comprehension come over her face.

"That's why you think I might have poisoned Mrs. Corrigan. Why, that's ridiculous. What would I get out of it? Rick and I aren't married."

"I'm sure that's a minor point that you intend to deal with, Eunice. I'd suggest you do it quickly because guys like Rick don't know how to hold on to money and unless you have some official standing and control, he'll blow it for sure."

She turned her back to me as she put my now-empty suitcase in the armoire.

"I'm surprised you didn't leave here when Rick told you I had seen him in Vancouver," I said.

"That would be foolish of me. I know you're going to tell Detective Berkowitz about me and Rick. All you learned is that we have a connection which I agree could make my presence here suspicious. But there's no proof that I even knew of Mrs. Corrigan's allergy to peanuts, let alone acted upon it. Running away would be like an admission of complicity. Since I'm innocent, I'll stay right here, available for police questioning."

Then she smiled. "Is that all, Miss Rhodes? I think you're unpacked. If you'll excuse me, I have other work downstairs."

For the first time, I felt sorry for Rick. If this woman wants something, she's going to do damn all to get it, no holds barred. Besides being extremely shrewd, she has the drive of desperation on her side. Her handling of Rick shows long-term planning and willingness to make big moves. Not every teacher would go virtually across the continent to take a job as a maid in order to attempt to achieve her goals. I'll turn over the facts on her to the very competent Detective Berkowitz and let her handle it from here. I always cooperate with the police—when it suits my purposes and timetable.

And when I came downstairs, there she was.

"Good morning," she said. "And how was Vancouver?"

I smiled. "Beautiful as always, but brief. And how was dinner with Abba?" I asked.

She was taken aback and then chuckled, showing very white teeth and a nice hearty laugh. "I forgot I'm not the only detective around here," she said.

"Elementary, my dear Watson," I said. "He's the only one who knew where I was going and was given full permission to reveal that fact to you alone."

I was relieved at her reaction. Usually I avoid disclosing my professional identity to the local police since they do not look kindly upon private investigators, let alone unlicensed ones like me. Of course if I lived in the sleepy little village of St. Mary's Meade and had a string of solved murders behind me, or dwelt on Baker Street and had built the career of Inspector Lestroud, I might be regarded as a valuable asset instead of a nosy nuisance. But unfortunately everyone in Palm Beach knew from Bootsie what I did for a living, so I lost the usual advantage of functioning sub rosa without being concerned about sharing my information. Having to deal with official antagonism would only impose difficulties that could hamper me, so cooperation would have to be the order of the day here. Phooey!

"May I ask if you've learned anything germane to this case?" she asked.

Ah, the new breed of educated law enforcement officers. "Germane"—now isn't that a classier way of saying "so did you pick up any shit I could use?"

I told her all I had learned. Her eyebrows went up when she heard about Eunice.

"I was just going in for breakfast," I said. "How about a cup of coffee?"

We went into the dining room and I was glad to see the sideboard filled with covered silver casseroles lined up on a series of hot trays. The household was functioning as always. I lifted the lids with the hand-embroidered mini pot holders Bootsie had made to protect fingers from hot silver knobs.

"I've never seen anything like those," said Detective Berkowitz, looking at the little holders as she sat down with a cup of black coffee.

"They're kind of cutesy-wootsey, but typical of Bootsie," I said as I lifted an egg benedict onto my plate. "She thought of everything for the comfort of her guests and had these made special. Growing up poor made her a sucker for anything she saw as genteel."

"I get the feeling, Miss Rhodes, that Mrs. Corrigan was one of those women who comes across as simple but is really rather complex," she said as she eyed my egg.

"You're quite right. Bootsie was one of those rare people whose mind constantly went to ways in which she could improve everyone's quality of life, down to the smallest details. Of course, having the money to implement those intentions helped. Which is why you're looking with surprise or is it longing at my egg benedict. Under that delicious hollandaise-sauce-covered poached egg is a hefty slab of fine smoked Scottish salmon rather than the usual pedestrian ham. Come on, go for it. And please call me Emma."

She got up and put one on her plate. "I'm Deborah."

Great. She's not one of those stiffs who insist on maintaining a distance from any possible suspects in the case, which of course, I am. She tucked into the egg gustily and looked up with pleasure. "Mmm, is this delicious. I had coffee and a bagel at 5 A.M.," she said apologetically.

Lovely. She's also an enjoyer. Abba must be in heaven. I like people who like things. People who appreciate good eating usually appreciate all sorts of sensual experiences. Another of the "Emma Rhodes Instant People Rating Rules" is that those who scan the menu in a four-star restaurant and then order broiled salmon or steak demonstrate a low sense of adventure and limited lust for life and usually aren't much fun.

I allowed her the uninterrupted pleasure of her breakfast and then, as she picked up her coffee cup, said casually: "The fact that you're here could indicate you're not totally sold on Jonathan Carswell as the alleged killer."

"It could," she said, sipping her coffee. "It could also indicate a need to tighten up a few loose ends and further solidify his guilt."

Good answer. Ambivalent. This is not going to be the open-and-shut "we've got the perpetrator so no need to look further" situation Tom Blair had feared. I left her as she headed for the kitchen to talk to Janet. Just the woman I wanted her to see.

After she left, I went into the kitchen. I asked Janet if all the servants knew of Bootsie's deadly allergy.

"Of course," she said heatedly.

"Everyone—including Eunice?"

"Everyone," she said emphatically. "Mrs. Corrigan may not have liked anyone to know because she hated to be sick and she never let on when anything bothered her. But she made sure she knew about everyone else's health problems. Before every one of our dinner parties, I had to check with the cook in every guest's home to find out if they had any special dietary restrictions. She was too sensitive to ask the people themselves." Her eyes filled with tears. "She was such a dear considerate person, there'll never be another like her again. For instance, Mrs. Pachurian has diabetes so when they're coming, I always end meals with fruit and cheese so the poor lady won't have the embarrassment of having to explain why she can't eat dessert. But I made sure no peanut ever came into this house, I can tell you. Now that you mention it, I once caught Eunice snacking on a bag of salted peanuts and boy, did I let her have it. She didn't like that, I can tell you," she said, smiling at the memory. "She's OK but she's a bit stuck-up you know—thinks she's better than the rest of us. She told one of the girls that she used to be a teacher. Maybe she was." She giggled. "The way she wears her hair in that silly old-fashioned bun on top of her head, she looks like my third-grade teacher."

Lie number one, Eunice. And a surprisingly foolish one because it's so easy to check. She claimed to have no knowledge of her employer's allergy. However, it's her word against Janet's and she's undoubtedly egotistical enough to believe that the word of a younger educated woman like her would be accepted over that of a simple older woman like Janet.

"Who came into the kitchen that day, Janet?"

"That's what the lady detective asked me," she said with a sigh. "But what could I remember? I'm so busy the day of a party that I never see nothing going on around me. I had the two dayladies helping me but they don't know nobody around here and believe me I keep them too busy to look up. Of course, the Count comes in and out to make himself a cup of tea, and Rivers is in and out for this and that. Mr. Jonathan is always here when I make my sausage stuffing. Since he's a little boy, he comes in to stick his fingers in the pot and lick out the bowl," she said fondly. "I always make more for him, and for all the friends and neighbors. But he would never do a thing to hurt his auntie. Those two loved each other always, it was a joy to see them together, believe me." Suddenly, she looked behind me and smiled. "Hello, Mrs. Pachurian."

"Lucy, how nice to see you," I said.

She had a bunch of vegetables which she dumped on the counter. She was dressed in a crisp navy blue linen Bill Blass dress and carrying a cream Coach bag. It was a warm day but she looked as cool as if it were November in Vermont. It's a knack some women have; they don't perspire, they don't even glisten. I'm told it's healthier to perspire, but I think I'd rather risk having less active sweat glands than having to look like a head of wilted lettuce whenever the temperature goes above eighty.

"Emma, it was you I actually came over to see."

"Why don't we go out to the terrace?"

"I'll send out some iced tea," said Janet.

We settled into chairs and a few minutes later, Rivers came out with a tray of iced tea and cookies.

"I just had to talk to someone who cared about Bootsie," said Lucy, her eyes filled with tears. "She was such a good friend and one of the most unusual people I've ever met. I'll miss her so."

"That's very much how I feel," I said. "How long did you know each other?"

"Actually, I met her before we bought the house next door. I was in Milo's showroom when she came in and we found out we were on some of the same committees for Good Samaritan Hospital and the Norton Museum and we became friends. She was always such fun, you know. Unlike the other women here she never took herself or her wealth seriously." She frowned. "Some of them didn't quite accept me because I was the wife of a shopkeeper, you see. But that never troubled me—I'd had enough of that with my family when I announced I was marrying Milo."

"How did you two meet?" I asked. "You do seem like an unlikely couple."

She laughed. "You sound like my family. I came here on a visit. My brother had his horse at the Polo Club and I came to see him play. Milo was there with a friend and I fell in love with him at first sight. He was so handsome, so different from the pale ginger-mustached men I knew. He had just opened a small store on Worth Avenue and was struggling to make it work. When I told my parents that I wanted to stay here and marry Milo, well, you can imagine. My father even suggested that I have an affair with him. 'People like us do not marry people like him,' he said. We're a country family, you see. For generations, we have been lord and lady of the manor in our village. I braved their wrath and married the man I loved," she said with a smile, "and I've never regretted it. Milo swore he would make me proud of him and he did. He took that little shop and built it into the most important source of antique rugs in southern Florida. We have a wonderful life and a wonderful son whom my parents adore."

"Where is he?"

"Colin is finishing up his last year at Oxford," she said proudly.

We went on to talk about all sorts of things. She wanted to know how I knew her cousin Alfred. I just told her I knew his stepmother and let it go at that. I could see she was dying to know more details. But the pleasure of dealing with people of her class is their good breeding prevents them from asking too many questions. I've never met an aristocrat who I could classify as a *yenta*, although the queen is coming close to looking like one. She wears her hair in a bouffant style now only available in small beauty salons under the El train in the Bronx, and is constantly schlepping a handbag. I once saw a documentary about her and she walked from room to room in her own home, always clutching her large pocketbook. I remember wondering what she had in there. She's never without an equerry to attend to her needs so what could be in the bag? Perhaps something too embarrassing to ask them for? Like a fresh Depends.

Then Lucy and I began reminiscing about Bootsie, each recounting examples of her iconoclastic behavior that kept us both laughing and giggling like schoolgirls.

"You know, when I die, I would want a memorial service just like this—people sitting around and remembering me fondly," said Lucy. She looked at her small Piaget watch and said, "Goodness, I must be going. Emma, you must come by to see my garden."

We didn't make a set date because I didn't know where

I'll have to be whenever. But I promised I would call her as soon as I had an open hour or so.

Abba came over that evening and he and I and the Count sat on the terrace. Abba sank into one of the upholstered rattan chairs and sighed contentedly.

"Why is this spot so fucking fantastic?" he said.

"Because Bootsie made it so. She used to say how decorators created interiors that lived out their fantasies—like English hunt rooms, Casablanca bar rooms, or French salons. She said when someone walks into her house, she doesn't want them to say—'Oh, Billy Baldwin did this.' She wanted them to take one look and say 'Bootsie Corrigan lives here.' Notice everything on this terrace is aimed at conveying comfort and pleasure. All the chairs face the marvelous ocean view, even if it looks a little like a shipboard lineup instead of a conversational grouping. And they're all deeply padded instead of having some sticklike things that must 'lighten' the arrangement. There's a table next to every seat. So it looks a bit cluttered, but it's so convenient to place your drink. What decorator would dare to upholster every chair in a different color? But Bootsie was colorful and bright. That's the look that's her—and it works."

"She was surely one of a kind," said the Count. "I miss her very much. She drew people to her like a bright flame. There are so many bad people in this world—why should anyone destroy one who brings so much joy to others?"

"Perhaps that's just why," I said. "Dark people often try to extinguish bright lights."

"Or maybe she's not bringing the joy fast enough to others," said Abba.

"You mean like money."

"Yeah, like John-boy or Rick. Or those 'moderate' bequests that may mean just a year's club membership to Tom Blair but can mean a great deal to some of the help.''

The Count shook his head sadly. ''Possessions and wealth can often be a heavy and dangerous burden.''

''The damn thing is nothing could have been easier than for anyone to drop a pack of powdered peanuts into the bowl,'' said Abba.

''Yes,'' said the Count, ''but not everyone had a reason to want my beloved Bootsie dead.''

I looked at him reflectively. Didn't he realize he was one of the everyone who had a damned good reason? Maybe because he didn't actually inherit the silver, he thinks that takes him out of the running as a suspect. But people will kill for expectations which don't always pan out into reality. And he surely had expectations.

''Hallo, everyone—I thought I might find you out here.''

It was our neighboring lordly visitor. He stood reflected in the moonlight looking like he just stepped off the courts at Wimbledon. White LaCoste shirt and white slacks topped with a blue tennis blazer.

''I like your jacket, Alfred,'' said Abba lazily. ''Savile Row, of course.''

Alfred looked amused. ''How did you know, Abba?''

''The four buttonholes,'' and he looked over at me and winked.

Alfred looked at Abba's hat. ''Just as your hat reveals its provenance—Israeli army—four bulletholes.''

We laughed, and I beckoned to him to join us. ''Sorry we're out of chairs. Pull one in from inside.''

''No, thanks, I think I'll just sit on the step here.''

Abba winced. ''Not in those fancy white pants! In Brooklyn, sitting on the stoop in your good clothes was a punishable offense.''

''My dear Abba—would you have me deprive my dry-cleaner of his livelihood? Actually, I came over to convey my condolences and offer whatever help I could, although I'm not sure to whom."

"Jonathan would be the proper recipient for your condolence wishes, but we here who share the sadness of her loss"—and I looked over at the Count—"thank you as well, Alfred."

I don't usually sound like a Hallmark card, but this was truly from the heart.

"Where is Jonathan now?" he asked.

"He's out on bail and went home, rather exhausted, as you can imagine."

He shook his head. "Losing your aunt, whom he absolutely seemed to adore, and then being accused of her murder—that's just too much to bear. I really feel for the lad. She must have been quite a woman, Cousin Lucy seems quite broken up over her death. I'll be leaving soon, going back home. I don't know what effect all this will have on the matter you and I spoke of, Emma," and he looked at me questioningly.

This seemed to be the cue for Count José to rise and say, "I think I'm a bit tired as well, so may I bid you all good night," and he went off into the house.

"That guy has more exit lines than Noel Coward. I've heard of a policy of noninvolvement, but what about normal human curiosity?" asked Abba.

"José is a gentleman, and gentlemen do not listen in on personal conversations," I said.

"Quite right," said Alfred approvingly. "The moment he sensed that the discussion was leading to matters that perhaps he should not be privy to, he took his leave. Quite proper."

"Then listen, Mr. Perfect Gentleman, how proper of you

was it to introduce a conversation that didn't include him? Wasn't that fucking rude?'' said Abba.

Alfred laughed heartily. ''Touché. I stand corrected. I think you are not the Philistine you hold yourself out to be, Abba, and perhaps the role you play is to hide the fact that you are actually a very kind and considerate person.''

''Well, you've been found out, my friend,'' I said, patting Abba's hand. ''I've always said that Abba is one of Nature's noblemen. He was born with manners which, after all, are only a form of consideration for others.''

''Shucks, fellas, you're embarrassing me. I'm flattered, but I'm more interested in hearing you two continue the discussion the Count's defection aborted. We've already established that I'm a *yenta*—so as long as I have the credentials, give me the benefits.''

''Is it all right to speak in front of him?'' asked Alfred.

I nodded. ''It's even all right to do anything in front of him. The man's a sphinx.''

''Oy, did you have to liken me to an Arab icon?''

''Not if you can point out any Israeli representation for someone who doesn't talk . . . an impossibility in your country, wouldn't you say?''

''The problem of the restoration of the candelabra has now taken on another complication,'' said Alfred. ''Who will you deal with to get it back, Emma?''

''I only promise to produce results; that doesn't necessarily include discussing the means,'' I said.

He looked at me with admiration. ''I do believe you will indeed.''

He arose and said, ''Well, it looks like there's not much I can do here at the moment. Will you have a farewell lunch with me tomorrow, Emma love? I'm leaving in the evening.''

''Pick me up at twelve-thirty,'' I said with a smile.

He leaned over to kiss me and left.

"Another one of your smitten-from-Britain lads," said Abba.

"And when's your next date with the lovely and talented Deborah?" I asked.

He jumped up. "Tonight. Policeman's hours—I'm meeting her at 10:30."

"How's it going?" I asked.

He smiled broadly. "Great. She likes me. She's got family in Israel. And I think I'm crazy about her." And he left.

I went upstairs and headed for my room. As I walked along the bedroom corridor, I noticed that the excitement of the day had apparently disrupted the usual routine of the sisters McClintock. There was an uncollected broom leaning against a wall, and as I passed the Count's room, I noticed that his unemptied waste basket was standing outside his door, apparently overlooked by the dayladies. I am truly curious about the Count. I'd like to know what goes on behind that charming facade. Oh, I've considered going through his room—but he never seems to leave the house. How lucky can I get? The opportunity has just thrust itself upon me. I picked up the basket and took it into my room. Going through garbage pails is not exactly my finest hour, but hell, it's better than a Dumpster.

With all his correspondence, I figured the thing would be jammed. It was. Luckily, he was an excitable writer who crumpled and rewrote a lot, which meant lots of his unfinished letters were there. Women tend to save correspondence but most men read and toss. I sighed contentedly. There was much to read, so I settled down in the easy chair, switched on the lamp, and began to go through the pile. Of course, the letters were all in Portuguese, but having a house in the Algarve, I've become quite proficient in the language.

Most of the mail was to and from his brother and sister in Estoril. The family did not seem to be as impoverished as he had indicated. Then why was he willing to hang on in the demeaning role of Bootsie's man on call? There were allusions to honor and family which were puzzling. And then there was a heavily embossed piece of stationery that seemed to come from some high official. I began to read it and suddenly found myself sitting upright. I continued reading, and then got up, phoned Alfred and the airport, and started packing.

IX

⤜⋄⤛

DAMN IT, HE'S a toucher—not to mention a talker. Who would have expected that of the elegant aristocrat? I could deal with both problems anywhere else but on an airplane. At a dinner party, you escape his chatter by turning your attention to the person on your other side. And if it's constant hands-on activity, which is not necessarily sexual but can be awfully annoying, one can usually just move away. But here we are, two seats side by side, and since Lord El Cheapo never flies any other way than Economy Class—we're almost in each other's laps. I fly Business Class. I know that means I'm probably paying five hundred dollars for three meals (I have done that on the ground, too, actually) plus the attentive pampering of the airline personnel and the comfort of larger seats but so what? I make it a rule to never make dollar-to-dollar comparisons with different expenditures. If you do that, you'll live like a monk and never even take cabs. Except for a marvelous old friend of mine who calculated and thus excused every possible luxury expense by saying "but it's only twenty or thirty or whatever number of martinis."

Well, Alfred was intelligent and witty so at least I wasn't being subjected to trivia and inanity. And I was getting information about Lord Gerald's character. It's always good to know as much as possible about the person with whom you will be dealing—and I expect that will be dear old dad.

When we arrived at Heathrow at 6 A.M., I had phoned ahead to my reliable cabdriver Desmond who was waiting there at Arrivals. My original plan was to drive down to Winchester with Alfred; Thompson their chauffeur was at the gate as well. But the prospect of another few hours sitting next to Alfred was out of the question today. Besides, I had a few things I had to do in London so I went off to my flat and told Alfred I'd be in touch.

I prefer taking a day flight so that I arrive in the evening and go to bed in order to somewhat reset my internal clock. But Alfred had already booked this flight so here I was at practically dawn, which meant I would have to force myself to stay awake until at least ten tonight so that I could have a fresh start tomorrow. The phone was ringing as I entered. I didn't rush down the long entrance corridor to the living room phone because I knew who it had to be and that he would persist.

"Emma, love—welcome to London."

"Who spotted me this time?" I asked with a smile as I sank into the easy chair next to the phone table.

"Actually, it was Detective Sergeant Parnell himself who happened to be on duty at the airport today looking out for a bad guy. He said you were with a bloke who seemed to be doing some treacly talk on you, as he put it."

"Ah, the drawbacks of having a relationship with a Detective Superintendent of Scotland Yard," I sighed.

I heard his smile through the phone. "Well, that's progress. I didn't know we were having a relationship."

"You're still in my little black book, Detective Superintendent."

He laughed. "Of course. But how many are in your little white book?"

Caleb Franklin had reached the top ranks of Scotland Yard even though he was black and a graduate of Harrow and Cambridge—all classic no-nos for that conservative and traditional organization who regarded public school and elite university graduates with distrust and blacks with prejudice. He was charming, brilliant, and my sometimes lover.

"How about dinner tonight?" I asked.

"With the demands of my profession plus my whirlwind social life, you think I can be available at a moment's notice?" he asked indignantly.

"Six o'clock OK?" I asked.

"Sounds fine to me."

"I know it's earlier than usual, but I expect to pass out with jet lag at ten and I know there will be a number of things we'll want to talk about and do before."

"I'd say that sounds reasonably accurate," he said.

I checked the fridge to see what George, my trusty concierge and friend, had put in there. I had phoned him from the plane so that he would expect me, though I know the flat is kept instantly livable as befitting the needs of my peripatetic lifestyle. Maria comes in weekly to air the place out, clean, and try to keep my terrace garden alive. Forget flourishing, I have come to accept this as a somewhat losing battle since there is obviously more to growing shrubs and flowers than regular watering. The basics were in the fridge—butter, milk, Chardonnay wine, Hovis bread, eggs, coffee, and a slab of Stilton cheese. I walked down to Waitrose, the upscale supermarket a few blocks down the King's Road, and bought pâté, a two-inch-thick steak, a package of frozen cooked saffron basmati rice, a pound of mesclun salad, and a few fruit tarts.

My flat in London is the *pied à terre* of my three residences. The apartment on Fifth Avenue in New York is my formal abode and is large, well-furnished, and the repository for the elegant and costly baubles I am given by grateful clients. The exquisite little Picasso of the musicians, which was a gift from Donna Isabella, Marquesa de Mantua, hangs in the dining room. The seventeenth-century French desk I received from Elizabeth Eddington is in the library. Yes, I have one of those marvelous rooms filled with gleaming dark wooden bookcases filled with books, no *chatchkas* allowed here. There are two deep real leather chairs with good reading lamps and adjacent tables bearing the controls to the room's stereo system. There's a large standing globe of the world, and a table bearing the entire set of Oxford English Dictionaries. I know it sounds like the set for the opening of Masterpiece Theatre but it's the most lived-in room in the place when I'm in residence. The villa in Vila Do Mar Portugal is a white stone and red tile-roofed cottage hanging over the ocean and is furnished in early Algarve, which means lots of dark wood and leather chairs, many colorful couches, and marble and tiles everywhere. But my London flat has one couch, one table, one bed decorated in pure Habitat, which is Lord Conran's store on the King's Road featuring light oak woods and peach, cream, and pale blue fabrics. The cushions are pure down, the linens the finest percale. It's luxury on a small scale. The place is not made for entertaining anyone but me and a few more. Both living room and bedroom have sliding glass doors on to the best part of the flat—the huge terrace that overlooks London rooftops. It's small, it's serviceable, it's bright, and I love the place. Of course, like all my abodes, it's totally wired into the latest communications systems—phone, fax, computer, copier, and answering machine.

I phoned Lady Margaret and told her on which train I would arrive in Winchester tomorrow. I could hear her restraint in wanting to know the fate of the candelabra, but breeding won out and she asked nothing. Which is just as well because that's just what I would have told her—nothing. As I've told you, the great advantage of my pay-nothing-now arrangement with clients allows me the luxury of speaking only when I have something to tell.

At five-thirty I put up the charcoal fire on the terrace. I made a marinade of Worcestershire sauce, soy sauce, and red wine and put the steak in it to soak. At six, when the coals were white-hot ready, I put the steak on for five minutes on one side, five minutes on the other and then took it off, wrapped it tightly in aluminum foil and placed it on my Hot Tray which was set to medium/high heat.

He rang promptly at six-thirty and I buzzed him up, left the door on the latch and went out to sit on the terrace. "I'm out here," I called when I heard the door open. He came flying out in the usual gust that Caleb Franklin moved in and I felt the lift that his presence always brought. I looked up at him and once again wondered why anyone would be against miscegenation when it could produce such wonderful results as Caleb Franklin. A descendant of the slave who came to London with Benjamin Franklin who educated and then freed him, Caleb is the namesake of this ancestor who married a schoolteacher and begat a long line of educators. Tall and broad-shouldered, he carried himself with an innate sense of authority that made you immediately aware you were in a presence. His dark brown eyes sparkled with intelligence and his smile could light up a room. In other words, the guy was a knockout and if bothered to take the time to notice, women were falling at his feet all around him.

He stopped in front of me and we both looked at each other and smiled. Then he lifted me from the chair, encased me in his arms, and kissed me until we both needed to breathe.

He looked around. "Are we entertaining the neighbors again?"

"Only Mrs. Smigott in 4B."

"Tell her to get a life," he said.

"I have—she did—this is it."

"I dropped the Veuve Cliquot on the table inside. Shall we, while it's still chilled?"

We walked inside and he opened the first bottle. I took the iced flutes from the freezer and we took everything into the bedroom. First things first. After a lapse in seeing each other, our initial coming together is usually almost ferocious. This is followed by a champagne-sipping break, and then a more gentle love-making.

"I'm hungry," I said as we lay there contentedly in each other's arms.

He laughed. "You're not supposed to be. You're supposed to be thoroughly fulfilled and satiated and somewhat radiant."

"I am all those things, but I'm still hungry."

He threw off the covers and jumped out of bed—Lord, what a great body—and began to get dressed.

"What's for dinner?" he asked.

"Steak."

He was too polite to register annoyance. "Oh. Why don't I go into the kitchen and get the broiler started."

"No need," I said as I began to dress. "The meat is done. It's waiting for us."

When I brought in the steak on a hot platter with the

meat juices mingling with the marinade, I saw him looking at it with the dreary anticipation of a man who expects he will be forced to pretend he likes well-done beef. When I began to slice it on the bias, of course, and revealed perfectly done medium-rare steak, he was stunned. When he put the first piece in his mouth and looked up at me with the look of a man who has achieved nirvana.

"This is fantastic—tender, juicy, everything a steak should be. How the hell did you do it?"

I described my procedure. "It's one of those Emma-time-saving-tricks I invented a few years ago. At five o'clock one evening, some friends who were invited for six called to say they couldn't make it before seven-thirty. I had a steak which I figured I'd do on the charcoal at six-thirty. But who wants to stand outside and broil in the dark at eight? So I got creative and did what I did tonight. The hot fire for five minutes on each side seared the juices in and gave it a nice brown crust. The sitting for hours on a hot tray cooked the inside slowly without overdoing it. Actually I had figured if it got overdone, they deserved it for coming so late. But as you see, it turned out great and it's been my modus operandi for serving steak without having to stand over a hot cooker while the guests are here."

"Emma, it's absolutely marvelous. But then I've come to expect the unexpected from you. You know you're spoiling me for other women."

"How many are there?"

"You want the total count?"

I nodded.

He thought for a moment and I was getting pissed. Caleb and I have no arrangement or even any sort of semi-formal relationship. We like each other, we enjoy each other's company, and we enjoy going to bed together. So what gives me the right to get annoyed if he's seeing other women? But who's talking about rights? We're talking pure emotion here. Which means that, irrational as it may be, I'd like him to live like a monk when I'm not around. What woman wouldn't?

He sighed. "You're it."

I tried not to look too pleased.

"An eligible hunk like you? They should be tearing down the doors."

"It may start out that way," he said with a smile, "but don't you watch the mystery movie channel? Inspector Jane Tennant's lovers take off because they cannot accept her crazy hours. Inspector Frost is always forgetting dates when duty calls and ends up losing his woman. And poor Inspector Morse's couldn't ever even get started. Ours is a profession with twenty-four-hour demands that cause potential lovers to back off and wives to leave."

"But you're mad about it," I said.

"I must be," he said, "but then, I'm mad about you, too. I wouldn't want to give either one up."

"Who's asking you to?"

After dinner, we went back to the terrace to have our coffee under a starry moonlit sky. We sat there in compatible silence for a while. Then he looked at his watch.

"Do you have to be someplace?" I asked.

"No, I just wondered if it's brain-picking time yet."

I sighed. "You know me too well. How can you tell?"

"I can hear your little gray cells going and I know you didn't just drop into London for no reason. If you were planning a long sojourn you would, I hope, have informed me in advance so that we could have made some plans. Your precipitous arrival means you're on a case, and you probably need some information from Scotland Yard."

"Isn't it wonderful how having a Detective Superintendent as a lover obviates the need for unnecessary explanations? Of course you realize the fact that I would like some details checked in no way reflects upon the pleasures of this evening. I could've done it all by phone,'' I said.

He reached over to touch me. ''Love, I long ago learned there's no such thing as a free lunch—or dinner, as the case may be. I'm not at all bothered. Your work, like mine, Emma, is a vital part of your life. I care for you, Emma, and I'm glad I can help in any way possible. Fire away.''

''I'm looking for a man named Rivers. He surfaced in Vancouver British Columbia in the winter of 1977, totally destitute with a little retarded boy in tow. He is in his sixties now and still speaks with a Liverpool accent. I have the feeling that he was running away from the mother country for some illicit reason. I know it's a long shot and I don't know if you keep records that long, but I thought I'd ask.''

''That's before my time, of course. I'm not certain if we keep data from that far back, unless perhaps if it was a very high-profile case. But I have a better source—the amazing Detective Sergeant Parnell. I think he still remembers the brand of pablum his mum fed him. I'll get back to you in a day or two.''

X

❧❦❧

I ALWAYS MARVELED at how, in England, a small city can have the quaint charms and intimate feel of a village. Winchester is one of those treasured towns where, just steps off bustling High Street, you will come upon a fifteenth-century pub facing on a verdant ancient square or a graveyard filled with history. Where you can whip around the corner from your busy office at lunchtime to attend mass in a tiny twelfth-century church nestling in between two timber houses. I love to walk along the banks of the Itchen, a favorite place for bathing parties in Victorian days. The river wends its way serenely through the city, under old bridges, in front of ancient red brick buildings that used to be places of commerce and are now lived in by prosperous lawyers and bankers. I had asked Thompson to meet me a half-hour after the train's arrival so that I would have time to wander about the city and rediscover its pleasures.

What makes Winchester so fascinating to history buffs like me are the many changes the city has undergone since the year c. 41 when it was established by the Romans, with

each new settlement leaving its mark. After the Romans
left, the dark ages brought Alfred the Great to be followed
by Norman Winchester when William the Conqueror took
over. Medieval Winchester saw the building of Winchester
College, followed by Tudor Winchester which brought
Henry VIII to the great castle.

Winchester was actually an important city for the clergy
in the sixteenth century until King Henry VIII decided to
dissolve its three monastic foundations and four friaries. It
seemed that it might regain its former royal importance in
the seventeenth century when Christopher Wren was com-
missioned by Charles II to build a major royal castle, but
the project was abandoned and Winchester never became
an English Versailles. Winchester Cathedral, made even
more famous in song, is a major tourist attraction, which is
why I avoid it. To me, vast elaborate cathedrals are merely
monuments of excess that testify to the wealth rather than
the devotion of the people of that era. I prefer to sit quietly
in the tiny St. Swithun-upon-Kingsgate, a wood-framed medieval church built around 1148 above one of the four Roman city gateways and listen for the long-gone voices of
common folk who had worshipped simply in its rough-
hewn pews. I walked from there to the High Street where
hundreds of years ago Roman soldiers marched, and pilgrims walked, and felt a sense of history that never fails to
thrill me. Growing up in a country where stores along the
main street are usually in ordinary buildings, it's fascinating
to see shops tucked into ancient structures with names like
Godbegot House, a group of gilt-encrusted fifteenth-century
tenements that belonged in the 1050s to Queen Emma, wife
of King Canute and mother of Edward the Confessor. I
looked up at the large clock presented to the city in 1713
which hangs from a turret over the High Street; the curfew
bell still rings at 8 P.M. every evening as it has been doing

for 900 years since the days of William the Conqueror.

As I walked along the short and narrow streets of Winchester, I liked to rub my hands along the walls of churches and ecclesiastical buildings which are made of local flint stone embedded in concrete and last forever. You can tell the importance of those who had lived within by the patterns of the flint stones which are somewhat helter skelter when lesser mortals dwelt there, but are carefully flattened, shaped, and honed for persons of power. If I had more time, I would take a walk through Winchester College which is probably the most elite school in England and home to the famous Winchester Choir. Admission is said to be gained by one of two ways. Either you are the son of a graduate, or you have the voice of an angel.

Winchester has four gates: I had told Thompson to meet me at the Westgate which is about 600 years old. I like to find the grooves down which the portcullis could be rushed in sudden emergency and also the five openings down which missiles could be dropped on those attacking the gates. I was standing on the roofwalk viewing the entire city when I spotted the huge Bentley draw up downstairs. Thompson spotted me at once and smilingly held open a door for me.

"Good morning, Madam."

As the car pulled into the driveway of Medthorpe Hall, I saw three people emerge from the house and stand on the front steps.

"Emma, how nice to see you," said Lady Margaret as I stepped out of the car. We kissed the air in the vicinity of our cheeks, and she turned toward the man standing at her side.

"This is my husband, Lord Gerald," she said with pride and affection and I felt relieved. The marriage was still intact. "And Alfred, of course, you've met." He kissed me on the lips.

"Welcome to our home, Emma," said Lord Gerald.

What a nice man, I thought. He was a big comfortable bear of a man with a shock of sandy gray hair atop bright blue eyes and a ruddy complexion that indicated a man who spent a lot of time outdoors. He had the look of a kindly person who would think slowly but would ultimately reach the fair conclusion. Well, this promises to be a pleasant day. Of course, I haven't met the virago yet.

"Mother will lunch with us later," he said, as though reading my mind.

I stood admiring the building. "You've had busy ancestors," I said. "The West Wing looks like Henry Holland, and I'd guess Wyatville did the North Wing. It's lovely."

He beamed at me. "Right. You certainly know your architects. The original was built in 1683 but subsequent generations had to put their own mark on the place, don't you know. Even the gardens have been done and redone."

"But luckily you ended up with Capability Brown," I said with a smile, looking out at a panoramic view of the lake and exquisite gardens.

His eyes widened. "Now how did you know that?"

"It's that romantic natural look he always managed to capture. None of that formal topiary and formal arrangements," I answered.

I may sound like a bit of a suck-up, but it isn't as though I spent hours in the British Museum to research his estates. I'm a history buff, as I mentioned earlier, and I'm aware that all stately homes and castles are amalgams of evolving styles due to the egos of succeeding generations of owners. The first lord builds a huge elaborate Tudor castle in the 1570s as a standing testimony to his successes. He passes on, and the next lord can't wait to put his own brand on the place, so he tears down the south front and west front and rebuilds in the current style. He bites the dust, and the new occupant hastens to establish his imprint by adding a new wing and redoing the gardens. And so on for generations until the place becomes a composite of architecture and design throughout the ages and it's a fun challenge to spot who did what and when. So if I give Lord Gerald the pleasure of knowing that I appreciate the fine details and beauties of his possessions, what's wrong with that? And if that awareness makes him feel more kindly toward me in order to possibly ease the way in our upcoming negotiations, who's being harmed?

Margaret was positively overjoyed. I guess she was rather apprehensive about his acceptance of this woman with the odd profession whom she had hired. He tucked my arm in his and led the way into the house.

I gasped with pleasure when I entered the heroic Entrance Hall.

"Adam!" I said.

Lord Gerald clapped with delight. "Emma—you're a marvel."

It was instantly apparent that the entire decor had been done by the famed Robert Adam who worked on stately homes in the late seventeenth century and left a heritage of beauty throughout England. He aimed at consistency and would continue a motif throughout the house that created a pure unity of design. Ox skulls in the frieze in the Hall reappeared again over the door and fireplaces. As we walked into the house, I saw exquisite pieces of furniture by Thomas Chippendale whose superb talent raised English furniture design to levels of sophistication and beauty that ultimately gained acceptance over the more elaborate products of France.

"You're very fortunate, Lord Gerald. Your ancestors had

marvelous taste. I have been in some stately homes where you wonder about the sanity of the current resident's forebears, let alone their aesthetics.''

"Gerald's father was quite a connoisseur of the arts," said Margaret proudly as we stopped in front of a pair of early Turner watercolors.

"May I offer you a sherry before lunch?" asked Gerald as we entered a small sitting room with long windows overlooking the gardens.

Alfred had already walked over to the tantalus and was pouring himself what looked like a large brandy which brought a scowl of disapproval from his father.

"A trifle early, isn't it, Alfred?"

"Not if one's been up since six," he said coolly as he siphoned soda into the glass. "I took Branches out for an early morning ride.''

The vibes in the room indicated that this contretemps was not a singular occurrence and my estimation of Alfred dropped heavily. I'm a great believer in familial relationships and grown children who don't get along with their parents present question marks to me. Especially when they're Alfred's age, by which time conflicts should have been resolved. This could mean accepting the folks for who and what they are, warts and all, or if that's impossible for you, getting the hell away from home. But here was big Alfred, hanging around the family home and acting childishly snippy.

Lord Gerald turned to me with a smile. "I apologize for my son's manners, Emma—may I pour you the glass of sherry he should've done before pouring his own drink?"

Alfred's face took on a deep flush and he walked over and sat down heavily. What on earth is going on here? Margaret looked troubled and jumped to her feet.

"I'll see to lunch," she said and left the room hurriedly.

Obviously this was a scene she had found best to exit.

I sipped my sherry quietly, it was marvelous, and looked out of the windows.

"What a glorious aspect," I said as I looked at the banks of flowers cascading down to the lake. "I would think you must find this hard to leave. Do you get to London much?"

"No, London has little charm for me now. I admit when. I was my sons' ages, I found it exciting. I still keep a flat there but I rarely use it. This is home to me."

"Lunch is ready," said Margaret. A butler appeared behind her and came over and put my unfinished sherry on a silver tray. "Wilford will bring your drink in, Emma—this way."

We entered the intimate family dining room that Margaret had mentioned to me and it was, as I suspected, huge. My entire London flat would fit into the far corner. A gleaming Chippendale table was set with silver, crystal, and flowers. The walls were covered in pale green silk and the ceiling was decorated with scenes of historic battles. It wasn't until I was almost seated that I realized someone was already at the foot of the table. The dowager duchess, of course.

"Mother, may I present Miss Emma Rhodes? Emma, this is my mother, Lady Sibyl."

"Do pardon me for not getting up, my dear," she said, "but these ancient bones make movement a bit of a chore. They tell us we achieve wisdom with age, but they do not inform us that we also acquire arthritis."

She must have been a handsome woman, but age had not treated her well. She would probably be in her early nineties now and her hands were gnarled and her back was bent. She had the blue eyes of her son, but whereas his exuded niceness, hers had a piercing quality that made me wonder if she knew I forgot to rinse out my pantyhose last night.

Lunch was crabcakes with light lobster sauce and brown rice, accompanied by a mixed green salad vinaigrette. It was superb and I was about to comment on its excellence when the dowager duchess said:

"In my day, Miss Rhodes, we would have fed you something more substantial like a slice or two of mutton or our home-cured ham—you look like you could use a few more pounds on you. But my daughter-in-law believes in this stylish nouvelle cuisine although I must confess I saw nothing wrong with the vieille cuisine."

Referring back to my opinions on handling familial relationships, with this mother I think getting as far away from home as possible would be the only means of survival. I could see Margaret's face tightening as I waited for one of the men to tell off the old battleax. I guess it will have to be me.

"You mentioned that as we get older, we get wiser, Lady Sibyl. And so we have gotten wiser about food. We've learned that too much meat affects both our health and longevity. It's not stylish, Lady Sibyl. It's just smarter. You should be grateful to Margaret, she's trying to keep your son alive and well."

"There, you see, Mother? That's what I've been telling you," said Lord Gerald.

The old duchess looked at me narrowly. Apparently she wasn't used to being challenged. Tough noogies—it's about time someone took on the old bag. I saw Alfred smiling.

"You're not afraid to speak your mind, are you, young woman?" she said.

"No more or less than you, Lady Sibyl," I said.

She made a loud strange sound which I realized was a

laugh. "You're no fool and you have what the young men in my generation used to refer to coarsely as guts. I respect that. And now that I know you're not some kind of a charlatan, I will leave you and my son to whatever business you came here to discuss." And she got up and left the table.

"I must apologize for my mother, Emma," said Lord Gerald.

"If you opt to take on that responsibility, Lord Gerald, I think you'll be very busy. A lot of old people seem to feel age entitles them to remove the guards on their tongues that used to keep them civil and polite. Maybe they're right. I've often thought that when I reach ninety, I'll eat desserts, drink malteds, stop dieting, and allow myself the pleasure of telling everyone what I think of them. What the hell, if you can't kick over those lifetime restraints when you're ninety, when then?"

"When then, indeed," said Lord Gerald heartily. He arose from his chair. "I think now would be a good time for us to have our little business discussion. The sitting room would do nicely, I think."

The three of them took seats and I stood leaning against the desk in front of the windows. They looked at me expectantly and I let the silence go on for about thirty seconds. In my business, a little drama never hurts.

I looked at Margaret. "Our deal was that, within two weeks, I would find the silver candelabra and return it to you. It's now a little over one week." I let a pause hang in the air.

"I have the candelabra."

Margaret gasped and Lord Gerald said, "Well done."

"I will turn it over to you—if you wish me to."

"Why ever would we not wish you to?" asked Margaret.

I turned to Gerald. "Lord Gerald, I understand this candelabra has great historic significance to your family, as well as some sort of mystic significance."

He shifted in his chair. "Well, I don't know about the mystic part, that's more my mother's line of country. But it most certainly holds an important place in the traditions and history of my family."

I looked surprised. "But I was given to understand that its presence in this house was vital in order to effect the successful fulfillment of certain events that are dear to your heart."

"Well, not really," he said, looking uncomfortable.

"Come, Father," said Alfred. "For god's sake—you went on forever about needing that damned piece of silver to ensure that Cassandra produced a son, and that I made a run for M.P."

Gerald looked a bit sheepish. "Perhaps I did. But my good wife here has made me see that the whole thing smacked of superstitious nonsense and that neither wishing or witching will make anything come true."

"Good for you, Margaret. And for you, Gerald."

"I'll second that," said Alfred.

"Which means we are now left with only the historic importance of the candelabra."

I reached into my bag and brought forth the letter I had found in Count José's wastebasket plus another larger document on the same cream-colored embossed stationery.

"I am told that the provenance of the candelabra is that it was one of a set of four owned by King José the First of Portugal who gave two to your ancestor in gratitude for having performed a heroic service and thenceforth your family's fortunes prospered. Correct, Gerald?"

He nodded. "That's why we must keep it here for succeeding generations."

"As a symbol of the heroism of your ancestor that

should inspire pride in the family for those to come."

"Just so," he said proudly.

"And this is the story that has been passed down for hundreds of years."

"Yes." He looked puzzled.

I opened up the large document and said, "Now may I read you the real story as it appears in the files of the Portuguese Institute for Historic Restoration located in Lisbon. It's in Portuguese so let me translate it for you."

"In the year 1735, King José the First had four magnificent silver candelabras made with the goal of leaving them to the state as his contribution to the National Treasure. When two of the candelabras needed repair and had to be taken back to their maker, Thomas Termain in Paris, the king chose an Englishman who had become part of his court and whom he had come to trust implicitly. This man was known by the name of 'Vicam' which is the way the Portuguese would pronounce Wykham since there is no W in the Portuguese alphabet. Senhor Vicam left with the two candelabras and a guard force of five men in October of 1775 headed for Paris. The bodies of the guards were found a year later in a wood outside of Paris. Thomas Termain reported receiving and repairing the silver and returning it to an Englishman who fit the description of Senhor Vicam and who was never seen or heard from again. King José was furious and frustrated. He could not give the remaining candelabras to the state since it would be a stain on the honor of his family to give only half of a set. And so to this day, the two candelabras are on the national roster of stolen treasures for which the search goes on forever."

There was a stunned silence in the room. "I also have an English translation that I had made for you, Gerald. If you wish to verify my translation and facts, I have here the phone number of the head of the Institute. I have spoken to him and he would be glad to take your call.''

Gerald looked like someone had hit him across the head with a two-by-four. He rose heavily from his chair, took the number from me and went to the telephone table at the far corner of the room. We heard the murmur of his conversation and sat silently until he returned. He looked stone-faced.

''How did you come across this information, Emma?'' he asked in a quiet voice.

''Count José do Figuera has been living with Bootsie Corrigan for over a year. I just recently learned that he is a descendant of King José the First and he has the first two candelabras. Unlike your family whose fortunes rose with the acquisition of the candelabras, his family's fortunes dwindled over the years. However, no matter what levels of dire financial need they reached, they would not sell even one of the pieces, which your ancestor apparently did in order to start his empire. It has been the Count's family's mission for these hundreds of years to restore the honor of their family by finding the other two candelabras so that they may give them to the State National Treasure.''

''But how did he know that Bootsie had the candelabra?'' asked Alfred.

''Quite accidentally. They met in Estoril and she happened to mention her silver collection and when he heard her description of the candelabra, he followed her to Palm Beach and became her lover. Although it wasn't his intention, he fell in love with her and stayed on. When she promised to will him her entire silver collection, he felt his mission would be completed in time.''

''But I understand she's been murdered,'' said Margaret. ''Good lord, I hope he didn't do it for those miserable candelabras that seem to cause nothing but trouble and unhappiness,'' said Margaret.

"He is now a bereft and almost broken man. Not only did he lose the woman he loved, but now also the two candelabras he has devoted his life to locating in order to salvage the honor of his family."

Gerald became agitated and started pacing back and forth. "I realize that once I take the million pounds from Sotheby's, I no longer have any rights to the candelabra nor can I have any influence over its disposition. Do I understand that at this moment you are the owner of the piece?"

"Yes."

He looked at me skeptically. "There are only two ways you could have gained possession of it. Either you stole it, which I cannot believe is true, or the owner gave it to you, which I find equally incredible."

I laughed. "I'm lousy at second-story work but I'm very good at persuading people to do what I believe is right."

"You mean you convinced the owner to hand it over to you—an object worth one million pounds—for no compensation whatever?"

"I didn't say that nor will I say any more. I never discuss or divulge my methods."

"I should think not," said Lord Gerald. "From what I can see, they verge on the magical. If too many people knew your techniques, we might all of us be in jeopardy. Now that you have it, what do you intend to do with it?"

"My first step was to offer it to you since that was my deal with Margaret and I never go back on a deal. The second step was to dissuade you from taking it. If that succeeds, my final step will be to turn it over to the Count."

"You mean sell it to him, don't you?" asked Alfred.

"How can I sell a person what is rightfully his?"

Lord Gerald smiled broadly. "Good show." Then his face became solemn. "Will you please tell the Count how dreadfully sorry I am that the honor of his family has been stained by the dishonorable behavior of one of mine?''

Sometimes I have a hard time keeping a straight face when I hear all this honor-and-nobility-of-my-ancestors crap that has these people treating an event that occurred three hundred years ago as if it happened yesterday. Change the clothes and the accents and they could be the Hatfields and the McCoys. My dad refused to talk to his cousin Ned for one year because he forgot to come to my grandmother's funeral. But I don't recall it being referred to as a stain on our escutcheon, just that Ned was a feather-brained schmuck. And the feud lasted a year, not a century.

I smiled. ''Now that you get to keep the million pounds that Sotheby's took in, Margaret won't have to visit the East Tower anymore.''

They both laughed and he walked over and put his arm around her.

Margaret looked positively radiant. ''Well, we must celebrate at dinner tonight. Emma, I know you planned to stay overnight, so please let me invite a few guests and we'll make it a small party.''

Why not? One case is now completed and I have almost two weeks to go on the other. It's time for a little break.

''Good. I'm always up for a party,'' I said, hoping this last-minute approach doesn't mean she'll just round up the usual prospects which usually include the vicar, the doctor, and some horse-faced local ladies and their deadly dull golf-playing husbands.

She did a lot better. It was Mark. He was standing at the foot of the stairs as I came down at six in my ice blue silk shantung Victor Alfaro gown with the plunging neckline and tulle underskirt.

''Emma—you're the only woman I know who can look elegant and adorably sexy at the same time.''

Mark, Earl of Chelmsford, was the man with whom I was wildly in love last year. He wanted us to marry, his mother wanted us to marry, and his father wanted us to marry. You'll notice there is one vital omission in that list—me. Being his wife would eventually make me the Duchess of Sandringham, a role that would force me into a lifestyle I did not consider appealing although my mother was enchanted at the prospect of being able to lord it over bridge tables throughout Westchester as she dropped little mentions of "my daughter the duchess." The real problem between us was his elitist lord-of-the-manor attitude which I found offensive and he promised to control. But how can a guy who looks like a Ralph Lauren model, is the first son and heir of one of the most important dukedoms in Britain, and was brought up to believe that he and his ilk are far above the common folk ever possibly change? Expecting to alter a man after you marry him goes against all the advice in those important how-to-snare-a-man guidebooks like *Cosmopolitan* and *Redbook*. We had a few contretemps and decided to cool things for a while. And here he is.

"Hello, Mark." I must admit my heart or whatever organ it is that seems to be affected when you run into a guy who gets to you, did a little tango inside. He wore his superbly tailored formal clothes with the easy urbanity of a man who has been dressing for dinner since he's fourteen. As I reached the foot of the stairs, he kissed me with what started as a light social meeting of the lips but grew into an open-mouth job that held us together for long enough for both of us to emerge somewhat shaken.

"Emma, I love you. And you still love me."

I couldn't refute his statement. Luckily, Alfred appeared and eliminated the need for us to go any further into this touchy topic. "I see you two old friends have found each other.'' And I swear, he smirked. "How about joining me for a pre-prandial drink?''

We followed him into the sitting room, and this time I felt sherry wouldn't do it for me. "Is a bloody mary possible?'' I asked.

"But certainly. Matter of fact, I'm renowned for my bloody marys. My secret ingredient is horse radish,'' he said as he began to assemble the ingredients with the kind of dedication you get from a real drinker. "How about you, Mark?''

"Scotch with a splash and two rocks for me. I'm easy to please.''

"That's the least likely thing I'd ever say about you, Mark. From the time we were children, you were always the one who demanded perfection.'' And he looked over at me. "As I see you still do.''

"What brings you to Winchester?'' asked Mark.

"A case,'' I said.

"Of course, I'm sorry, you can't reveal the details or the client. I should not have asked.''

"You're almost family, Mark. I don't think it would hurt to say that Emma has just resolved a little matter for my step-mum and she and father now regard Miss Rhodes here as wonderwoman,'' Alfred said as he handed me my drink. "It's an opinion I must say I share. And if you hadn't gotten there ahead of me, I think I would be trailing after Emma like a lovesick lad.''

And that's just where you would stay, my boy—trailing way behind. Personal chemistry is a strange thing. He had nice regular features and a pleasant manner, but his constant reach-out-and-touch-someone that might be enjoyed as affection if you cared for the guy is icky and majorly irritating when you don't. I remember one of the worst experiences of my teens was when Benton Berlin took me to a movie and throughout the entire picture kept running his thumb across the top of my hand until I thought I'd belt him in the balls. I think he'd read somewhere that there was sexual significance in palm action and had just gotten his erogenous zones wrong.

Mark looked at me with a proud and proprietary look that I enjoyed.

"She's quite a girl is Emma," he said.

"Oh, there you are." Lady Margaret was at the door. "Come on, children, dinner is served."

We followed her into the dining room and were introduced to the other guests. We were ten altogether. There was Sir Robert and Lady Constance Lascelles, both lawyers who lived in London and came down to their country house in Winchester on weekends. Sidney and Rosemary Green owned the large bookstore on the High Street and were obviously good friends of both Gerald and Margaret. I was interested to note that a disgruntled-looking dowager duchess no longer sat in the hostess seat at the foot of the table facing Gerald; Margaret now occupied that place. I might go in for marriage counseling as a sideline.

Dinner was lively as all the people were intelligent and articulate and the wines were excellent—the perfect ingredients for a good dinner party. I was amused to note that Lady Sibyl kept eyeing me with baleful looks. I assumed that her son had told her the entire story of the silver candelabra and she was now blaming me for being the bearer of bad tidings. I could understand her unhappiness. When you're ninety years old and have cherished a romantic myth involving the honor of your family, it's not easy to accept that your proud beliefs were based on fraud and deceit. I can't say I felt sorry for her. Not when she was sitting there with a half-million-dollars worth of emeralds and diamonds around her neck and a very attentive grandson next to her.

But she had the mien of a malcontent, and life would never please her.

We had just completed our entrées and the cheese wagon was being wheeled in when Wilford, the butler, entered with an air of restrained excitement. He whispered something to Lord Gerald, who sat up immediately as Wilford handed him a phone. All conversation ceased as we all looked at Gerald in alarm. What kind of emergency would induce him to perform an act of such rudeness as to take a call at the dinner table? He seemed to be totally unaware of our presence and listened intently. Suddenly, his face turned pink and took on a look of absolute incredulity as he put the phone down.

"Ladies and gentlemen. That was my son Neville. He called to tell me that his wife just gave birth to twins"— and we all held our breaths—"two boys!"

Bedlam broke loose. Alfred jumped up and ran over to his father to pump his hand. Voices up and down the table were shouting "Congratulations!" "Bloody marvelous!" "Here, here!" "Well done!"

Wilford came back in with a footman following him with bottles of champagne and glasses.

"Wilford," said Lord Gerald, "champagne for all the staff as well—bring them all in."

Soon the room was filled with white-aproned maids and liveried footmen and an air of noisy joy and excitement as everyone seemed to be talking at once.

"My god," I said, "this must've been what VE Day was like!"

Gerald had arisen and Margaret was at his side. I heard him say, "My darling, you were so right," and she beamed up at him. "Two boys. I can't believe it. We have two grandsons."

"I'll send flowers immediately," said Alfred as he started to leave the room.

"Right, yes, of course," said Gerald. He looked at me and said with a smile, "He is a good man, isn't he? I am indeed blessed." He looked over at Lady Sibyl who was sitting impassively in her seat. "Poor mother. She so hates to be wrong."

"I wouldn't worry about her. She's the type who'll find her righteousness rationale quickly. Maybe the stars were in proper orbit. Who knows?"

After dinner was over and all the guests had left, Mark, who stayed behind, sat with me and Alfred. They were sipping brandy, but I had had enough alcohol and was doing fine with plain soda water. With my OK, Alfred told Mark the entire story of the candelabra. When he came to the part of his father fearing that his two most important desires would never come true without the infamous talisman, I said:

"Number one made it to the top of the charts. What's going to be about number two?"

Alfred shrugged. "First place, we've never had the kind of family money to mount a campaign."

"But now you do, thanks to the candelabra," I said.

"True, that obstacle has been overcome. But there's another that is, I believe, insurmountable."

Is he a cross-dresser? Has someone taken photos of him wearing ladies' panties?

"He wants me to run for M.P., but on the Conservative line."

"So?" I asked.

To my surprise, he answered, "But I'm Labor—I always have been. He simply cannot countenance having a son representing Labor."

"That's it?"

"I don't think you realize the seriousness of this issue," said Mark. "In country families like ours, the Labor Party has always been regarded as the enemy. To someone like Lord Gerald, joining them would be regarded as a betrayal and a defection."

"I see." And I did see. In the United States, accepting change is part of our national character. As every new wave of immigrants arrives, we pick up some of their language, their food, and their ways and it all gets fed into the hopper of our subconscious without a ripple. Since most of us are the children, grandchildren, or great-grandchildren of immigrants, we're egalitarian and not too hung up on national traditions. The British upper classes, however, had been steeped in isolation for so many years that they developed an intractable belief in their own superiority. Change is not regarded as a challenge but rather as a threat, and tradition reigns.

"I assume you tried to reason with him."

He grimaced. "*Tried* is the operational word. He just won't listen."

"Margaret is most likely on your side. Has she ventured her opinions?"

He shook his head. "She has enough in her plate getting along with Grandmama. This is not the time for her to take on a major issue like this."

"I'll bet he'd listen to Emma," said Mark. "Older men adore her." Then he looked at me with a fond smile. "But then, younger men go a bit batty for her too."

"That's a capital idea," said Alfred. "He has tremendous respect for you. Would you, Emma? Talk to my father to get him to understand my point of view?"

Did he ever push the right button! Who says flattery gets you nowhere? I couldn't resist such a test of the Rhodes Powers of Persuasion.

"OK, I'll give it a shot at breakfast. What time does your father come down?"

"Quite early." And he made a face. "How he can eat kidneys and sausages at six-thirty in the morning is beyond my comprehension. Tea and toast at eight-thirty is my speed."

I looked at my watch. "I'm off to bed, gentlemen. I've got to get back to London tomorrow and fly to Palm Beach tomorrow night."

"Can I come along?" said a plaintive voice. It was Mark.

"To London or Florida?"

"Both."

I'll have to talk to Caleb, which could be awkward with Mark around since they do not love each other. But I could accomplish my business with Caleb via phone. As for Florida, Abba will be busy with his beauteous detective, and it might be nice to have a companion of my own. Why not?

I was alone at the table eating my boiled egg when Lord Gerald arrived in the dining room. He looked surprised to see anyone there.

"Well, good morning, my dear. It's nice to see there's someone else who enjoys an early breakfast."

That may be, your lordship, but that someone else isn't me. Ordinarily, at this obscenely early hour I'd be turning over, cozily anticipating at least another hour of sleep. And then I'd be off to my health club for an hour workout. Only then would it be time for breakfast.

I watched him load his plate with mushrooms, kidneys, bacon, sausage, and eggs and I marveled at his indestructible digestion. He sat down and I noticed *The Times* on the table at his seat. I knew he'd be dying to read it, but good manners would prevent him from opening it while I was there.

"Where's Lady Sibyl?" I asked.

"Oh, she breakfasts in her room."

That's a plus.

I looked at the paper. "Well," I said. "Now you have a young Labor government. I think change is always healthy in politics after the existence of a long-entrenched party."

"Perhaps, but not if we are replacing them with radicals," he said a little heatedly.

"Then wouldn't it be good to insinuate some more temperate clear-thinking members into these so-called radicals to prevent missteps and excesses?" I asked innocently.

He stopped a forkful of mushrooms that was headed for his mouth and said thoughtfully, "Hmm, never thought of that."

"I understand Alfred has an interest in politics. If he's looking for a constituency, I do hope it's Labor. He can get so much more done that way."

"Emma, we are a conservative family and have been so for generations."

"Do you want your son to sit in Parliament?"

"Very much so."

"Why?" I asked.

"Because I want him to contribute his excellent mind to improving the future of England."

I looked at him silently for a moment. "Then wouldn't he be in a better position to do so if he were working within the party in power?"

He looked at me with a slowly dawning smile. "Young woman, I have a feeling I've been cleverly sandbagged."

"Has it worked?" I asked.

"Quite effectively, I'd say," he answered. "And now that you have convinced me that Alfred should run on the Labor ticket, would you mind if I opened my *Times*?"

"Not at all," I answered.

As he unfurled the paper, he said, "What greater proof do I have of my son's political acumen than the fact that he sent you in as his advocate?"

XI

THE LIGHT WAS flashing on my answering machine when I walked in. It was Sergeant Parnell. I phoned him back and luckily caught him at his desk.

"That yob you asked the Gov about—Rivers. I recall the case right well."

There's nothing like having friends in high places, I thought with delight. But then it's often handy to have friends in low places, too.

"I were just a new lad on the force then but it were a very big story. This chap Rivers were the sales manager of a chemical company in Liverpool. Important job, you know, company thought the world of him, big future and all that. Had a house in one of them new estates for young folks on the way up, him, his wife and son. Only the little boy was funny in the head, what they call retarded but his dad adored the little tyke. Happens the missus didn't feel the same way. Neighbors said she downright hated the poor little thing. Seems she was one of those beauties who fancied everything she had must be perfect. Well, they fought a lot about the kid—she wanted to put him away somewhere and Dad wouldn't hear of it. Neighbors used to hear them at it all the time. Then they started to hear crying and screaming during the day, and folks noticed bruises on the wee lad. The missus claimed he fell, or some such. One day Rivers come home from a trip a bit early and found her beating the little lad with a broomstick, and everyone heard her screaming how she wanted to kill him because he were ruining her life and he'd be better off dead anyway. Two days after that, Dad walked in and found her holding the boy's hands over the stove. Well, he went right mad and smashed her head in with a hammer that were laying on the counter. He were remanded for murder and found guilty."

"Guilty!" I exclaimed. "With those circumstances? What jury would convict a father trying to protect his child?"

"I quite agree—we all did. But his lordship the judge tells the jury what to do here. And this one in particular is a tough old sourface. Says it's murder plain and simple and no man has the right to take another's life unless his own life were in danger, which it weren't. And he puts on his little black cap and sentences the poor man to hang. Well, there were a big uproar, I tell you. The newspapers full of the injustice of it all, and people writing letters and parading around Old Bailey with signs, but it do no good. The law's the law."

What a story. I was listening, dumbfounded. Poor Rivers, what a horrifying ordeal.

"How did he get out of it? Was he pardoned?"

I heard the sergeant laugh. "Well, you might say that. But not officially. You see, he were being transferred to another prison for the hanging while his lawyers were trying to appeal, which nobody thought he had a hope for. As I says, there were lots of folks out there who were on his side. Well, right outside Tidbury, doesn't the prison lorry hit into a vehicle that seem to come out of nowhere and it's a big brouhaha and Rivers somehow gets gone from the van and, well, they can't find hide nor hair of him. Tidbury is on the Sea, you see, and it were thought that a boat was waiting.''

"You mean it was a planned getaway, and the accident was prearranged?'' I asked.

"So t'were thought, miss.''

"But I assume he was handcuffed and probably foot padlocked. How far could he run? And there was more than one guard in the van—probably a few. After all, he was an important prisoner. How come they couldn't find him?''

There was a silence at the other end and then a little throat-clearing. "Most folks don't think so, but coppers have feelings just like everyone else. If ever a woman deserved to die, that one did. And if ever a court didn't do justice, this was it.''

"You mean the guards didn't look too hard?'' I asked.

"Oh, I'm sure they looked as hard as they could right enough. But it were figured that a car were there to take him away.''

"What about the boy?''

"He had been with family. When social service went looking for him, the relatives said they sent him out of the country to family in Canada. Oh, there was a big dustup about improper supervision and all that, but the folks claimed they thought it best for the boy to be gone from the newspaper oiks who were at them and the boy day and night. And there weren't none who didn't agree.''

"Did anyone ever hear from Rivers again?''

"Oh, there were what we call 'sightings' here and there—someone says they seen him and the boy in Vancouver. But by that time, public opinion was making him the hero and the judge the villain. Don't think there was any politician would dare to suggest hunting him down.''

"So case closed," I said.

"Officially—never."

"But unofficially?"

He laughed. "I reckon anyone daft enough to go after a twenty-year-old case like that would be looked at as a bit balmy. ''

"No, I guess it wouldn't exactly be a career-builder."

"Rivers must be an old man in his sixties. So even if anyone knew where he was," he said pointedly, "what joy would there be in putting him away now?"

"Quite right, Sergeant. And thanks so much for telling me all this."

I made myself a pot of tea and put on a CD of Verdi's *Nabucco*. It was thinking and mulling time and *Va, Pensiero, Sull' Ali Dorate*, the chorus of the Hebrew Slaves in Act Three, always seems to soften my soul and mind. One of the most beautiful and moving pieces ever written by this greatest of operatic composers, legend has it that he added it while the opera was being rehearsed for opening night and wasn't certain if it was worthy of inclusion. The chorus tried it out while the opera house workmen were putting finishing touches to the hall. As the chorus began, all the workmen stopped to listen, and upon completion, there was a moment of silence followed by the men cheering "Bravo, Maestro"—and Verdi decided to keep it in, fortunately for opera lovers. Every time I hear it, I get a vision of the first time I saw it performed. When the third act curtain arose, you saw a stage filled with hooded figures, all kneeling with their backs to you. As the music began, they slowly turned around, rising and lifting their hoods with the lights shining full on their faces as they sang. It has to be one of the most powerful scenes in opera.

As I sat on the couch sipping tea, I couldn't get the picture of Rivers out of my mind. I tried to reconcile the image of the tormented man of twenty years ago with the self-assured authoritative major domo I knew. One thing was clear: this was a man who had, like men in a war, been pushed to the end of his endurance and been tried and tested as few do—and had survived. Which means he had the confidence in his strength and abilities, and the fearlessness thus engendered. He would always be able to do whatever he felt had to be done.

The ringing phone yanked me out of my reverie. It was Abba.

"Greetings, sweetheart. Better get your pretty tush back here. There's been another mysterious death, as those police assholes down here call it."

I went cold all over. It may be part of my business, but I will never get to be sanguine and relaxed about killing.

"Who? And how?"

"One of the McClintock sisters. I don't know which—I could never tell them apart. They found her dead on the floor of her kitchen."

"What makes them think it wasn't a natural death—heart attack, for instance?"

"Sis insists she had the heart of a lion and the physical health of a twenty-year-old. Says no one in their family ever died under the age of ninety. Their doctor concurs. They're doing an autopsy."

"I get the feeling you suspect foul play too."

"First place, in my business we never accept anything as 'natural,' and we're usually right. There's a stink about this whole fuckin' thing. When a person who has a connection to a murder victim suddenly dies mysteriously, we'd have to be *idiotym* to ignore it."

"I'll see you tomorrow. Oh yes, I'm bringing a friend

with me. He just wants to visit for a while.''

There was a silence and a sigh. ''OK. Who?''

''Mark.''

''*Oi veh.*''

XII

~∿~

THE BENTLEY DROPPED Mark at The Breakers and me at Bootsie's. There was plenty of room for him to stay at the house, but (a) it wasn't my right to invite him to a place that wasn't mine, and (b) I was working on a case and didn't want sexual distraction.

"So where's His Putzship?" asked Abba who was at the house when I arrived.

I told him. "He'll be over tonight."

"I can't wait."

I ignored him. "God, it's hot. It must be in the nineties."

He shrugged. "For we children of the desert, this is balmy. How about a swim?"

I went upstairs to change into my bathing suit and there was Eunice unpacking for me again. We exchanged polite greetings, and I noticed there was a subtle change in her demeanor, a greater assurance than I had seen before. When I went down to the pool, I saw why.

"Well, hello there, Emma." It was Rick Bolton, spread-eagled on a chaise around the pool looking like a beached whale. His skin was pale white and there was far more than there should have been; unlovely love handles and a large gut hung over his Speedo trunks and he had long colorful tattoos of what looked like snakes on his legs. All and all, a most unappetizing sight.

"You're in pretty good shape all over," he said with a leer.

I was wearing my Gucci brown ombre spandex bikini.

"That's because I always make the time to work out—something you obviously haven't been able to fit into your busy schedule," I said sweetly. Then I gave him my slow once-over appraisal accompanied by pointed silence, which usually makes the subject look for the nearest beach cover-up. He did.

"I came home for Auntie's funeral," he said.

Sure you did. "Have you seen your cousin?" I asked.

"Shitface John-boy? Yeah. Why?"

"Well, it is his house now so I guess he's the one you'd have to ask for permission to stay here."

His face turned red and angry. "Hey, I'm family, you know. Who the hell are you?"

"I'm an invited guest," I said with a smile.

And I dove into the pool.

After swimming a few laps, I climbed out to find Abba and Rick eyeing each other suspiciously.

"Abba, this is Rick Bolton."

"I figured," he muttered.

"Rick, this is my friend Abba Levitar, another invited guest."

They glared at each other. It was obviously hate at first sight. Abba took a dive into the pool and began swimming laps.

"How long do you plan to stay, Rick?" I asked.

"Until I get my money," he said.

"With all the questions about Bootsie's death, probating the will may take some time," I said.

He lay back on his chaise and smiled. "I'm not in any hurry."

"Emma! I thought I heard you."

It was Tom Blair who emerged from the house together with another man.

"Emma, this is Kevin Birnbaum."

He was wearing chinos and a pink LaCoste shirt that clung to every roll of his considerable girth. His slacks were worn high, just inches below his slightly protuberant breasts. His deep tan and shapeless body made him look like a Tootsie Roll that had been out in the sun too long. Then he smiled, and you forgot the rest of him. His face and eyes projected a keen intelligence that indicated this man would never miss a thing and you'd like him for a friend, but never for an enemy.

"Kevin, this is the Emma Rhodes I told you all about."

"Not all, Tom. You told me she was smart—you didn't tell me she was also gorgeous."

Tom smiled. "Maybe I'm too old to have noticed."

"No man is that old, Tom," said Birnbaum.

"This is fun," I said. "It's like listening to your own eulogy. I assume this is going to be somewhat of a business meeting, so let me put on my business clothes." And I slipped on my brown see-through coverup.

We walked over to the far end of the pool and sat down at an umbrella-shaded table.

"Tell me the details about the late Miss McClintock, Tom. Which one was it?" I asked.

"Meg," he said. "There's not much to tell. They found her lying on the floor in her kitchen, quite dead. No weapon, no external damage to the body. The coroner ruled her death as poisoning."

"What kind of poison? Were her tissues and blood cherry red?" I asked.

"I really don't know the details. The M.E. said it looks like poison but they haven't been able to identify what kind."

"Any signs of forced entry?" I asked.

He shook his head. "No need. Sister Pat said they've lived here all their lives and never locked their doors and she's not going to start now."

"That's a lovely sentiment. Unfortunately, it also makes a lovely epitaph," I said. "Are the police tying Meg's death with Bootsie's?"

"I haven't spoken to Detective Berkowitz about it. I don't know."

Birnbaum had been listening carefully. "Emma, you're obviously familiar with unnatural death, I see."

"Unfortunately, it's often part of my business."

"Just what is your business?" he asked.

I explained.

"Tom told me you were investigating the case."

"That's not quite accurate, Kevin. My goal is merely to find the real murderer."

"Isn't that the same thing?" asked Tom.

"No," I answered. Tom looked puzzled.

Kevin smiled. "What she means is she's not going into the background of relationships between the victim and the accused, she's not going to go through his high school yearbook to find out what the other kids thought of him, she's not going to try to find out if he was sexually abused by an uncle when he was five."

"Exactly, Tom," I said. "That's the attorney's job in order to plead his client's case before a sympathetic jury. All I'm out to do is find the real murderer so that the client whose case Kevin pleads will not be Jonathan."

"I wish you luck," said the attorney with a smile. "However, I must proceed with the assumption that you won't succeed and prepare to protect Jonathan from prosecution. Which means I'll have to hire a private investigator."

"Right," I said. "Please tell him about me so that we don't get in each other's way."

He nodded. "Of course. Obviously you feel our client did not do the dastardly deed. May I ask what made you come to that conclusion?"

I told him about Jonathan's unconcern about money which ruled out his obvious motive. He's a teacher and to my knowledge is not involved in any project that requires an infusion of big money. Also, the brilliant method of introducing the deadly substance in a heavily trafficked public place which in a sense is like Poe's *The Purloined Letter*, in which the sought-after object is made invisible by its very visibility, would never be Jonathan's style. He is too button-down and unimaginative to have conceived of such a dangerously clever concept.

"And do you have any particular favorite in mind for the position of murderer?" asked Kevin.

"There are so many candidates it looks like the New Hampshire primaries."

He laughed. "Good."

I got up. "Gentlemen, unless there's anything else I can help you with, I'd better be on my way."

I showered and dressed and then went to the garage at the far end of the estate to pick up a car from Bootsie's fleet. Besides her Bentleys she maintained a few lesser vehicles for when she went out on some do-it-yourself errands, and also for the use of her guests. I took a Honda Civic and headed for Lantana. This little town is a short distance from Palm Beach, just over the Intracoastal Waterway but light years away in character and wealth. Its one claim to fame is that it is the publishing home of newspapers with the largest circulation and the lowest level of journalism in the country: the *National Inquirer* and the *Star*. I drove through streets of mobile homes, shanty-like cottages, bars, and stretches of dusty tracts of open land. I kept an eye out for my destination, the school where Melissa and Jonathan worked. The streets seemed quiet and unpopulated. I passed the huge women's prison, a large shopping center with the ever-present Publix supermarket and Eckerd drugs, and then turned a corner of Lantana Road and came to a vast open tract of land that had earth-moving machinery and heard a surprising din. The area was filled with people shouting and carrying placards. They were all responding to someone on a platform who seemed to be inveighing the crowd with rhetoric that obviously aroused them. I slowed down to try to read their signs and suddenly I stepped on the brake so hard, I thought my air-bag would inflate. The speaker was Melissa.

I parked the car and walked over. There was a large permanent sign at the front of the property that read "Coming Soon! Winn Dixie Supermarket, Blockbuster Video, Clark's Cafeteria, FEDCO Drugs."

Then I listened to the chant that had started as the placard-carriers, led by Melissa, began marching toward two well-dressed men who stood in front of the idle machinery.

"One-two-three-four, we don't need another store."

The crowd was mostly black and Hispanic women. I stood aside and began to read their posters.

> "Give our kids a place to play
> Give our kids a place to stay!"

I joined the group in the back so that Melissa wouldn't see me and listened to her confrontation with the men.

"Ms. Trabert," said one of the men quietly. "We sympathize with your desire to have a complex for children here that would include a gym, playground, and daycare center. But as we've told you before, we're not Donald Trump—we're just ordinary marginal businessmen who own land that we must rent at a profit or we'll go broke. We can't afford to donate it. But if you can find the money to either buy the land from us or build your complex and pay us rent—we're sure our incoming tenants will accept the withdrawal of their leases for such a good cause."

I listened to her rude retort which was the usual unreasonable response of "cause people" who firmly believe every property owner is wicked and wealthy. I was stunned at the force of her fury. This coming from the timid, quiet Melissa? Boy, did I have the wrong number! I slipped away with her words to the real estate men ringing in my ears— "Where would we get that kind of money?"

I arrived at Jonathan's school just as it was letting out and saw him emerge with a cluster of smiling children around him. I waved and he came over.

"They obviously adore you," I said.

"They're good kids," he said shyly. "What are you doing here, Emma?"

"I just wanted to chat with you about a few things and thought I'd pick you up and take you for coffee somewhere."

He led me to a small store-front coffee shop with a sign that read "Comidas y Bebidas." The owner greeted Jonathan like an old friend and led us to one of four tables that were set up behind the establishment under the shade of a tree.

"Cafe con leche OK with you?" Jonathan asked.

I nodded. "Fine. How are you holding up?"

He looked sad. "When I saw that movie *The Fugitive*, I didn't really understand how Harrison Ford felt when he was innocent and nobody believed him. Now I do. I feel so helpless."

"But not hopeless. You have three deterrents to injustice on your side—Kevin Birnbaum, me, and Detective Berkowitz."

"Detective Berkowitz? But the case is now with the D.A. It's out of her hands."

"But not out of her mind. She's a very capable and conscientious officer and I have it on good authority that she's not entirely sure they have the right man. Remember, too, that she's now working on Meg McClintock's death which the police have to view as somehow tied in with your aunt's murder—they never accept the existence of coincidence in such cases. Since you're not being considered as a suspect in *her* death, it has to raise questions about you being the perpetrator in the first one."

I didn't tell him that Abba and Detective Berkowitz were spending every spare moment together and that the murders had inevitably worked their way into pillow talk.

The proprietor arrived with our cafes con leche and placed a plate of cookies on the table with a smile.

"Mmm," said Jonathan, "Torticas de Moron—*gracias*, Jorge. You must taste these, Emma. They're named after Jorge's town, Moron, in the Cuban province of Camaguey where this recipe originated."

I tasted one and it was deliciously lime flavored. "These look eminently dunkable, Jonathan," I said as I slowly lowered one into my cafe con leche. He watched me carefully.

"Congratulations, Emma, you've passed the dunking test. There aren't many of us who have mastered the fine art of dunking."

I bowed my head in acknowledgment of his praise. "I know, it's all in the timing—to know just when the cookie is saturated but still firm enough not to break off when you lift it out of the cup."

"Exactly!" he said as he proceeded to do the same thing. We both smiled at each other.

"I just saw Melissa," I said.

"Where?" he asked.

"On a vacant lot off Lantana Road. She had quite an audience."

"Oh yes, that's her child care center project," he said casually.

"You mean she has others?" I asked.

"Oh yes—she's fighting with two grade schools to have after-school activities for children whose parents work and don't get home until six. She wants the schools to also offer dental and medical care and dinners for the kids."

"Sounds like a good idea," I said. "Why are they fighting?"

"The schools hardly have enough budget for books let alone what Melissa wants. They say they'll gladly do it if she provides the funding."

"That sounds reasonable," I said.

He smiled. "Not to Melissa. She doesn't believe them. She says if they cut the salaries of all the deadwood bureaucrats at the Board of Education, they'd have enough money for everything."

"Sounds to me like Melissa doesn't believe anyone."

"Well," he said, "she does get a little carried away with her ideas. She doesn't trust people in authority or people with money."

"How did she feel about your aunt? Why didn't she ever ask Bootsie for donations to her projects?"

"She did, but Auntie turned her down. Auntie wasn't

big on trusting people either. The people she didn't trust
were what she called Dumb Ass Do-Gooders. To quote her,
'they don't know shit from shinola about running a business
and if I give them money, they'll piss it away on misman-
agement.' She only gave money to efficient established or-
ganizations like the Red Cross and the Policemen's
Benevolent Association." He grimaced. "I hate to say anything negative about Auntie because she was such a great
gal, but she did like her glory, which means she only gave
large sums to groups who could give her accolades and
recognition."

"How did Melissa take these turndowns?"

"Well, at first she was angry. But I explained to her that
Bootsie grew up very poor and had the need to have her
giving acknowledged by society. Melly's family were quite
well-to-do and were old money, so she never really understood Aunt Bootsie."

"What's her background?"

"She grew up in Grosse Pointe, Michigan. Her father
was an executive with Ford. Her great-grandfather founded
the local country club and there is a Trabert Wing in the
museum."

"So she's now assuaging the guilt for her life of inherited ease by taking up cudgels for the poor and downtrod-
den," I said. "A common enough story. Why doesn't she
ask her family to contribute to her worthy causes?"

"Oh, she doesn't talk to them and they gave up on her
years ago."

I didn't quite know how to put what I was now going to
say, but what the hell.

"Don't you find it a trifle trying being with someone
who is so humorless and driven?"

He laughed. "Oh, she's not that bad. We have so much

in common, and I do admire her. She's noble and very committed.''

''Nobility can be tough to live with. And I didn't hear the most important word of all, Jonathan—love.''

His face turned serious. ''Sometimes I think I love her. I don't know.''

''I've been in love, Jonathan'' (I didn't tell him how many times; it might cut into my credibility), ''and believe me, when it hits, you know it.''

''We're planning to get married,'' he said.

''When?'' I asked.

''When this whole awful thing is over and I'm officially cleared.''

And officially a billionaire.

At this point, let me caution you amateur sleuths reading these pages that because someone seems obviously guilty doesn't mean, ipso facto, that they're not. I know that mystery books tend to offer a lot of red herrings and the reader concludes that the writer is being tricky. But as any law officer will tell you, persons who appear to be the most guilty usually are. Unfortunately for those of you who love to try to guess whodunit as early on as possible, there are, as I told Kevin Birnbaum, a whopping plethora of suspects. And the fact that I've shown you how each has good cause to commit the murders does not mean he or she didn't do it.

Which leads me to Rivers, the redoubtable butler.

XIII

WHEN I ARRIVED back at Bootsie's house, Rivers advised me that there was a message for me from a Mr. Mark Croft.

"Hello, my darling," was his opening line. "Can we have dinner this evening? I hear this place Ta-Boo is rather smart."

We agreed that he would pick me up in his rented car at seven.

Just as I was about to corner Rivers for a small chat, the doorbell rang and he went to respond. It was Abba.

"If you're selling Israeli Bonds, I already gave at the office," I said.

"What do you think—I'm an Avon lady selling door to door?" he said as he gave me a big bearlike hug and kiss. "I made a presentation at a synagogue in West Palm Beach last night and we got pledges for a quarter million dollars."

"Wow—that's marvelous, Abba," I said.

"Not bad," he said. "That means we'll probably end up with one hundred thousand."

I was puzzled. "But you said a quarter million."

"That's pledges, not cash. What happens is these *gonser knockers*, translation: big shots, get up and call out these five-digit figures to impress the audience. You know, 'Mr. and Mrs. Sylvan Ginsberg pledge ten thousand dollars.' Everyone applauds, Mrs. Ginsberg smiles proudly. When the bill accompanying his pledge card arrives at Mr. Ginsberg's home or office, he responds with a check for one thousand dollars. What are we going to do—sue him? A thousand bucks ain't tin anyway, so we send him a thank you and never tell him we think he's a chintzy son-of-a-bitch."

"Is this a Jewish thing?" I asked.

He got indignant. "Of course not. It's a charity-raising thing. You ought to come and hear me sometime, *bubele*. I'm a master—I play the audience like a violin. By the time I get finished with my horror stories, the men are so guilty that they didn't have to go through such hell and the women are so awed by my bravery that they fall all over each other to outpledge each other."

"Let's go out to the terrace," I said. "I'd suggest the pool, but ratface Rick seems to have set up camp there."

We sat down and I turned to him purposefully.

"So what's new on the McClintock murder?"

"The M.E. is sure it's poison but he hasn't been able to identify it. Maybe she ate my grandmother's *cholent*."

"What's that?" I asked.

"It's a meat-and-potatoes stew that orthodox Jews make to avoid cooking on the Sabbath. Since they're not permitted to turn on the stove, they put the pot on the lighted burner before sundown on Friday and leave it on a low flame until sundown on Saturday. It just cooks and cooks, fat, meat, whatever. It's Jewish cassoulet. A police captain I knew in New York went to a law enforcement symposium at the Concord Hotel in the Catskills and innocently ordered *cholent*. Nobody warned him that only veteran Jewish stomachs could handle it, with a little help from Alka-Seltzer. He woke up in the middle of the night with massive indigestion and the doctor told him it was the closest thing to a heart attack he had ever seen."

"Does your delectable detective have anyone in mind as the alleged perpetrator of this crime?"

"No. The two sisters were universally liked—they didn't have an enemy in the world. As for motive, it sure as hell couldn't be robbery because with all the millionaires in Palm Beach, who would bother with a house where the most valuable thing is a collection of souvenirs from Disney World? It had to be someone she knew because she must've eaten or drank something with the killer in order to consume the poison. There wasn't a cup or dish visible anywhere, so our nasty visitor had to be a pretty cool customer who took the time to wash, dry, and replace the glass in the cupboard."

"I assume the police are looking for a motive?" I asked.

He looked at me indignantly. "What do you think? My Deborah is a dorkbrain? She figures that the good sister obviously saw something in Janet's kitchen that she wasn't supposed to see—like the murderer mixing pulverized peanuts into the stuffing. She didn't mention it to the police because she probably didn't realize its importance and besides, she was a nice lady but a bit of a dumb fuck. But the murderer was afraid she would become aware of the meaning of what she had seen and eventually tell all. So he or she popped her."

I smiled.

"What are you grinning at?" he asked.

"*My* Deborah?"

He threw up his hands. "OK—so I care for the woman and I'm being a little proprietary. Is that a crime?"

"No," I said, "neither is it a crime to use the big L word."

He looked shocked. "Me? Say I'm in l—l—l . . . you see, I can't say it."

"Men! Why ever not? All you do is start by putting your tongue against your top teeth to make the *l* sound, then lower it to make the *o* sound . . ."

"Wiseass broad! My history with that word hasn't been great. The two times I told a girl I loved her, one stuck her tongue out at me and the other went to the dance with someone else."

"How old were you when these traumatic events took place?" I asked.

"Six and sixteen."

"Vulnerable ages. No wonder you've been irreparably damaged. However, I can't picture Deborah responding in either one of those ways if you told her you loved her."

He looked uncharacteristically troubled. This was an Abba I had never seen. He was always so sure of himself and on top of things, it was strange to see him looking uncertain.

"Suppose she doesn't love me?" he asked.

Ah! When it comes to warfare, strategy, and derring-do, he's a lion. But when we come to emotions, he's a pussy-cat. Time for me to enlighten him.

"Usually you have some sense of how she feels. I assume you've been to bed together. Or does your religion require premarital virginity?"

"Actually on paper, yes. But that's one area where we've become totally assimilated, thank God. Yes, of course we've slept together."

"I have no desire to probe into your sex life, Abba—

but couldn't you get some feeling about her true feelings then? I'm sure you've had enough loveless, purely sexual coupling to tell the difference.''

He smiled. ''Yeah—it's different with Deborah. I think she cares for me. But how can I be sure? If I tell her I love her and she doesn't feel the same way, I'll be making an ass of myself.''

I sighed. ''Listen, lover. You're a big boy now. It's time to take some emotional risks. That's part of life.''

He sat up straight in his chair. ''You're right. I'll do it. We're having dinner tonight.''

''Great. Mark and I are having dinner together—how about joining us?''

''The last time I double-dated was my senior year in college,'' he said. ''Will we go to the malt shop after?''

''Come on, it'll be fun. We'll come back here after for a nightcap and then I'll plead weariness and retire upstairs and Mark will go home and you'll have this romantic setting facing the moonlit ocean to make your declaration.''

''You mean his lordship won't want to retire with you?''

''Oh, he'll want to, all right, but he knows such intimate behavior is off limits at the moment.''

He looked at me incredulously. ''Are you telling me that there be no nooky for the nonce?''

I shook my head. ''Abba, your way with words never ceases to amaze and charm me. Have you ever thought of writing scripts for porno films?''

He snorted. ''Scripts? Nobody talks in those X-rated movies. He says 'hello' and the next ten scenes show his blue-veined rigid schlong in action. I didn't take two semesters of writing courses to turn my talents to such banal shit. But don't change the subject, my girl. How long will this boinking ban with his lordship last? From my observation, such strictures often cause the punisher to suffer as much pain as the punishee."

I laughed. "Now look who's changing the subject! How about my plan for our double dining tonight? Come on, don't tell me a man who has been through two wars, escaped from an Arab prison, and hunted and brought to justice three concentration camp commandants is afraid to face one nice Jewish girl?"

He looked abashed. "All right, all right. What restaurant are we going to? I can't afford Lutece-South. Remember, I'm not one of the landed gentry who stands to inherit an estate bigger than Rhode Island. The only land my father left to me was a plot next to him in Mt. Hebron Cemetery."

"We're going to Ta-Boo. It's a lively place, and prices are pretty fair."

"Good. Because so far I've only taken her to places like Bradley's Saloon where twenty bucks buys you a pretty good dinner. If I take her to a fancy spot, then she'll get the idea that I'm serious about her. Right?"

Mark and I were at the bar when they arrived. He had been a bit disappointed when he heard we wouldn't be alone, but he perked up when he heard we would be dining with a woman detective. "Just like Jane Tennant in *Prime Suspect*," he said.

Abba was wearing a blue blazer, tan slacks, a blue chambray shirt, and a red paisley scarf, for God's sakes—almost the identical outfit to Mark's except for the difference in tailoring which amounted to probably about two thousand dollars. Deborah looked lovely in a Jones-New York ivory linen suit and olive green silk blouse and I wore a white silk Claude Montana jump suit.

Abba looked at the busy bar and said, "I've never seen so many old farts with young chicks. Look at those *alte cockers*, they have gold chains hanging down to their belly buttons which is about three inches above where their dates hemlines end. It reminds me of a joke I just heard.''

I groaned. Abba was not famous for his joke-telling.

''This 87-year-old guy tells his golf foursome that he just got married. 'She's 32,' he says proudly. 'So how did you get her to marry you?' they asked. 'I lied,' he answered. 'I told her I was 97.' ''

We all laughed, and it did break the ice a bit. The conversation was tentative at first since Mark and Abba were a little leery of each other, their last encounter having been a rather unfortunate one.* But after consuming one bottle of Chardonnay with our first course, everyone relaxed. Then Mark coaxed Deborah into talking about some of her cases and he was enthralled. She was a combination of femininity and forcefulness that you find only in women who are completely at ease with themselves and therefore everyone else. She was quick, she was smart, and she had a ready laugh. Just right for Abba. I looked at his face that was filled with love and thought, well, that's two of us who agree. Now all we need is the critical third party. And then there's the little obstacle of geography and careers to deal with.

By the time we got to our main course and were working on a bottle of Merlot, everyone was so relaxed that I felt free to bring up the current case.

''How's the M.E. doing on his search for the poison that killed Meg McClintock?'' I asked.

''Who's Meg McClintock?'' asked Mark.

I gave him a brief version of the facts and I could see he was intrigued. I hope he wasn't on his way to becoming a crime junkie which could make him quite a pest. Maybe

*IMPOLITE SOCIETY

he'll want us to become Nick and Nora Charles from the old William Powell and Myrna Loy movies.

"You can't identify the poison?" he said. "Maybe it's curare—I read once that it's hard to detect."

"Yes, Mark, it breaks down fast and leaves almost no trace in the body, but it leaves external signs like petechial hemorrhaging."

"You know, when I was a little boy, we had an old gardener who taught me all about plants and he warned me that many were lethal. For instance, autumn crocus is poisonous as are foxglove, larkspur, and peonies."

Deborah looked uncomfortable. "I don't like to talk about current cases in front of civilians," she said, looking at Mark and smiling to ease the rigidity of her statement. "However, I can tell you the toxicology people are on it and they'll locate it eventually."

"OK, *sharmuta* my love," said Abba, "we'll change the subject. Mark, what was it like growing up in a house with sixty rooms and twenty servants?"

"Compared to what?" asked Mark with a smile.

"Compared to someone like me who grew up in a five-room apartment with one bathroom and played in the street with a gang of kids."

"Actually, I didn't grow up in the house because I was sent away to school at eight." He smiled sadly. "I would have adored staying home and having a number of playmates to frolic with. I assure you that the number of rooms, bathrooms, and servants have no bearing upon a child's happiness. Now let me ask you some questions. Did you see your parents often?"

"Morning, noon, and night, breakfast and dinner, seven days a week. Except when I was in school or out playing. On weekends, full time. That's when we went to visit uncles, aunts, and cousins."

"That must have been lovely," said Mark wistfully. "I saw Mother and Father only on holidays. Upper-class British children have a rotten childhood but we spend it only with others who are undergoing the same vicissitudes so we sort of suffer through together. Then we grow up and find out how much better off we are than the rest of the country and life gets very easy and enjoyable. You, however, have it the other way 'round. You have a pleasant childhood but then you grow up and your struggle begins."

"But children aren't prepared for suffering whereas grownups are better equipped to handle it," I said. "I think sending kids away from parents who love them and putting them into the hands of strangers who don't, and subjecting them to mistreatment of bullies which is inevitable, is tantamount to child abuse. The only ones who should bring up children are their parents."

"Hear, hear," said Mark, raising his glass and then leaning over to kiss me. "We'll never send ours off, will we, darling?"

"Did I miss something?" asked Abba.

"Nope. Mark always starts to fantasize when the clock strikes midnight. Why don't we all go back to my place for a nightcap?"

Mark insisted on picking up the entire check. "Emma invited you and in my country, that means it's our treat."

I had discussed this with Mark beforehand. I knew Abba's expense account didn't run to the kinds of wines Mark would order. Abba made the proper protests but I could see he was relieved. He had recognized the labels on the bottles.

When we arrived at the house, we all had a drink on the terrace and then I followed the promised arrangement and pleaded weariness, sending home a puzzled and disappointed Mark, who obviously had other plans. I went to bed and fell asleep quickly. What seemed like minutes but was actually two hours later, I was awakened by knocking on my door. It was Abba.

"She loves me, she loves me!" he said, grabbing me and twirling me around the room. Luckily, it was one of the rare times when I wore a nightgown because the air conditioning had been set on frigid. Usually I sleep in the buff because I consider it lunacy to get dressed to go to bed. I move around when I sleep, and pajamas pull under the arms and at the crotch, and nightgowns end up around my neck.

He sat on the edge of my bed, absolutely exultant.

"So what happens now?" I asked, stifling a yawn.

He looked surprised. "What do you mean?"

"What usually happens when Jewish boy meets Jewish girl—they get married and live happily ever after."

He laughed. "Maybe twenty years ago. But not these days. My life and career are in Israel, hers are here. She has a marvelous future—do you know she moved ahead faster than any other woman in the department, and there's even talk of the possibility of her becoming the first woman commissioner of police in Palm Beach, maybe even the entire state?"

"That's wonderful," I said, not meaning it. The women's movement has a lot to answer for. "You have a wonderful professional future, she has a wonderful professional future. What about your future together?"

He looked surprised. "I'll be going back next week and she has vacation time owing so she'll be coming to Israel next month. And I can always find reasons to come over here. We'll probably end up spending more time together than most couples—those commuter guys who get home at eight every night and play golf on the weekends, or those working couples who are in the office until ten. The main thing is we love each other.''

Coming up with rationales for our behavior is one of the most creative human activities. Convincing ourselves is quite another thing. So there won't be any little Abbas and Deborahs running around in the near or probably distant future. I was disappointed—he'd make such a great daddy. But we live in an era of choices, and if that's hers and his and it works for them, why then I'm happy for them. But deep down inside, I'm a little sad.

XIV

~<~

IT WAS ANOTHER glorious perfect Palm Beach morning so I took my robe and towel and walked to the beach. Although the beaches are all public property, which means anyone can swim anywhere, accessibility or lack of same is what makes some beaches virtually private. Bootsie's estate took up a few acres of beachfront. The only other ways to get to the ocean in front of her estate other than from her property were to walk a mile or so from an adjacent stretch of beach or come by boat. None of which has ever happened. I laid my robe on one of the chaises under an umbrella that were part of Bootsie's permanent installations and checked the sign. Ever the superb hostess, Bootsie had a crew clean the beach of flotsam, jetsam, and seaweed every morning and post swimming conditions for the day. The sign indicated the temperature of the air and water and the safety conditions of the surf.

I know it's foolhardy to go into the ocean alone since even strong swimmers can get caught by a sudden undertow, but the exhilarating feeling of having an entire ocean to myself made it worth the risk. I first checked along the water's edge for the possible presence of those colorful little blue balloons that are actual lethal Portuguese men o' war whose sting could paralyze you. Then I plunged in and started to swim parallel to the beach at a lazy pace. The water was refreshingly cool, just the way I like it. Floridians only go into the ocean in summer when the temperature is tepid. Yuch! I came out and stretched out on a chaise for a while, and then returned to the house to shower and dress and have breakfast. What a life!

Since the Count, Rick, and I were the only residents at the moment, there were no prepared dishes on the sideboard, so I walked into the kitchen and gave my order to Janet.

Fortunately, I was finished with my toast and eggs and was lingering over coffee when Rick walked in. He barely looked at me and headed for the kitchen. I guessed he was one of those ''don't-talk-to-me-until-I've-had-my-coffee'' types. You know, the kind who snarl at you and then proudly acclaim, ''I'm not a morning person.'' I don't buy those excuses—politeness is mandatory no matter when. He came back in with a cup of coffee and waited for Janet to bring in the food he'd ordered. Something about the way he dragged himself indicated he had had a snifter too many the night before.

''Good morning,'' I said loudly, dropping my spoon noisily on my saucer.

I chuckled inwardly as I saw him wince at the noise. There's no better way to begin the day then to irritate someone you can't stand. I didn't bother to start a conversation because I knew words would have to wait until he had some food. After he finished his three eggs and bacon with five slices of toast—that gut and love handles didn't come from nowhere, he earned them—I broached a topic.

''How long do you plan to stay here, Rick?''

He grunted. "Don't know. All that money that's coming to me and the bastards won't give me a nickel. I can't leave this fuckin' place because I'm broke. It's like I'm a prisoner."

"This place isn't exactly too shabby. You even have your girlfriend here. I can't see where you have too much to complain about."

"Aaa, she's a drag. Always telling me to be patient. I understand this town is crawling with tasty pieces of ass and here I am stuck inside with an old bag who acts like my mother."

Poor Eunice. She did her job, now who needs her? So much for gratitude.

"When do you think that old fart lawyer will be giving out the money?" he asked.

"A will usually takes some time to probate, and in this case, when the circumstances of the death are questionable, it will probably take even longer."

"Sonofabitch, don't I always have shitty luck."

"It wasn't too great for Bootsie either," I said, trying to contain myself from tossing my coffee into his ratty face.

"She was an old broad anyway, and she had it plenty good for pretty long," he said with a sneer.

What could I do to give this little creep a hard time? Of course.

"You realize, Rick, that if you killed your aunt, you don't get a penny because a murderer by law is not allowed to benefit from his crime."

He jumped up in his seat, his face red with alarm.

"What the fuck are you talking about? I didn't kill her. The fuzz can't pin this one on me. Shit, I wasn't even here."

"But your sweetheart was. If Eunice did it, you could be held as an accessory."

He was actually sweating now. I know this may sound

like I'm not a nice person, but I was really enjoying this. Wouldn't you?

"Why the fuck would Eunice pop her? What's in it for her?"

"You, of course. Not only would you get the quarter of a million dollars, but if Jonathan is convicted of the crime, the entire billion-dollar estate passes to you."

"It would?" His eyes widened. Apparently the thought had never entered his head. You could see his slow brain working out the details. First his face showed delight when he realized he could inherit everything. Then a shadow came over him as he then realized he'd get nothing if he's found responsible for Bootsie's death.

"But if I got all the money, what's that got to do with Eunice?"

"Everything, if she's your wife."

"My wife?" He laughed. "You gotta be kidding. I don't need no ball and chain. And if I did, you can bet your butt it wouldn't be her."

"So you say. But the police don't know that. Eunice coming here to work for your aunt—why would an educated woman like her go all the way to the other end of the continent to take a job as a maid unless she had a special motive? You have to admit, the whole thing looks suspicious, as though you and she planned it."

By now he was white as a sheet. It's understandable; Rick was from a class of miscreants who spend their lives operating on the edge of the law. They see themselves as victims of a police force who view them as possible perpetrators of all sorts of crimes. But this wasn't just some petty misdemeanor that could bring jail time; it was a capital case that could put him away for life. I was scaring the hell out of him. I know it's mean, but I was really enjoying watching him squirm. It's not as though my scenario was far-fetched; it actually was quite feasible. Detective Berkowitz thought so when I ran it by her yesterday.

"You know that lady detective," he said in a panic. "You talk to her and tell her I got nothing to do with this. If Eunice decided to pull the plug on my aunt, I didn't know nothing about it—I didn't have nothing to do with it, I swear." He got up from his chair and started walking around the room repeating, "I swear, I swear."

I believed him. But that still left Eunice as a possible perpetrator. Rick said he'd never marry her but I can't believe that she would plan and execute a murder without some certainty that she would tangibly benefit. She must have some assurance that she and Rick would be husband and wife. Or could she be so self-delusional that she had convinced herself he loved her?

"Good morning."

Speak of the devil, it was Detective Berkowitz.

She smiled at me and then turned to Rick, who was holding on to the chair to support himself. His face was a study in abject terror.

"Mr. Bolton, may I have a few words with you?"

I left the dining room and took my coffee out to the terrace.

"Good morning, Emma."

It was the Count who was sitting in a chair reading the newspaper.

"Good morning, José."

The poor guy had aged about ten years since I saw him last. He looked so pathetic that I felt like assuring him that everything would be all right and that he'd get his silver candelabras. But would he? His dejected posture could be from sadness at losing them, or from losing Bootsie and a very pleasant lifestyle, or from the knowledge that he killed her in vain. He had the opportunity and the motive. Was he the murderer?

"Beautiful day, isn't it?" I said, ever the snappy conversationalist.

"The climate, yes," he said. "But the atmosphere, the heart of this house, is sad. It misses the joy brought to it by Bootsie."

He was right. There was an absence of life and the bubbling spirit of Bootsie's ebullient personality. A house is, after all, just a building. Its spirit and soul are imbued by the occupants.

"I miss her most dreadfully," he said.

His face turned dark. "I made a most tragic mistake, and I am guilty of a terrible sin."

My God. Is he going to confess to me? I don't have to read Miranda to him—I'm not a cop. But I would feel the responsibility to report his words to the authorities.

"I was greedy," he said. "I wanted those candelabras so much that I let my feelings for Bootsie be forgotten. I was actually angry at her for forgetting to leave them to me. Can you imagine such venality? I truly loved her, and she was so wonderfully kind to me. Then she is wickedly deprived of her life, she who enjoyed so much every moment of living, and I feel nothing but sorrow for myself. I am ashamed. This is one of the times when I regret having given up Catholicism. My wife used to pray for the salvation of my soul. Perhaps she was right. I could confess to the priest and do penance and feel comforted. Religion can be such an emotional support. Now, I have nothing to help me through this very difficult time."

He looked absolutely wretched. Unless the man was the most consummate actor since Laurence Olivier, he was telling the truth. I felt sorry for him.

"Don't beat up on yourself too much, José. We are all

only human. What you felt was only natural. If she promised them to you, then you certainly had the right to feel disappointed, even slightly betrayed. But knowing Bootsie, you have to realize her intentions were for you to have them but she was a great one for procrastination. Someone who loved life as she did tended to avoid discussions about death."

He sighed. "I knew that. But how could I remind her all the time to put me into her will? It would seem so—so *com porco*, like a pig."

I'll bet that didn't stop Miss Eunice from nagging her employer to add her lover to the list of legatees. Her determination precluded any such niceties as consideration or sensitivity. Too bad the Count didn't go to gigolo-training-school. I'm sure they'd include a course on "How to Ensure Your Quid Pro Quo for Services Rendered."

We chatted for a while and then he went back to reading the paper and I just sat enjoying the view.

"There you are, Emma. I thought I might find you out here."

It was Detective Berkowitz. José began to rise, ready to deliver one of his polite exit lines.

"Don't get up, José," I said. "I want to take a walk—the detective and I will take a turn around the gardens."

I told her about my conversation with the Count. She listened carefully and nodded.

"You believe him, I gather?"

"I once asked a psychiatrist friend how he was able to distinguish the important from the non-important when a patient was spilling his guts on the couch. His answer was that experience had taught him to detect the emotional sound of truth. Yes, Deborah. I believe him."

She smiled. "Well, that's something. Eliminating suspects is a step forward."

"Where does that put that major creep Rick Bolton?" I asked.

"With his girlfriend, very much in the running, I'd say. If guilt were assigned by reverse popularity, that is if the most obnoxious suspect were adjudged the perpetrator, he'd head the list." Then she smiled. "Unfortunately, it doesn't work that way. Often the most sympathetic character has committed the crime. Which is why police, like doctors, have to distance themselves emotionally from their cases."

We sat down on a bench facing a bed of red petunias and blue ageratum.

"This place is absolutely gorgeous," she said, looking admiringly at the plants and the far view of the ocean.

"Working in Palm Beach," I said, "you must see a lot of this kind of opulence, I should think."

"Not really. There's not too much crime happening along Ocean Boulevard. Most of our business comes from West Palm, Lantana, and over on the western side of the county. So I don't get to peek behind the walls of these mansions too often. Of course, we were all over the Kennedy place when the alleged rape case happened, but there was hardly any opulence there." She shook her head in wonder. "The place was a shambles—just a rabbit warren of little dark rooms. And dilapidated! It looked like a single-occupancy hotel for the homeless. When you come down here on vacation, you'd think you'd want luxury, not discomfort. The first time I went in there, I wondered what my grandmother would have said if she had seen it. I think she might have started to vote Republican. She was one of those fanatic fastidious housekeepers whose house always smelled of Clorox and furniture polish. When we opened the door on Passover after the seder to admit Elijah, we used to yell out 'Elijah, don't forget to wipe off your feet on the doormat!' She considered anyone whose home wasn't spotless to be subhuman. Here you had acres of beautiful beachfront, and the house not even air-conditioned. I couldn't imagine anyone accepting those sort of shabby living conditions, let alone the millionaire Kennedys. I wonder what Hyannisport looks like.''

"I grew up in Rye," I said, "a community heavily populated with old wealth. They live in large million-dollar houses that have well-kept exteriors but inside, nothing has been touched for thirty or more years. The original ancient kitchens, worn upholstery, shabby rugs and furniture—it doesn't seem to matter. It's regarded as genteel.''

"What do you think it is?'' asked Deborah. She looked at me. "I don't mean to sound prejudiced, but is it a *goyishe* thing?''

"No, I don't think so. I think it's more an old money thing. If you've had it for generations you have no need to display or prove your wealth by ostentation. Refurbishing comes under that heading.''

"But how about comfort and cleanliness?'' she asked.

"Old furniture is perfectly comfortable, often more so. As far as cleanliness, that's the province of the help and you get to accept the low level they provide. What's your choice? Remember, there's no Mr. Hudson around to ride herd on them and their jobs are not at risk if they forget to dust the hunting prints. Your grandmother may have gotten great satisfaction out of having a spotless oven, but can you imagine a maid boasting with pride about how well she scrubbed madame's kitchen floor today?''

"I guess I never thought about it that way," said Deborah.

"Pigsty or not, I understand the Kennedy place sold for 4.9 million dollars.''

She grimaced. "What some people will pay for the Camelot myth.''

"Where did you grow up, Deborah?" I asked.

"New York. Long Island. Little Neck, in a house that would fit into that corner of the garden."

"What brought you down here?" I asked.

"My grandmother and then my parents moved down here when my dad retired. They live in Hallandale. Actually, I left the police force in New York City to come down here." Then she added, "I was an inspector."

I was stunned. The only way one gets the title of inspector in New York City is by having it bestowed upon you for outstanding performance. It is a discretionary award from the higher-ups and is not given lightly. I looked at her with interest wondering—what's her story?

"What brought you into police work?" I asked. "It's not the usual career move for a nice Jewish girl from Long Island."

"I was about to take my master's degree in social work, when I was offered a job as investigator for the Corporation Counsel of the City of New York. That involved working with detectives on cases of people suing the city. It sounded interesting so I thought I'd give it a shot. Apparently I was good at it because one of the detectives I worked with handed me an application for the police exam. I never had any intention of going into law enforcement, but I decided, what the hell. I passed, and started out as a patrolperson riding in a two-person police car in one of the toughest neighborhoods, in Harlem. My parents were petrified and unhappy but I found I loved it. I kept hearing 'for this we sent you to college?' They were afraid to tell my grandmother who was a communist; to her, the police were fascists. But every day was like an adventure. It was exciting, never boring, and I liked dealing with people. I found, to my surprise, that police work is 90 percent social work—you become like a counselor, almost a priest to the neighborhood. You help marriages and families stay together, and when someone is distraught and needs to talk to someone—they call the police, we're there day and night for them."

"When did you decide this would be your career?"

"During my first week on the job. I took every promotion exam as it came along and went to Sergeant to Lieutenant to Captain."

"What was your rank when you left?"

"I was commander of the precinct that I first started out in."

I looked at her in awe. "Are there any other woman commanders of New York City precincts?"

"No."

"It's a wonder they didn't do a CBS movie of the week about you."

She smiled. "There was a producer who nagged me for a whole year to do a TV series about me. But I refused."

"Why?"

She grimaced. "It might do a lot for his career, but not for mine."

"What made you give it up to come down here?"

"The climate and my family. I hated the cold winters and I wanted to be near my family—my parents and grandmother weren't getting any younger. When I was offered this job here, I took it. It's a small department, but a very good and modern one. And they made me an offer I couldn't refuse."

"Do you think you may be their first woman police commissioner?"

She smiled. "I'm not ready yet for a job that's basically administrative and political. Right now, I like being where the action is."

This is an extraordinary woman who is highly committed to her profession and will never give it up. I certainly can empathize with that. What does that bode for a relationship between her and Abba?

She got up looking at her watch. "I have to go. I'll see you later."

She left just as Rivers approached me. He was holding a sheaf of papers that looked like mail.

"Madame, I wonder if you will be seeing Mr. Blair soon?"

"As a matter of fact, I was planning to go there now."

Absolutely. It's a decision I made two seconds ago.

"I have the house correspondence—bills and things—that I gather he will handle. Would you be kind enough to bring them to him?"

I took them. "No problem," I said. I put them into my large shoulder bag that functions as an attaché case and a portable trunk, and walked to the garage. Exercising a great deal of control, I waited until I got into the car and drove two blocks before I inspected the envelopes. They were bills. The only ones that interested me were from three doctors. I know Bootsie hadn't been ill—so who were they for? Luckily the doctors' billing people were short of saliva and I was able to open the flaps by carefullly inserting the handy-dandy nail file I always carry for such and other law-breaking occasions. I know, opening mail is not only a violation of privacy but a federal offense. But that's only if you get caught.

The bills were for Rivers, the first from a urologist for extensive prostate tests and treatment, the second from an oncologist, and the third from a radiologist for radiation treatment. Rivers was not yet on Medicare, which meant that Bootsie paid his medical expenses. He apparently had prostate cancer. Today, that's no longer a sentence of death. It depends on how early the disease is detected and many other factors. My uncle has lived with prostate cancer for ten years and is on the golf course every day. I have known others who have been operated on and are totally cured. I also know others who have died.

When I arrived at Tom Blair's office and asked to see him without an appointment, the receptionist looked at me as though I had asked her to cut her fingernails, which were one inch long and painted purple.

"Mr. Blair is a very busy man," she said indignantly. "He never sees anyone without an appointment."

I'm always bemused at the proprietary way receptionists and secretaries (whoops—I'm not being P.C.—administrative assistants) guard their employers zealously and regard them as revered creatures doing incredibly vital work, even if they're running toilet paper factories. (Not that I'm degrading the importance of that essential product.) No wonder so many guys leave their wives for their secretaries. It's hard to be treated like a god in the office and then to come home to be told to take out the garbage and why the hell didn't you hang up your pants.

"Just tell him Emma Rhodes is here to see him," I said with a smile.

Her face took on that mulish look that not-too-bright people take on when they're being pushed. The only way to get a mule's attention was to hit it on the rump with a two-by-four. Since I hadn't come equipped, I had to resort to other measures.

I just walked right past her into Tom's office, with her screeching, "You can't go in there."

"Emma—what a nice surprise," said Tom, rising in his chair just as the door opened and Miss Purple Nails came storming in.

"It's all right, Tina—Miss Rhodes is always welcome here, even without an appointment."

Her limited brain didn't know how to cope with this

radical deviation in accepted procedure. She was shaken and as she left the room, she looked at me accusingly as though I were responsible for a major upheaval in her otherwise placid daily life.

"Tina tends to be a little excessive in her loyalty," Tom said.

"Keeps out the riffraff," I said.

"What brings you here, my dear? Did you come to share this old man's morning coffee break? I was just about to go out to our coffee maker and make myself a cup." He sighed. "I remember when my secretary used to bring it to me. Now I'd be accused of sexual discrimination if I asked. Emma, can I bring you a cup or is that reverse discrimination? One has to be so careful these days. Tina came in last week and began to cry. Her mother was ill and she was worried. My instinct was to put my arm around her to comfort her in a fatherly fashion, but I didn't dare for fear of being accused of sexual harassment."

"It may seem wrong and unnatural when you have to curb good instincts," I said. "But not if it helps to curb base instincts. When I was a young summer intern in a big nameless Wall Street law firm, I was bending over a file cabinet when one of the partners walked by and responded to an age-old male instinct—he goosed me. I was mortified and furious but he thought it was hilarious. My instinct was to knee him in the groin, but I realized that wouldn't enhance my future chances of being taken on as a full-time associate, so I gritted my teeth and smiled at the bastard. If now everyone has to bend over backwards, an apt choice of words under the circumstances, in order to create awareness of the kind of seemingly innocent but horribly demeaning behavior women have been subjected to in offices for years—then so be it."

He made a small bow. "Well said and I shall no longer

carp at my loss of services. Now how about coming to the coffee station with me and making your own cup? To make the trip more alluring, there are donuts.''

We sat at his desk munching and sipping, and I handed him the mail. He shuffled quickly through it, and his eyebrows went up when he saw the opened envelopes.

''Would you believe that doctors use envelopes with cheap glue so that the flaps never close right?''

''Knowing many doctors' attitudes toward money, I might consider that a reasonable explanation,'' he said with a smile.

''Rivers has prostate cancer.''

''I know,'' he said.

''Did Bootsie know?''

''Yes. He is undergoing treatment and the hope is that he can be cured. We don't know yet.'' He looked at me. ''Does this have any import in your search for the true culprit?''

''Maybe,'' I said.

I left his office and waved to Tina with a big smile. ''Ciao!'' If looks could kill, I'd never have made it out the door.

XV

~~❧~~

I FOUND RIVERS in the kitchen sitting at the huge butcher block table in the middle of the room having a cup of tea with Janet. He jumped up when I came in.

"Don't get up, please, Rivers. I'm sorry to have disturbed you. Whenever you're finished, I'd like to talk to you."

Janet arose. "We're done. And I was just about to go to my room for a bit of a lie-down anyway."

She left the room and I took her place at the table.

"Would you like a cup of tea, Miss Emma?" he asked.

I didn't really. But it would establish the easy casual tone I needed for this interview so I said yes. He made a whole thing of ascertaining my tea needs—"Milk? Sugar?" When he finished and sat down, he looked at me expectantly. There was no apprehension, only curiosity. It was the look of a clear conscience, but this is a man who has been to hell and back and has undoubtedly learned to control all show of emotion.

"You know, Rivers, that I've been retained by Mr. Jonathan to clear him of murder charges."

"Yes, we all know that. I'm sure you will be successful because there's no possibility whatever that he killed his aunt," he said emphatically.

"Did everyone know about Mrs. Corrigan's allergy to peanuts?"

"All the staff did. As did the McClintock sisters. The only ones here who to my knowledge did not know were Mr. and Mrs. Pachurian and her cousin."

"You were in and out of the kitchen that day while Janet was preparing the dinner. Who did you see there?"

"As I told the police, Eunice and the McClintocks. Then there was the boy from the liquor store with a case of Gamay. Manuel the gardener brought in the flowers. Mrs. Pachurian dropped by to bring the parsley and thyme from her garden that Janet uses in the stuffing. Oh yes, the laundry and cleaners made deliveries."

"Are all these delivery people regulars?"

"Yes—wait, no, the laundry chap was someone I'd never seen before."

"And you told all this to the police?"

"Yes—except about the new laundryman. But they didn't ask me that," he said defensively.

I smiled. "Then that's their mistake, not yours."

He relaxed.

Time for a new tack.

"What do you plan to do after this whole affair is over?" I asked. "You must've figured out that the household won't exist any longer."

"Yes, I know. Mr. Jonathan won't want to live here— he's a very modest sort of gentleman and I suspect this sort of grand life would never suit him. Besides, I'm ready to retire. Between the money Mrs. Corrigan left me and social security—yes, I'm an American citizen and she paid into the system for me always—I shall be quite well off indeed.''

''And I hope you will also be quite well,'' I said.

He looked startled.

''Yes, I know about your cancer,'' I said. ''I also know that it can be quite curable.'' I told him about my uncle and the other prostate cancer survivors I knew.

He smiled ruefully. ''Thank you for your encouragement,'' he said. ''But I'm afraid my case may be too far gone. The doctors have given me very little hope.''

His face registered no sadness, no anger, no fear—just total acceptance.

''What will happen to your son?'' I asked softly.

He was surprised. ''You know about Charlie?''

''I know all about you, Rivers.''

He looked at me sharply. ''All?''

I nodded.

''How?'' he asked. ''Even Mrs. Corrigan didn't know everything.''

I told him of my source and much of what Sgt. Parnell told me. He smiled when he heard that no one had any intention of hunting for him. ''I didn't think the coppers would be coming after me after all these years.''

''Just for my own curiosity, did you have help in your escape?''

He smiled in remembrance. ''T'would have been fair impossible without it. The minister who came to visit me— after all, I was about to die—slipped me a note telling me that there were folk who wanted to free me, and to be ready when and where. Nevertheless, I was fair shocked when our van smashed into the other one. I couldn't see anything, of course, I was in the back with the guards and we were all thrown about on the floor. Suddenly, someone broke open the door and pulled me out and two of them, there were, fairly dragged me to another car that was waiting and took me away. It all happened so fast, I was in shock, I tell you. They took me to a small boat and transferred me to a ship that took me to Vancouver. I kept asking for Charlie and they told me he'd be there waiting for me. And he was. He was the most wonderful sight I ever saw," and his face illuminated with the memory.

"Do you know who the people were who carried out the whole escape?"

He shook his head. "Not to this day. I have always wanted to thank them for my life and Charlie's, but they said it was too dangerous for any identification or for any contact to be maintained. I thank them every day in my prayers, and I've taught Charlie to do the same."

"Where is Charlie now?"

"In Boca Raton living with a wonderful family who take fine care of him. He's a sweet lad, very loving. I spend my day off with him every week and phone him every day. He has a job," he said proudly. "He takes the bus every day by himself to the Association for the Handicapped and works there until five. They tell me he's a very good worker. He gets paid, of course. It's not very much but it gives him some self-esteem. Of course, I pay the people he lives with."

"I assume you've made provisions for him?" I asked.

"You mean after I die? Yes, of course. All my money will go into a trust fund that will take care of him forever." He looked at his watch. "If that's all, Miss Emma, I really must go. I have to do my ordering."

The phone rang and he picked it up. "Yessir, just a moment please, she's right here. It's Colonel Levitar."

"What's with that 'Colonel' bullshit?" asked Abba.

"I mentioned it once not even in front of Rivers but he finds out everything. And you know how impressed the

British are with rank. To what do I owe the pleasure of this
call? Between your bond selling and your love life, I don't
get to see you too much."

"Well, *hamoodie* my love, today's your lucky day. I'm
free. How about lunch at Charley's Crab in about fifteen
minutes?"

"We'll never get a table."

"Are you kidding? In my uniform?"

I groaned. "Not the bullet-torn hat again."

"Stop complaining. It works, doesn't it?"

He was already seated when I got there and the waiter
and the *maitre 'd* were fawning over him.

"I ordered for you," he said. "The special today is
grilled pompano."

"Great. But no wine or I'll be zonked for the afternoon
and I'll be needing all my faculties today."

"What's up?" he asked.

I told him about Rivers. "He knows he will probably die.
Which means he needs that two hundred fifty thousand dollars Bootsie left him to take care of his son. Which means he
needed her dead."

"Did he know about the legacy?"

"Yes. Tom Blair told me she had the unlovely quality
of letting everyone know how much she was leaving them
so she could enjoy their gratitude in her lifetime."

Abba looked thoughtful. "This guy has killed before to
protect his son."

"Exactly. He had motive and means. I tell you, this case
is crawling with suspects. But it can't be Rivers."

"Why not?" asked Abba.

"It would be too corny if the butler did it."

"Hello, you two." Milo Pachurian stood at our table
smiling.

We invited him to pull up a chair. "I really can't. I'm

here with some clients. Emma, I just wanted to ask you if you knew when Bootsie's house will be closed. If Jonathan intends to sell the furnishings, I'd like to buy back my rugs.''

I told him I had no idea about the ultimate disposition of the property and he left.

"Pompous little prick, isn't he?" said Abba. "Notice how he referred to his 'clients.' Most shopkeepers—and that's all he is—refer to people who buy from them as 'customers.' *Lawyers* have clients.''

"Milo is very full of himself, no doubt. But it must be tough on the ego to live among all these leisured million-aires and billionaires while you have to scrounge daily to make a living—no matter how good a living it is.''

"There are lots of guys who spend their business lives kissing ass," said Abba. "Isn't that the American way to climb the corporate ladder—brown-nosing the guy above you?"

"As always, Abba, your choice of words is precise, al-beit a bit graphic.''

"So what's your next step, my sexy sleuth?" he asked.

"A little chat with Eunice and Rick. There are some niggling details that need clarification.''

"And what do you hear from the young lord?"

I smiled. "The usual. He loves me.''

"He's really not a bad guy. Deborah liked him, too." He looked at me appraisingly. "I can tell from your ex-pression that you really care about him. For god's sake, why don't you marry him? Being a duchess has to be a bit of a blast. Going to all those hunt balls, tea with the queen. It's a little girl's dream.''

"But I'm not a little girl anymore. Having to act the part of lady of the manor, subservient to the lord, of course—how can I live with that?"

"Times have changed in England, *hamoodie*. Take a tip from Cherie Blair, the new first lady there. During her husband's campaign, she walked behind him and kept her mouth shut. Now that he's prime minister, she's back to her career as a judge and can be herself. The role of prime minister's wife can be put on and taken off, just like her judicial robe. That's what you can do. Assume the duchess role when needed, and drop it to be yourself the rest of the time."

"Can it be that simple?" I asked.

"Who said simple?"

I thought about what Abba said as I was driving back to the house after lunch. The whole idea of marriage scares me, let alone one filled with ducal responsibilities. I love my life. I enjoy the total freedom of doing what I want when I want to without requiring approval or acquiescence from anyone else. I wince when I ask a married friend to join me in some activity and she responds with "sounds great, but I'll have to check with Bill." I enjoy meeting different men and having romances—I know it sounds almost adolescent, but there's a lot of fun and pleasure in courtships. Sure it's nice to have someone to snuggle with and wake up in bed with—but why does it always have to be the same man? I frequently am asked "but do you want to be alone all your life?" Yes, as long as I always have accessible men and I can't see why that supply should ever dry up, no matter how old I become. You hear of couples dating and mating well into the nineties. Then there's the question of children. There are times when I see a particularly adorable child, or run into some nicely behaved and bright kids, that I think fondly of begetting some of my own. But unfortunately, all the drawbacks of parenting are tangible and the advantages are intangible. It's easy to understand the disappointment at being unable to go skiing in

St. Moritz because your child got sick. But it's hard to appreciate the joy and pride one feels when your kid stars in the school play. True if I were married to Mark, we'd be floating in nannies, there would be none of those sleepless nights, and the loss of freedom would be minimal. But I don't know if I'd want someone else to bring up my children. The days of the trained and faithful old nanny who stayed with you until she died are gone. Today's baby tenders are more likely to be young things who quit regularly, or ladies from the islands who don't have any sense of familial commitment. When I see these types of nannies with impassive faces pushing strollers filled with joyless-looking children compared to the kids with mommies who are loving and involved, I wonder if I would have the heart to turn the rearing of my child over to some unconcerned stranger.

When I got back to the house, there was a message from Mark. I phoned him.

"Darling, I just received a call from home. I'll have to fly back to England tonight. Can I come over and spend the afternoon with you?"

"What's wrong? Is everybody all right?" I asked.

"Nothing serious. Just some infernal property matter that must be attended to immediately."

"Bring your swim things—we'll go to the beach."

When I opened the door, my heart jumped again as it did every time I saw him. Not only was he handsome, but he had that suave air of total assurance that comes from an upbringing of privilege when you are treated from the cradle on as though you exist on a higher plane than most other mortals. We went down to the beach and ran hand in hand into the ocean. There's something very sensuous about being kissed and held body to body in water. Afterward, we lay upon our chaises in the shade of an umbrella.

"Have you given any thought to us?" he asked.

"A lot."

"I know you think I'm a bigoted prat. To my dying day I'll regret my inexcusable outburst against Detective Superintendent Franklin and Abba. I can't help the way I was brought up, but I can change. I believe I already have. You must realize I had never had any social relationship with a Jew or a Black. To us, such people had useful functions, but were in no way ever considered to be our equals. Since that ghastly evening, I've made a concerted effort to become friendly with members of both groups and it's been like a revelation. I know that sounds patronizing, I don't mean it to be. I've actually become quite close with Sidney Goldfield who is on the local council with me and through him, a number of his friends and family."

I started to laugh. "I know. Some of your best friends are Jewish."

He looked puzzled.

"That's a common apologia of people who claim not to be anti-Semitic. I don't mean it for you, Mark. I believe you're sincere and I'm delighted. For you as well as me. You mentioned the town council. Does that mean you're starting to become interested in politics?"

"Yes. Not because of Mother's encouragement, but because I'm getting to realize it's a way to make a difference in this world. Even if it is often a dirty game, it's the only game that gets you the power to do anything."

We were on adjoining chaises and I leaned over to kiss him.

"What was that for? Whatever it was, I must remember to do it again."

"That was for the new emerging Mark who I approve of."

"You mean I'm becoming a *mensch*?" he said with a

twinkle in his eye. "Shocked, are you? It's a word I picked up from Sidney's mother. She called me that. I was a bit disconcerted until Sidney explained that it means a real solid person and is actually a very nice compliment."

I don't really want to get married, but he's making it harder and harder to keep saying no. Now he's making it even more complicated, and in some ways more appealing. He's offering me the chance to be the wife of a duke and also of a politician.

I sat up on my chaise and turned to him. "Mark, let me get through with this case first. I've got to keep my head and emotions clear until it's settled. Then I'll give the whole idea of our marriage my total attention and will give you my answer. Deal?" and I held out my hand.

He sat up with a broad smile, grasped my hand and said, "Deal!"

Then he rolled over to my chaise and took me in his arms. Have you ever made love on a chaise longue with a detachable pad? It's not the most comfortable thing in the world, but so what?

He couldn't stay for dinner and I couldn't drive him to the airport because he had a rental car to return, so we said our goodbyes at the house after he had showered and changed in the pool cabana. I was saddened to see him go, but a bit relieved to have the distraction removed. I went up to my room to change and then came down and headed for the kitchen. Pat McClintock was there as I thought she might be.

"Hello, Pat," I said. I had already conveyed my condolences and sent flowers. "How are you doing?"

She looked at me with a small smile and kept shelling peas into a large bowl.

"Keeping busy," she said. "Doing what the Lord expects us to do. And I've started to keep a written book about the days so that when I meet Meg again in Heaven, I'll be able to tell her what she missed. She'll want to know everything that happened after she left us and I'll surely never remember.''

Once again I envied the comfort of faith.

"Pat, would you mind if I asked you some questions about when you found her?''

"If it'll help find out who did that terrible thing, I'll be glad to answer questions until the moon comes up,'' she said firmly, not missing a pea-shelling beat.

"Exactly where was she lying?''

"Right inside the kitchen door. I'll never forget that sight till my dying day.''

I was surprised. "Not inside the room?''

"No. She was right next to the door.''

If she had a drink with someone, wouldn't she be either standing at the sink or sitting at the kitchen table? Then how did she imbibe the poison? The absence of a glass or two on the drainboard meant nothing since the murderer could have washed and put them away.

"What do you think she was doing at the door? If she felt sick from the poison, might she have been going to a neighbor for help?''

"No,'' said Pat emphatically. "The Roberts and the O'Neils on either side of us work, there's no one home there during the day. If Meg felt poorly, she would have gone to the phone to call the doctor.''

I thought for a moment, trying to get the picture. "When you opened the door, was she blocking your way? Were you able to open it fully?''

"Oh yes, she was just inside but clear of the door.''

"As though someone rang the kitchen doorbell, and Meg answered it opening the door wide. And the person stepped inside.''

"They'd have to, wouldn't they, if they were going to poison her."

"You would think so," I said thoughtfully.

I looked over at the stove. "That looks like a large roast for three people, Janet."

"But you'll be five. Mr. Jonathan is coming and Mr. Blair."

That sounded interesting. "What time is dinner?"

"In about half an hour," she said.

Dinner was pleasant if you managed to ignore Rick's deplorable table manners. Afterwards, Jonathan, Tom Blair, the Count, and I took our coffee out to the terrace. They had a touch of brandy with theirs. Rick went off somewhere and the Count, as usual, went upstairs to his room. He seemed to be sinking into a depression and I wished I could help him. Perhaps later.

"I spoke to the D.A. today. He's holding off on trying the case against you, Jonathan," said Tom.

"That's good, isn't it?" asked Jonathan.

"Of course."

"I imagine the McClintock murder has made them reconsider Jonathan as the killer," I said.

"Yes," said Tom.

"Thank goodness I was teaching school at the time she was killed," said Jonathan.

We heard a lot of shouting and Rick came tearing over to us, followed by Eunice.

"Hey, Mr. Blair—you're a lawyer. She says she's my wife. But I never married the bitch."

"Who and what are you talking about, Rick?" asked Tom. "Calm down, please."

Eunice appeared. "I'm afraid he's referring to me," she said quietly.

"What's common-law marriage?" Rick asked.

"It's a marriage relationship created by agreement and usually cohabitation without religious or civil ceremony," said Tom.

"Cocksucking lawyers can't talk English. What the fuck does that mean?"

"If a man and woman live together and hold themselves out to be man and wife, that is called common-law marriage and is recognized by some states as a bona fide legal marriage."

"I told Rick that when we stayed in a hotel in South Carolina some months ago registered as husband and wife, and visited with my whole family to whom I introduced Rick as my husband, that qualifies us as common-law spouses," Eunice said.

"If those are the terms acceptable by South Carolina I'd say yes, you are married."

"But we're in Florida now," said Rick.

"In this country, every state must give full faith and credit to the laws of another. If South Carolina terms you man and wife, so does Florida and every other state in the union."

Eunice smiled.

Rick looked horrified. "Holy shit." He snarled at Eunice. "You tricky cunt. You did that whole thing, dragging me down to your fucking family reunion, just to trap me, didn't you?"

"I'm also the one who convinced your aunt to leave you a quarter of a million dollars," she said angrily. "If it weren't for me, you'd still be crashing at another friend's house every night. How long do you think they would let you do that? I gave you a future, and security. You owe me."

This is better than *As The World Turns*. Jonathan, Tom, and I sat there like an audience at a performance. The two of them seemed to forget we were there. I figured we wouldn't interfere unless there was violence. Even then, I'm not sure. He was in such lousy shape, I think she'd take him in a minute.

She turned soft and loving. "Rick, I love you and I know you're really fond of me. We've always gotten along well. We could have a good life together. I'll always take care of you and I'll handle the money so that it will keep growing into a million dollars eventually. I'm good at handling investments. I did it for my mother for years."

At the mention of a million dollars, Rick's greedy eyes lit up. I could see his slow mind working. Maybe this wouldn't be such a bad thing. Nothing says I have to be faithful to the old bitch. I could fuck around all I want and she'd be home taking care of the place, cooking, cleaning, doing my laundry. I'll be rich and rich guys always play around. He looked at her and said, "Well, maybe—I'll think about it" and stalked off.

"That sort of changes things, doesn't it, Eunice?" I said.

"What do you mean?"

"You lied to me. You told me you weren't Rick's wife and therefore had no reason to kill Bootsie since you personally wouldn't benefit. Now it's apparent that you had an excellent motive for murdering his aunt."

She looked at me serenely and said, "Prove it" and walked off.

"My, my," said Tom Blair. "That is a very unpleasant lady."

Abba snorted. "She's a tough bitch and if Rick weren't such a scumbag, I'd almost feel sorry for him."

"She reminds me of those insects who devour their young—or is it fish?" I said. "But you have to admit, she planned everything pretty neatly."

"Not quite," said Tom with a smile. "He could always divorce her."

"But then he'd have to give her some if not half of the money."

"Maybe he would, if they lived in Connecticut or New York. But in Florida, we have something called Equitable Distribution which means a divorced spouse is only entitled to the money made during their marriage. Inherited wealth is exempt from marital settlements. In other words, he wouldn't have to give her a cent."

We all laughed. "Whoops! However did she slip up on that? Wouldn't I love to see her face when she finds out," I said.

"How about Rick?" asked Abba. "Does he know he could divorce her and only have to give her half his back-pack?"

"I wouldn't think so," said Tom. "And I certainly am not going to tell him. I'm not his lawyer, thank God, and never will be."

"Who knows? He may never find out and they could stay together forever. I've seen marriages that lasted based on lesser reasons," I said.

"My Aunt Goldie and her husband," said Abba, "stayed together for forty years because his name was on the lease of their rent-controlled apartment on West End Avenue. She couldn't stand him because he insisted on wearing the same underwear two days in a row and turning it inside out, and he chewed Indian nuts in bed. She figured she could probably find another husband, but never a seven-room apartment with three bathrooms on the eleventh floor in a white-glove doorman building for under two thousand a month."

Tom turned to me. "Does this man make up these stories?"

"No, his anecdotes sound unreal because he comes from such a bizarre family."

"Bizarre?" said Abba. "That from a *shiksa* whose parents eat corned beef on white bread, maybe even with mayonnaise?"

Tom looked surprised. "Is that wrong, Abba?"

"*Oi veh.* Where do I begin?"

"I suggest you don't even start, Abba, or you'll have to explain why Jewish people eat smoked salmon with cream cheese instead of the proper way with minced onions, lemon, and capers."

"That's a base canard," Abba thundered. "We eat lox with cream cheese. Smoked salmon is a whole different dish."

"And that's only on an ethnic level. I haven't hit into your personal idiosyncrasies. Like pouring ketchup over the duck l'orange that nearly got us thrown out of Le Cirque."

"I'm used to it. That was the only way you could eat my mother's duck. The ketchup buried the grease."

"If we're into confessions about eating anomalies," said Tom, "when I was a child it was believed that spinach provided important iron for growing bones. The only way my mother could get me to eat the inevitably stringy sandy stuff was to mix it with chocolate pudding."

"Ugh!"

"I know it sounds terrible, but I still like it," he said.

I got up. "Well, much as I'm enjoying these personal revelations, I must go. I phoned Lucy Pachurian earlier on and promised I'd stop by to see her garden."

Abba eyed me with a cynical smile. "Sure, sweetheart. I know how much you appreciate nature. I didn't think you could tell a pickle from a petunia."

"Sure I do. Say, where can I buy half-sour petunias?"

XVI

❦

I DECIDED TO walk over to Lucy's rather than drive. Of course, I was taking quite a risk. Unlike the southern end of Ocean Boulevard with the aligned glitzy condos which have sidewalks filled every morning with white-haired walkers in lavender velour jogging suits, the northern end has no sidewalks. Anyone seen walking is apt to be picked up by the police as a suspicious character, unless she has a dog on a leash. But it was one of those dry, sunny days without the punishing humidity and a walk was appealing.

The Pachurians' red-tiled-roof Mediterranean home was far smaller than Bootsie's, but lest you start feeling sympathy for the poor neighbors next door, let me inform you that the house suffered in comparison only because it had just fifteen rooms as compared to Bootsie's twenty-five. The door was answered by a uniformed maid who, after asking my name, ushered me into a large white-tiled foyer with a round center table bearing a tasteful arrangement of fresh flowers. I followed her into a huge living room that was filled with the colorful charm of Colefax and Fowler chintzes. At the far end of the room was what I first thought to be a tacky photographic mural, until I realized I was looking through a glass wall into the garden. A riot of colors and shapes, flowers and shrubs—it was the most breathtaking garden I have ever seen, and the glass wall brought it right into the house.

"It's enchanting," I said.

The maid smiled with the proprietary pleasure that evidences a warm relationship between servant and madam.

"Yes, Mrs. Pachurian works on it all the time." She led me through the kitchen which was a large blue and white ceramic-tiled wall room, with a huge cooking center with stove and sink in the middle of the room. Hanging from racks above it were ropes of garlic and onions and six or seven herbs that were being dried in bunches. A woman was sitting at the sink paring vegetables.

"Hello, Pat," I said. It was Pat McClintock.

She didn't seem surprised to see me and just nodded her head and went on with her work. We went out the kitchen door and there was Lucy kneeling in the ground working on a small bush. When she saw me, she arose, pulled off her garden gloves, and said with a warm smile,

"Emma, I'm so glad you could come. This is my pride and joy."

"As well it should be," I said. "It's exquisite."

"Would you like me to show you around?"

"Of course."

She led me around what seemed like acres of gardens, explaining the names and often the origins of many of the flowers.

"What's that funny-looking thing?"

"Bloodroot."

"And isn't that pokeweed?" I asked.

She looked surprised. "Why yes, how did you know?"

"I had a friend who used to grow it."

As we walked around, she commented to a man who was working, "Juan, don't be afraid to be a little rough with that—nicotiana can take it."

"And where's the vegetable garden that yields all that great produce?" I asked.

"We'll come to it soon. I have that close to the house. In England, we call it our kitchen garden," and then a few minutes later, "Here it is."

This was not just a small plot growing the usual tomatoes and herbs; this was about forty feet of garden. I saw cucumbers, string beans, squash, carrots, cabbages, onions, and potatoes. "What's this thing with the big leaves?" I asked as I started to reach for it.

"Don't touch it," she said sharply. "I didn't mean to startle you," she said apologetically, "that's castor beans. It's rather delicate and is a young plant and shouldn't be handled."

At the end of the vegetable garden, right next to the house, was a small building.

"Your potting shed?" I asked.

"Yes," and she started to walk by it.

"Could we go inside?" I asked.

She looked hesitant.

"I'd love to see it. I always feel you can tell a lot about a gardener by the condition of her potting shed."

"All right."

As we walked in, I inhaled appreciatively. "Mmm—I love the smell of manure and fertilizer. It's so evocative."

"Was your mother a gardener?"

I laughed. "What? And risk her manicure? My mom is a woman of great and many enthusiasms, but gardening is not one of them. Although she did try when I was a child and we had just moved into our house in Rye from our apartment in New York City. She got a book, and followed the instructions to the letter. She had the gardener cordon off a designated area chosen for its prolonged full sunshine, had him turn over the earth working in pounds of manure. No fertilizer, this was to be a totally natural organic garden. The book was from Rodale Press, you see. Then she went to a seed store and bought and planted. I'll never forget, we waited patiently and finally the excitement when seedlings began to pop up, and finally grow! Then the marauders came. I think they just sit back watching and waiting for the moment of fruition. The birds ate all the strawberries—I went out in the morning with a big pail and they were all gone. Rabbits ate the carrots and cabbages. Even the raccoons somehow got involved. Then came aphids, slugs. Soon, the garden was a mess and we had nothing to harvest. That was the end of my mother's sortie into horticulture."

Lucy laughed. "I know. Constant vigilance is required, but you learn how to keep away the destroyers and interlopers organically without resorting to pesticides. For instance, slugs can be discouraged by putting sand around the plants. Marigolds among the vegetables keep some bugs away. But basically, if you keep developing your soil to make it healthy, like filling it with worms who impart important nitrogen, the plants become strong enough to repel the damages of invaders."

I shook my head. "My mother's enthusiasms tend to be shortlived because, although she dearly wants to enjoy the results of a specific pursuit, she could never muster up the intense dedication it takes to achieve it."

"That's just what it takes—true dedication. We English are, as you undoubtedly know, avid gardeners. Of course, we have all the ideal conditions—lots of rain, some sun, and soil that has been gardened for hundreds of years. I grow vegetables because there's absolutely nothing like the taste of freshly picked produce. As for flowers, I look upon them as gifts from God. When you look carefully at a bloom and you see the intricacy of its design, the subtlety of its colors, you marvel at the divine force that must have created it.''

I looked around the potting shed. "This is so well organized, Lucy." There was a large counter where some newly potted seedlings stood obviously waiting to be planted. Tools were hung on the walls; there wasn't a single one lying around or just leaning. Bags of manure and peat moss were stacked in bins. The shelves had bottles neatly arranged in rows. There was a large jar of what looked like the castor beans I saw on the stalks outside. And smaller bottles of white powders. Then I noticed the building was really L-shaped and I turned the corner into another area that looked somewhat different. There was a refrigerator, a washing machine and dryer, and a large stone tub. The shelves held large enamel pans, glass measures, empty bottles, and bottles filled with powders, glass funnels, and mortar and pestles.

"What's all this for?" I asked.

She got a bit flushed. "I guess you could say this is my laboratory. I do my experimentation here."

"You mean like creating hybrids, grafting, stuff like that? I am impressed, Lucy. That takes a great deal of skill."

"It's my hobby," she said shyly. "I haven't been wildly successful, but I'm getting there. Come, let's go into the house. I'm dying for a cup of tea. Pat makes the most marvelous scones and she just made some this morning."

She excused herself and went upstairs to wash up and change and then we sat in the living room sipping tea and chatting. She told me about her childhood which, like most

English aristocracy, was financially privileged but emotionally bankrupt.

"After spending my life with people who revered impassivity, you can imagine what a delightful shock it was to meet someone like Milo who wore his feelings at his fingertips. Sparks flew out of his eyes," she said, laughing. "He would explode in fury, then be adorably contrite. I knew at once this is the man I wished to spend my life with. I knew that marriage to him might be like a roller coaster, but it would never be boring. And I was right," she said with satisfaction.

I walked back to Bootsie's house, refusing Lucy's offer to drive me. She was amazed and somewhat amused to hear I had come on foot.

"How refreshing, Emma," she said. "In England, walking is a large part of our lives. Here, the only kind of walking they do is that horrible power walking. One only walks with a specific purpose, never just for the love of the activity."

When I returned to the house, I phoned Detective Berkowitz.

"Deborah, have they identified the poison that killed Meg McClintock yet?"

She told me they had not.

"Tell them to test for Ricin. It was a favorite and virtually undetectable secret weapon of the Soviet KGB. Don't ask me why—it's a hunch."

As soon as I hung up, the phone rang. It was Jonathan.

"How are you doing, Emma?"

Uh, uh, he's committing a no-no—he's hinting for a progress report.

"Fine, Jonathan."

I find the best way to deal with overeager clients is to pretend I don't know what they're talking about, which would force them into making an overt inquiry, which they're usually loath to do since they know it's not permitted under the Emma Rhodes Rules of Client Behavior.

"Everything OK at the house? Do you need anything?"

"No, Jonathan," I said sweetly, "thank you very much but Rivers and Janet are taking good care of the three of us."

"Three? Oh, yes," he said in a disgusted voice, "I forgot Rick is there."

"I wish I could," I said.

"Well, I can't deny him the right to stay in Aunt Bootsie's house. After all, he is family."

"That doesn't put you under lifetime obligation, Jonathan. I do believe that one should try to accept relatives, warts and all. However, when the warts outweigh the warmth, I say dump 'em. I have a couple of cousins who were terminally obnoxious and I complained to my father. I'll pass on to you my dad's words of wisdom. 'Emma, being a relative does not require a relationship.' "

"You're right," he said cheerfully. "You're always such a source of support and encouragement. Couldn't we get together soon?" he asked wistfully.

I hardened my heart. "Let me see how my time goes, Jonathan, and I'll get back to you."

The phone rang again. This time it was Tom Blair.

"Emma, my dear. Would you give me the pleasure of entertaining you for dinner this evening at my home?"

I wondered who else would be there, but there's nothing ruder than asking for the guest list before accepting an invitation. The inference is that the company of the host is not sufficiently entertaining without an accompanying chorus. When anybody does that to me, I reel off a list of the most objectionable people the potential invitee knows, which ensures refusal and my mandate to put her or him on my non-guest list forever.

"Jonathan and Melissa will be here as well."

It couldn't be collusion because Jonathan just got off the phone. Oh well, it will give me a chance to see how wealthy retired widower lawyers live in Palm Beach. I'm always up for that. I guess when you come down to it, Abba is right. I am a *yenta*.

It was a splendid high-rise building overlooking Lake Worth. The view from the huge wraparound terrace on the tenth floor, where we had our cocktails, was spectacular. And the crabmeat fritter *h'ors d'oeuvres* were sensational. The passing boats with their illuminated masts made a fascinating parade. We watched the bridges open every time a craft with a high enough mast passed, thereby tying up east and west vehicle bridge traffic. We wondered why no one has invented a telescoping mast that goes up and down like an antenna so that an entire bridge mechanism wouldn't have to be put to work and all those car drivers would not be inconvenienced.

The apartment was somewhat overfurnished in old world elegance. It looked like someone had brought in the scaled-down contents of a house but couldn't quite leave behind some treasured pieces. Unlike most modern building layouts that have L-shaped dining rooms, Tom's had a full-sized separate dining room where we sat at a highly polished Duncan Phyffe table set with white lace place mats and gleaming crystal and silver. We were waited on by Silvana, a Cuban woman of what the French call "a certain age."

"Silvana has been with us for how many years?" Tom asked her as she placed the bowls of cold avocado soup before us.

"Thirty-three," she said with a smile.

"Silvana raised my two sons, took care of my wife in her last illness, and takes good care of me now. I don't know what I would do without her."

"Oh, Mr. Blair, like I told you, I know five young *chiquitas* who would move in with you tomorrow to take care of you and your money," and she laughed loudly as she returned to the kitchen.

The conversation got around to Rick and his pervasive and annoying presence.

"Why can't Jonathan just tell him to leave?" asked Melissa.

Tom shook his head. "I don't think that's wise at this time. Jonathan is not yet owner of the house and Rick is a legatee. When Jonathan is totally exonerated, as I hope and expect he will be, and takes full possession of the estate, he can then toss the bum out."

"I will be exonerated, won't I, Emma?" said Jonathan, looking at me longingly.

"I hate to make definite statements until I am absolutely sure, Jonathan. That's why I resist client entreaties for early opinions and predictions. All I will say is the chances are good."

I saw Melissa's lips tighten.

"Don't you think Jonathan is entitled to more detail than that? After all, he is paying you a lot of money. Don't you think you owe us something more?"

Should I let her have it? Why not? She's one of those smug know-it-alls who needs comeuppance once in a while. And I do so enjoy puncturing pomposity.

I smiled at her sweetly. "I owe you squat. Jonathan hasn't paid me a cent and won't until I conclude the matter for him. The very reason for my high success rate is these terms allow me to operate in total discretion without having to report to anyone, thereby jeopardizing the secrecy I need to do my job. If I divulged details of my suspicions at this time, you might reveal that information to someone tomorrow, and they would pass it on and so forth until it would reach the wrong ears and the entire case could be destroyed.''

"I would never tell anyone. What do you take me for?'' she said indignantly.

"A zealot who firmly believes it's just to use any weapons at all to fight injustice and hypocrisy. Let's say tomorrow a 'good friend' mentions how 'worried' she is about poor Jonathan being headed for prison or worse. We all know smarmy hypocrites like that. I'll bet your instant reaction would be to scorn her phony crocodile tears by assuring her of his innocence and proving it by naming the suspects whose names I've given you in strict secrecy. It's human nature. And yours, Melissa, is to proclaim whatever facts you need to prove a point.''

She turned red.

Maybe I went a little too far, but boy, it was fun. Perhaps I'd better make a little nice.

"But don't get me wrong, Melissa. I thoroughly admire your work. I saw you operating at the shopping mall site and I think your goals are admirable. We need people like you.''

The red turned to a lighter flush of pleasure and she looked mollified.

"However, your work and mine are antithetical to each other. Mine requires secrecy, and yours demands full disclosure. So why don't we let it go at *'vive le difference'*?'' and I smiled in as friendly a manner as I could muster.

The rest of the evening went swimmingly and Melissa actually kissed me good night. I didn't leave until I had gotten the recipe from Silvana for those fantastic crabmeat fritters. Would you like it?

Sauté a very finely chopped large onion in oil. When golden, add a tablespoon of chopped parsley and a 7-ounce can of crabmeat (picked over to remove pieces of cartilage). In a large bowl, sift 1 cup of all-purpose flour with 1 teaspoon of baking powder, 1 teaspoon of salt, and ½ teaspoon of freshly ground pepper. Pour in 4 lightly beaten large eggs, add the crab mixture and mix by hand until thoroughly blended. Refrigerate the bowl, covered, for at least 2 hours. Then deep fry until crispy brown by dropping small spoonsful into hot oil and drain on paper towels. Serve immediately, or leave in a 275° oven until ready to serve.

At breakfast the next morning, just as Count José and I were finishing our coffee, Rivers came in to announce that Detective Sergeant Berkowitz was here to see me and he had put her in the sitting room. When I entered, she jumped up.

"How did you know it was Ricin?" she asked.

I dropped down in a chair. "I didn't know. I guessed— and I'm almost sorry I'm right."

It's all due to my photographic memory. I don't know about other photographic memories, but mine doesn't work like Dustin Hoffman's in *Rain Man*. I don't have instant total recall of everything I read, only those items that interest me.

"I read an article in the *New York Times* last year about a man who was jailed for possessing 130 grams of Ricin, which they called one of the deadliest poisons. It said that a speck of Ricin, jabbed from the tip of an umbrella, was used by Soviet agents to kill a defecting Bulgarian official at a London bus stop in 1978."

"What made you think it was Ricin that killed Miss McClintock?"

I sighed. "Ricin is made from castor beans. There's a

specific recipe for it and it can be made anywhere and distilled into a white powder. It's often made by sheep farmers in Montana to control coyotes. It's 6000 times more potent than cyanide."

"So? We're not in Montana—we're in Florida. There are no sheep farmers here."

"But there are home gardeners who grow castor beans."

She looked at me sharply. "Do you have someone specific in mind?"

"I suggest you talk to Lucy Pachurian. You may have to get a warrant to search her potting shed."

She gasped. And I felt like crying.

"You'll find a jar of castor beans and a jar of white powder that I believe to be Ricin on the shelf."

Detective Berkowitz looked at me sympathetically. "In your business as well as mine, Emma, it's not a good idea to develop feelings for anyone involved in a case."

"I know," I said sadly. "Until the case is over, you never know who might turn out to be the bad guy. It's one of those lessons that your mind tells you to learn, but your heart doesn't always listen."

She was about to leave when she turned back. "Emma, I think I'd like to have you along when I talk to Mrs. Pachurian in her home. Would you mind?"

"That depends—will I be able to speak or will you have me sit there as a dumb bystander?"

She laughed. "I can't imagine you sitting dumb at any time or any place, Emma. OK—it's not exactly kosher procedure, but I'll bend the rules a bit."

We rang the bell, and Lucy answered the door. When she saw Detective Berkowitz she turned white. She spotted me standing behind Deborah and her hand flew to her mouth.

"Hello, Mrs. Pachurian," said Deborah politely. "May

we come in and talk to you for a few moments?''

She recovered quickly. Standing there in her pale yellow linen pantsuit with a lime-colored silk kerchief around her neck and tan Kenneth Cole sandals, she looked the epitome of cool.

She smiled and held the door open. ''Of course, please come in.''

The three of us sat in the living room looking out on that beautiful garden. The whole thing was so unreal it was as if we had stepped through the looking glass. It was too bucolic a scene to be viewed while discussing murder. We all sat smiling at each other as though we were there to discuss the next fund raiser for the hospital.

Lucy sat in a chair facing Deborah and me on the couch.

''Now how can I help you, Detective Berkowitz?'' she asked, ever the composed, perfect hostess.

''Mrs. Pachurian, we have just discovered what poison killed Meg McClintock. It was a little known but lethal substance called Ricin.''

Lucy looked calm and unconcerned. ''Very interesting, but why are you telling me this?''

''Because we have reason to believe that you know this poison. In fact, that you have some in your possession.''

Lucy's eyes flicked to me for a second.

''I think you're mistaken, Detective.''

''Mrs. Pachurian, I could get a warrant to search your garden and potting shed within minutes.''

Lucy was silent but her mind was obviously working, a fact that didn't escape the detective.

''I have two of my men standing guard at the shed now awaiting the warrant. So there would be no chance for you to remove anything.''

''My gardener may have some of the poison you mention. I don't know what he has there.''

"Do you grow castor beans, Mrs. Pachurian?"

"Yes."

"Ricin is not the kind of poison you pick up at your local hardware store, Mrs. Pachurian. It is distilled from castor beans and made into a lethal powder. Suppose I ask your gardener if he did this."

Lucy sat rigidly silent.

"Mrs. Pachurian, when we find the castor beans and Ricin in your potting shed, which you know we will, and your gardener denies any knowledge of its presence, our conclusion would have to be that you made the Ricin."

"All right, perhaps I did. I needed it to get rid of the predators and pests who were destroying my garden," she said firmly.

"You told me you only do organic gardening, Lucy," I said. "You said you don't kill pests, you deter them."

Lucy looked at me accusingly. This is not the favorite part of my profession.

"Sometimes I make exceptions."

"What kind of pests do you try to kill?" asked Deborah pleasantly. "We don't have coyotes around here. Rabbits? Raccoons?"

She looked horrified. "Oh no. I'd never kill those creatures. They're just doing what God intended them to do, finding food to survive. They don't mean any harm."

"And what harm did Meg McClintock do?" asked Deborah.

She drew herself up in great hauteur and said, "The woman was a busybody—a nasty gossip. We have many of her kind in our English villages and they may seem like sweet old ladies but actually they are vicious harridans who often inflict great harm."

"Did you think she would tell someone she had seen

you put the powdered peanuts into Janet's bowl of stuffing?'' I asked softly.

I felt rather than saw Deborah stiffen.

Lucy looked at me coldly. "Really, Emma, what on earth are you talking about?"

"Was Bootsie also a bad person?" I asked.

She said nothing. The inbred control of her class kept her face totally impassive. I would have to find the right button to press in order to pierce that veil of arrogance.

"What I can't understand is why you would ever want to hurt Bootsie. She was your friend. She was a wonderful person, everyone loved her."

She was stone still, but I could see color rising in her neck. So I pressed on.

"Why, there was nothing Bootsie wouldn't have done for you—she had to be the best friend you'll ever have. She was so kind-hearted and giving."

I turned to Deborah to further extol Bootsie's virtues.

"She was an angel—she donated money to so many causes. If anyone was in need, she was always there for them."

Out of the corner of my eye I saw Lucy's face become livid.

"She was a fraud—she fooled all of you!" Finally unable to control herself any further, she spat out, "Your precious Bootsie was nothing but a conniving, wicked blackmailer. She was no friend of mine."

"Did you really seriously think she would tell the authorities that you were counterfeiting antique Aubusson rugs?" I asked softly.

I stole a glance at Deborah; she was too professional to react overtly but I saw her eyes widen.

Suddenly, all the calm, cool lady-of-the-manor mien dropped away and Lucy began to pour out her anger.

"You heard her that night at the Red Cross Ball," she said as though it was just the two of us having a discussion. "Remember how she kept hinting to Milo and me that she would tell the police about our rug business? You might not have picked it up, but it was plain to us what she was threatening. She just loved to play cat and mouse with us—it was really monstrous."

"How did she find out that you were converting new Chinese Aubussons into old French Aubussons?" I asked.

"She bought one from us and then did some research. She actually flew in the curator of a museum in New York who told her it was not genuine. Imagine her distrusting her good friends that way!" she said indignantly.

The nerve of some people.

"Do you know she made Milo give her one of our genuine Aubussons? It was worth almost a quarter of a million dollars, just for her silence. She was so greedy. She had seen a small rug in my bedroom and she asked to buy it from us at a pittance of what it's actually worth. That's what all that snide hinting was about that night—she was pressuring us to give her what she wanted. You call that a nice person? She was a malicious hateful woman. I knew one cannot keep giving in to the demands of a blackmailer. We just couldn't keep living with that sword she was holding over our heads."

She leaned forward and looked at me intently. "How could I let her destroy what it has taken my husband years to build? He was so anxious to prove my family wrong, he wanted to make a lot of money to show them that he could provide me with a life of wealth. He desperately wanted their respect and approval. And he got it, finally," she said with great satisfaction. "What right did that wicked woman have to take all that away?" She laughed, a joyless laugh. "I know you think she was some sort of saint. Everyone did. She was always so cheerful, so full of fun. But if you listened carefully, it was often at someone else's expense. Oh, she put on this gracious lady act, but she was a crude, cruel woman. But then, what could one expect from a woman who was raised on a pig farm in some godforsaken corner of Louisiana?'' she said contemptuously. ''We wouldn't accept her into the Jockey Club, of course.''

''Let me guess. You are on the Admissions Board?'' I asked.

''Yes, of course,'' she said proudly.

''Bootsie knew that?''

She nodded.

''Don't you think she may have been just a little miffed that her good friend and neighbor blackballed her entry into the club?'' I asked.

She was astonished. ''But her application was ridiculous in the first place. With her pedigree and background, how did she ever expect to be acceptable?''

''Your husband is a shopkeeper, Lucy.''

''But I am the daughter of an earl,'' she said.

Aren't the English aristocracy just the most endearing folks? It's that kind of repellent smug sense of entitlement that makes me hesitate to marry into that class and why I'm not ready to give Mark a ''yes'' answer—now or ever.

''I can see why you would be unhappy with Mrs. Corrigan,'' said Deborah smoothly.

Lucy turned to her with a triumphant smile. An understanding ally!

''You see why I had to put her out of our lives?'' she asked.

Deborah nodded. ''Of course. But you told me you didn't know about her peanut allergy,'' she said chidingly.

''Oh, of course I knew. She thought no one knew but we all did—you can't keep that sort of thing quiet around here. Her cook told my cook, and that's the end of the secret.''

"So you just sauntered into the kitchen that day and slipped the peanuts into the stuffing. That took a lot of nerve, Lucy, with all those people coming in and out," I said admiringly.

"Yes, it did, didn't it?" she said proudly. "I knew I had to do it then because andouille sausage is so strong a flavor it would mask any other. I just unloaded my bag of herbs on the counter next to the bowl of stuffing and no one noticed my dumping in a little bag of pulverized peanuts."

"Except Meg," I said.

"She saw me stirring it in. She asked me what I was doing and I told her I had taken a spoonful taste of the stuffing and was just sort of smoothing out the mixture. I wasn't sure she believed me."

"So you were afraid she'd think about it later and perhaps pass on her suspicions," said Deborah, nodding her head as though that was a perfectly natural conclusion for Lucy to have drawn.

Encouraged by this seeming approval of her actions, Lucy continued enthusiastically. "When she was working in my house the next day, she dropped one of her little nasty remarks. I came into my kitchen for something, and she was talking to my cook about the police questioning everyone. When she saw me, she got that crafty look on her face and said something about how she didn't tell the police everything she saw but was thinking about it."

"So you had to get rid of her," I said conversationally, as though it was the sensible thing to do.

"Of course. What choice did I have?"

She smoothed the folds of her jacket. "She was a malicious gossip. It was inevitable that her foul tongue would bring her grief someday. I look upon it as retribution for all the pain she has certainly caused."

"How did you administer the Ricin?" asked Detective Sergeant Berkowitz.

By this time, Lucy was so into recounting the narrative of her exploits that she was eager to tell everything. I've seen this before when the murderer starts to become proud of her cleverness and wants to draw admiration for her ingenuity. Ego triumphs over common sense as she loses sight of the fact that she is condemning herself with every word. But the urge to unburden herself is so great, the desire to share with someone else the difficult and dangerous deeds she has committed is so strong, that confession becomes a great relief and her need defeats all reason.

"I rang the bell and Meg answered. Her sister was in my kitchen at that moment so I knew Meg would be alone. I had a bunch of rhubarb that I had come ostensibly to bring her. She loved rhubarb. As she stepped back to let me in, I jabbed her with one of my insulin needles filled with powdered Ricin mixed with water. Then I left. It was really very simple."

Deborah arose. "Mrs. Pachurian, you are under arrest for the murders of Mrs. Corrigan and Miss McClintock. You have the right to remain silent . . ."

XVII

JANET HAD PREPARED a cold buffet that Rivers had set up at poolside. We sat around a large table in the shade of a tree as he helped us fill our plates with salad nicoise, marinated shrimps with artichoke hearts, paper-thin rare roast beef rolled around baby asparagus spears, mesclun salad with hearts of palm, thick slices of country ham with chunks of five-grain homemade bread, and mugs of cold vichyssoise. There were pitchers of chilled sangria, lemonade, and silver buckets with Chardonnay.

"I love victory celebrations," said Abba as he looked with delight at his heaped-up plate. "This is better than after the Six-Day War."

"We really shouldn't be celebrating," said Melissa. "After all, two people are dead and Mr. and Mrs. Pachurian are in for a bad time."

"Melissa, don't be such a self-righteous *fahbissineh*."

"That means sourpuss," said Deborah, smiling.

"Birth, death, and taxes are everyday facts of life. But good triumphing over evil is rare—and thus a cause for celebration. So don't rain on our parade by trying to make us feel guilty about enjoying ourselves for a goddamned good reason.'' And he shoved a beef-covered asparagus into his mouth.

"She can't help it," said Jonathan fondly, putting his arm around Melissa. "Her first thought is always for the other person. She hates to see anyone hurt."

Abba looked around. "Where's that little scumbag and his slimebucket bride? How come they're not out here for the free lunch?"

"Since there's no one else to whom I would ascribe those colorful but apt descriptions, I assume you mean Mr. and Mrs. Rick Bolton," said Tom Blair.

"Those are the cocksuckers to whom I am alluding," said Abba.

"I may sometimes abhor your profanity, but I always applaud your grammar." Tom gave a small bow of acknowledgment to Abba.

"They came by my office this morning and picked up his inheritance check. To be more accurate, his wife-of-the-moment picked it up and tucked it into her handbag. You know, a favorite Chinese curse is 'May you live in interesting times.' I would add to that the curse 'May you live with a nagging wife.' "

"I don't know," said Abba. "My Uncle Hymie lived with my Aunt Yetta for forty years and she was known in the neighborhood as The Nag of Nostrand Avenue. There wasn't a thing he did without her supervision and approval. In the winter people stood back from him on the subway because she made him wear a pouch of garlic around his neck because she said it prevented colds. In the summer, we all sat outside and drank cold lemonade but he had to have hot tea because she said that's what the English drank in the tropics and *they* knew, she saw it in *Lawrence of Arabia*. He couldn't play poker with the men at night because she said he was delicate and the night air in winter was bad for his sinuses. When she died, we thought he'd be a free man. The minute her *shiva* was over, the local brisket brigade of eligible widows attacked him, bearing pots and casseroles and jello molds. Hymie wouldn't look at any of them, not even the beauteous red-headed Shirley Kissel with the killer cleavage. All he did was cry and talk about his marvelous wife Yetta, what wonderful care she took of him, and there'll never be another like her. Thank God, we all said. But he mourned for and missed her for the rest of his life. So who knows what and who makes a happy marriage? There's an old Jewish proverb 'A worm in a radish thinks it's a rose.' Poor Hymie just didn't know any better.''

I looked at him. "Is this one of those mythical case histories you prepare for the Rabbinical Marriage Counseling class at the Hebrew Seminary?''

Deborah laughed. "So that's how he always has a pertinent story for every situation.''

"Much as we hate to interrupt your touching flow of questionable family remembrances, I think everyone would prefer hearing from Detective Sergeant Berkowitz about the final developments in our two murders,'' I said.

"OK,'' she said. "Let's begin with first hearing from you, Emma. You've explained how you knew about Ricin, but how did you know about the rug counterfeiting?''

"I have a friend who dyes fabrics for a hobby. When I walked into Lucy's potting shed lab, I recognized the equipment. The enamel pans, the glass funnels, the refrigerator and freezer. I noticed boxes of bloodroot and salvia for reds, crabapples for pinks. The big tub, the washing machine—it probably never dawned on her that I would be familiar with the process.''

"What's the washing machine for?'' asked Deborah.

"To age the rugs by agitating them."

"But what made you connect the dyeing process with old rugs?" asked Count José. "After all, it could just have been Lucy's hobby, like your friend."

"I remembered Bootsie's cryptic remarks to them when we were at the Red Cross Ball. Also, when I admired her Aubusson that hangs in the front hall, she was somewhat oblique about her dealings with Milo and mentioned getting it at a bargain price. Also, I was puzzled at the source of the Pachurians' affluence. There are no trust funds or inherited wealth; I checked into Lucy's family and they're barely able to cover the taxes on the family estates. Sure, I know the antique rug business can be very profitable. But real estate around here is way above that kind of money. And their style of living—she wears designer clothes, they have a domestic staff, and the house is not furnished with three-piece suites from Broyhill's. I mean, it's obvious there's more money coming in than could be produced by two rug shops."

"Actually," said Deborah, "Lucy viewed the fake Aubussons as a harmless victimless crime. As she and Milo chose to see it, the buyers were not being cheated because, since they believed their rugs were genuine, they enjoyed the full pride of ownership, and the pleasure of showing off their possession to all their friends."

"Convoluted reasoning, but beautifully self-serving," said Tom.

"But isn't it very difficult to make a rug?" asked Melissa.

"They weren't making the rugs, they were just doctoring modern-made Chinese fake Aubussons to make them look antique. Aubusson rugs used to be made in France from patterns made in the eighteenth century on paper called 'maquettes' which are worth a fortune today. For over twelve years, Chinese technicians experimented with replicating them and finally succeeded in making rugs that almost have the look, feel, and shadings of the real thing. It's very difficult—it often took twenty shades of red, for instance, to produce just the right red for a rose. Only a real expert can tell the difference. What Milo and Lucy did was to take the phonies and age them by putting dyes around the edges subtly to look like oxidation and wear. Going through the washing machine agitator pulled the yarns to make them look as though they'd been subjected to hundreds of years of walking feet.''

''Is the difference in price between the modern Chinese and an antique Aubusson so great that it's worth all that effort?'' asked Tom.

''You can buy a 9×12 Chinese rug for $10,000. A genuine antique Aubusson in that size would be $100,000.''

''Holy shit!'' said Abba. ''That's quite a markup. No wonder they're rolling in Rolls Royces.''

''But Auntie detected the counterfeit,'' said Jonathan proudly.

''Something about it made her suspicious which is why she called in an expert,'' I said. ''I suspect that if Lucy hadn't turned down her application for club membership, she would never have questioned the provenance of her purchase. After all, they were good friends and Bootsie had a firm code of friendship that included faith and trust. I'm sure she regarded Lucy's rejection as a betrayal of the friendship and that made her mad.''

Tom laughed. ''And when Bootsie got mad—my, my— I've been in tornadoes that were less turbulent.''

''So you got the wife for the two murders but what's happening to hubby?'' asked Abba.

''His case was turned over to OCVAN,'' said Deborah.

''What is that?'' asked Count José.

"That's NAVCO backwards," said Abba.

The Count looked puzzled.

"It stands for 'Organized Crime, Vice, And Narcotics'—it's the department that deals with white collar crime," said Deborah.

"I suspect the Pachurians will not be seeing too much of each other in the coming years," said Tom dryly.

"She must have loved him a great deal to kill for him," said Melissa.

Abba snorted. "*Motek*, my darling, I think you need a course in Reality One. It's time you stopped endowing people with nobility. She didn't do it for him—she was out to preserve her own social position and fucking fancy way of life. The thought of maybe having to shop in Loehmann's was enough to push her over the edge."

"Melissa always sees the best in everyone," said Jonathan.

"Not if they're landlords, I'll bet," said Abba.

"Speaking of that," said Jonathan shyly, "I've decided to keep this house and to live in it. After all, I grew up here, it's home to me. I've told Rivers and Janet they can stay on as long as they like."

"Wonderful!" we all chorused. "Bootsie would be so pleased."

Jonathan put his arm around Melissa. "That is, my wife and I will live here. We got married yesterday."

"Congratulations! *Mazel tov!*"

We all got up and kissed them and then Tom proposed a toast, and Abba proposed a toast and we were all feeling festive and happy.

Suddenly Count José arose and announced:

"You are wonderful people and I shall miss all of you. I am returning to Portugal tomorrow. There is nothing more for me here; I think it is time for me to go home," he said forlornly.

I looked at Jonathan and he nodded and whispered something to Rivers who went into the house. A few minutes later, Rivers came out carrying a large package which he gave to Jonathan.

"Count, I shall miss you too. You were a great source of happiness to my aunt and I thank you for it. So please, Melissa and I would like to give you this little going-away gift of appreciation."

The Count took the package and bowed slightly to Jonathan and Melissa.

"*Obrigado*, thank you very much." Then he sat down, leaving the closed package on the ground at his feet.

"Aren't you going to open it?" asked Jonathan.

The Count looked bewildered.

"The Count is a gentleman, Jonathan. Many people consider it poor manners to open a gift in front of the donor thus conveying that the object itself is unimportant but it's the thought that counts," I said. "When you think about it, it's a damned good idea. It prevents you from having to pretend delight when you find three pairs of purple satin jockey shorts with your monogram on the crotch."

"That's OK, José—I give you permission to open it here," Jonathan told him.

We all waited while José tore off the paper. When he saw the gift, he stared at it, transfixed. Then he jumped up and threw his arms around Jonathan and when he turned around, tears were streaming down his face.

It was the pair of silver candelabras.

It took him a few moments to compose himself. "*Que posso dizer?* What can I say to such a gift? *Obrigado, obrigado*, thank you, thank you. I cannot believe it. It is beyond my dreams."

"Emma told me the whole story and I feel these rightfully belong to you and your family. I think Auntie meant for you to have them, and had she lived, would have eventually given them to you."

Of course, then everyone had to hear the story so I told them.

José looked at me. "But how did you know?"

"One of the less attractive but frequently very profitable and informative parts of my job is to go through wastebaskets. Of course, I only deal in dry refuse; I draw the line at garbage pails and dumpsters. You pursue an extensive correspondence, José, and you throw out a helluva lot of letters. Most people tear up their personal mail before they toss it, but thank goodness, you don't."

He looked puzzled. "I never felt I need bother since they are all in Portuguese."

"So?" I said.

"Ah, of course. Your house in the Algarve. You know our language." He smiled. "I never thought my garbage could be so valuable and productive."

"Only in the right hands," said Abba.

José kept looking at the candelabras and touching them in awe, as though he couldn't quite believe they were there in front of him. "I cannot tell you how much these mean to me, my family, and my country."

He looked at Jonathan. "May I excuse myself? I must go upstairs and phone Portugal—I'll call collect, of course—so there will be someone from the government as well as my family to meet me at customs when I arrive. This is a memorable day in all our lives as well as for my country."

"Of course, but you don't have to call collect," said Jonathan, laughing.

He started to repack the silver. " Leave them here, José.

We'll take care of the packing. Go on upstairs and make your calls," said Jonathan. "Rivers, could you please re-pack these for traveling? The Count will carry them on the airplane."

As Rivers took them into the house, I commented on his unusual good humor.

"He looks almost exuberant, for Rivers. Usually he could pass for an usher at a funeral chapel."

"Maybe because I told him he could bring his son here to live with him," said Jonathan.

I was surprised. "I thought Charlie was staying happily with a family in Boca."

"Yes, he's been there for years. But only because Aunt Bootsie preferred that arrangement," he said a little shame-facedly.

I was silent as I absorbed what he said. "You mean she was uncomfortable with a retarded person?"

He nodded. "Charlie lived with us when he was a boy. But when he grew up, Auntie insisted Rivers find other accommodations for him. She said he frightened her. Lord knows why, he's the sweetest, most gentle guy you'd ever meet."

Abba noticed my distress. "It's disillusioning to learn that our friends have many faces, some of them not so nice. You have to realize that the Bootsie you saw was respond-ing to you only. And you being such an adorable *tsotskele* evoked only her good side. Apparently not everyone elic-ited the same positive reaction from her." He turned to Jonathan. "I mean no disrespect to your aunt, Jonathan. Just explaining the facts of life to young Emma here."

"Jonathan understands," said Melissa. "She wasn't al-ways so nice to me either."

"She wasn't supposed to be—you were an almost daughter-in-law. From what I've seen, the best you should expect from a mother-in-law is bare civility and honest recipes where she doesn't leave out a critical ingredient.''

Deborah looked at him appraisingly. ''You've just made some surprisingly insightful observations, Abba. Obviously you too have many faces.''

She doesn't know the half of it. I've seen the many sides of Abba, and some of them are frightening as they must be in his profession. He's courageous, forceful and decisive—and is ready to kill in seconds if necessary. If theirs is to be a real and lasting relationship, she will have to know and accept his many facets. The fact that she too is in law enforcement should make it easier. I looked at them with affection—they're so happy, so right together. If I could, I'd pray to the gods of love—I'm not sure if that's Eros or Ann Landers—to make this thing work for them.

He put his arm around her fondly, ''Ah yes, I am a man of many parts. The part you just witnessed is the psych degree from Brooklyn College.''

''Jonathan, giving those candelabras to the Count was a most generous gesture,'' said Tom. ''I'm proud of you.''

''It's the only good thing that came out of this whole horrible affair,'' I said. ''It was wonderful to see the Count's joy. It makes me feel positively euphoric.''

''There's nothing better than witnessing a *mitzvah*,'' said Abba.

''Good deed,'' translated Deborah.

''. . . especially when someone else paid for it!'' he said with a hearty laugh. ''Jonathan, you're a righteous person, and that's about the highest compliment a Jew can give.''

Jonathan was beaming with pleasure. ''I'm not finished spreading largesse.'' He reached into his beach jacket pocket and handed me a check. ''Emma, let me give you this with the grateful thanks of both me and my wife.''

I thanked him and peeked—it was for twenty thousand

dollars. I smiled as I thought how nicely it would fit in next to the check for twelve and a half thousand pounds I received yesterday from Lord Gerald.

"You know, Emma, I'm beginning to see that you're right—rich people can be just as worthy as poor people," said Abba.

"Yes, and they demonstrate their worthiness so much more eloquently."

That night, when I went upstairs to bed for the last time—I'll be going back to New York tomorrow—I found a large rolled-up object on the floor in my room. There was a yellow Post-it on it.

Where do you want us to ship this?
It's yours—you deserve it, with our deepest thanks.
                              Jonathan and Melissa

It was Bootsie's Aubusson.